I0690927

Spectral Revelations

A Karina Cardinal Mystery (Book 6)

By Ellen Butler

A Karina Cardinal Novel
K.C.

Power to the Pen

Dedication

To Clator

For providing inspiration when I was at a loss.

Prologue

Monday

The dumpster reeked of sulfurous rotten eggs, decomposing vegetables, and remnants of the restaurant's catch of the day. She pinched her nose, regretting the choice of a hiding place. Peeking around the fetid trash, she watchfully awaited her mark.

He'd have to come out sooner or later.

There was a waxing gibbous moon tonight, but the scuttling dark clouds covered any sort of light it may have provided. Due to town ordinances, the limited lights in the parking lot barely spread their glow farther than five or six feet.

The flickering light he'd parked beneath flashed bright one last time and went dark. It didn't matter; his white SUV sat like a beacon in the empty lot.

Finally, she heard the squeak of the back door swinging open.

The car beeped, and taillights blinked. He walked rapidly, carrying something in his left hand. His head swiveled back and forth, scanning the empty lot.

Silently, she pulled out of sight, going so far as to cover her mouth, even though she wasn't close enough for him to hear her breaths. The car door closed with a quiet clunk. She waited for the telltale sounds of an engine revving to life. Instead, she heard the back door creak again and poked her head out in time to watch it close behind him.

He'd forgotten to lock the vehicle.

She pulled the sweatshirt hood over her head and darted

across the lot to the SUV.

A small brown box sat on the passenger seat. In a trice, she had the box in her hands. The vehicle's dim overhead light revealed a flash of shiny metal.

The scrape of a shoe and a skittering stone were her only warnings.

She pivoted. "Surprised to see me?"

Chapter One

Wednesday

The cell phone sitting on the conference table sang out "Benny and the Jets" by Elton John. My mother's face popped up on the screen. I rolled my eyes in irritation before sending the call to voicemail and turned back to my computer.

"Did you just send your mom to voicemail? Again?" my coworker Rodrigo asked.

"Yes." He frowned, and I, for some reason, felt the need to defend my actions. "We have—" I checked the clock on my laptop, which read 4:20, "—ten minutes to finish this presentation before the team meeting. I don't have time to go down a rabbit hole with Mom right now."

I worked as a lobbyist at the National Healthcare Advocacy Alliance. We had a four-thirty meeting with our boss, Hasina, to review the strategy for our latest healthcare initiative with the Urban Health League.

Rodrigo shook his dark head and dusted off an invisible piece of lint from his beautifully tailored gray silk suit.

I readied myself for a lecture.

He didn't disappoint me. "If I did that to my mother, she'd lecture me for the next three weeks and threaten me with her *chanclas*."

"What's a *chanclas*? Did you finish the diabetes data on Atlanta and Chicago?" I asked, tapping away on my laptop. "I'm referencing it on the last page of my report."

"Already sent it out in an email to the team." He leaned back in his chair, stretching his arms above his head. His Puerto Rican skin tone remained tan, even though it was October. Not every man could pull off the lavender button-down with the bright green and black tie he wore. He was in his mid-twenties, and his beautiful wardrobe would have been *en pointe* in New York City. Unfortunately, he was a unicorn amongst the bland Washington, D.C. wonks.

"*Chanclas* are sandals or flip-flops. I know you took Spanish in high school. Do you remember none of it?" he gently chided.

"If you recall from our trip to Mexico, I can order *cerveza y piña coladas,* and ask where the bathrooms are. By the time I hit Spanish Three, I was so lost. My teacher took pity on me. The C she gave me was due to the extra credit research project she granted me, not because I actually earned the grade with knowledge of the language." I finished the final bullet point on my conclusions and started a grammar and spellcheck. "Why would your mom threaten you with a flip-flop?"

"It's a Latin thing. Italians threaten their kid with a wooden spoon, Latinas with a flip-flop."

I chuckled and corrected a spelling error caught by the computer. Spellcheck finished, I emailed it to the team and closed my laptop. "Done."

"Right on time." Rodrigo scooped up his computer and his afternoon pumpkin spice latte. We headed to the elevators. "You doing anything interesting this weekend?"

I pressed the UP button and sighed. "Rick and I are having dinner with Mike and his new girl."

He bit his lip to hold back a smile. "*That* should be interesting. What I wouldn't give to be a fly on the wall. Dinner with your boyfriend, your ex-boyfriend, and his new girlfriend."

You could consider Rodrigo my "work husband." He was as familiar with the men in my life as my sister or mother. Possibly even more so since we'd had the unfortunate luck of experiencing not one but two escapades together. His fluent Spanish had come in handy during our Mexico caper. When I'd been a suspect in the death of a senator, Rodrigo doggedly helped me pursue a lead that law enforcement dismissed. It wasn't either of our faults that the assassin turned the tables, chasing us up Interstate 95 with a dead woman in the trunk of his car, intent on adding us to his pile of victims.

Not wanting to give Rodrigo fodder, I responded, "I don't know what you're talking about. It's not like I've never met her before. Min Lin is a perfectly charming woman."

An engineer for Lockheed Martin, Min Lin was all things I wasn't: petite with straight black hair that hung at her jawline and serious dark eyes. I had wavy, long chestnut hair, emotional green eyes, and stood a solid five feet, nine inches in bare feet. I was fairly certain Min Lin's closet held only three colors—black, gray, and shades of beige. Like Rodrigo, I enjoyed colorful fashions, especially when it came to shoes.

I might have had an addiction. *Hello, my name is Karina Cardinal, and I'm a shoe-a-holic.*

Rodrigo followed me onto the elevator, giving a distinct snort to my description of Min Lin.

"What? She's perfectly fine—erudite and staid."

Rodrigo pressed number eight, and it lit up. "Last week at happy hour, I believe you compared her to a zucchini."

I rolled my eyes and said dismissively, "I remember we did shots to celebrate a win for Jennifer, but I don't recall saying anything like that."

"To quote: 'She has the sense of humor of a zucchini. When you look up the word "serious" in the dictionary, there is a photo of Min Lin.'" Rodrigo used air quotes to emphasize my comments.

Good lord. How many shots did I have?

"In Mike's defense, considering the shenanigans my—" cough, "—adventures put him through, perhaps a zucchini is exactly what he needs." The elevator opened, and our discussion ceased as we slipped into seats around the half-full conference room table.

The rest of the team filed in, seven in all. Finally, our boss, Hasina, strode through the door, her thick low-heeled pumps clacking against the faux wood laminate floors. She wore a mustard pantsuit that hung limp and wrinkled off her waif-thin figure. Neither the suit cut nor the color did anything for Hasina's olive skin tones. Gossip around the office had it that Hasina was in the midst of a messy divorce. The sleepless nights had deepened and spread natural dark circles beneath her eyes. Hasina was a good person, and a good boss, and I pitied her current predicament.

She placed a four-inch stack of files, topped by her computer, cell phone, and cup of coffee at the head of the table. "Are we all here?"

In response, Elton John cried out, "Benny and the Jets." My face flamed, and I quickly fumbled to swipe the call to voicemail. "Sorry. I'm putting it on silent now."

Everyone at the table pulled out their phones and switched the ringers off.

"No problem." Hasina took a moment to turn her phone off. "That wasn't Cathy from the Urban Health League, was it?"

"No." I shook my head.

"It's her mom calling," Rodrigo piped up. "*Again.*"

"Is it important? Do you need to call her back?" Hasina asked in a concerned tone.

"It's nothing important; it can wait until after the meeting," I assured her.

Hasina plopped into the chair with a slight sigh. "Karina, as team lead, you have the floor."

****

An hour later, the meeting broke up.

"Good job." Hasina loaded her materials back into a pile, sans a coffee cup this time; instead, she tossed it into the trashcan. "Are you attending Senator Wheelan's fundraiser tonight?"

"Along with Rodrigo." I nodded toward the door my coworker was exiting. "Will you be there?"

"I might stop by. It starts at seven?"

"Yes, but the senator won't arrive before eight. I planned to go home and change first, then get there about a quarter 'til," I replied absently.

Another voicemail notification popped up on my cell. That would make three from my mom, along with a text from my sister, Jillian, which read,

CALL MOM!!!!

"Perhaps I'll see you there." Hasina gathered her belongings and headed out the door.

"Um, yes. See you." *What on earth is going on?*

I returned to my office, closed the door, and phoned my mom without listening to the voicemails first.

"Hello? Is that you, Karina?" Mom answered.

"Hi, Mom, it's me. I saw you called … a few times. I was in a meeting with my boss. What's going on?"

"Have you heard from your Aunt Vera?"

"Aunt Vera?" I sat in my office chair and spun around to look out the window. "No. I haven't spoken to her since June, when Jilly and I went down to visit for her birthday. Why?"

Aunt Vera was my mother's first cousin, not her sister, making Vera my first cousin once removed. This was explained to me when I had a family tree project during seventh grade. I never forgot it. However, because she was of my mother's generation, we grew up calling her aunt rather than cousin. Mom always said Aunt Vera was the sister she never had.

"She was supposed to call me back about Thanksgiving and our girls' trip in February."

Every year, Mom and Vera took a girls' trip to someplace warm. It started when I was a junior in high school. Arizona spas, Florida beaches, and cruises to the Bahamas were just a few adventures the two had taken.

"We're cruising to Jamaica this time. I've got to book it this weekend if I want to get the discount on the room upgrade," she said in rush.

Mentally, I rolled my eyes. Mom was known as "the family planner," never satisfied until events were arranged down to the last detail. Mom and Dad were coming east for Thanksgiving, while my brother Tyler and his family would be attending Thanksgiving in Oregon at his in-laws' home.

"As far as Thanksgiving is concerned, Jilly and I have already discussed it. You and Dad can stay at my condo, and Aunt Vera can stay at Jillian's apartment. Turkey dinner is at my place. Tell Aunt Vera she's in charge of bringing her famous chocolate pecan pie. I'll get the whipped cream," I rattled off directions without pausing. "See, planning done. No worries."

"That is precisely what I'm trying to explain. I can't 'tell' Aunt Vera. I've been calling her since Monday night," Mom's tone sounded a bit frayed about the edges. "She knows we've got to book this trip ASAP. She hasn't returned any of my calls."

Well, that was odd. Aunt Vera usually returned a call within twenty-four hours, or at least sent a text. "Hm. Maybe her phone is on the fritz. Did you try her at work?"

"Yes, I called the main number, and I was passed to her boss. He said she sent a text to him. She requested time off to take care of her sick niece in D.C."

My brows furrowed in confusion. "What?"

"Exactly. Jilly's not sick. Are you?"

"No, of course not." I swung back around to my desk and

opened my laptop.

"I'm stumped."

"The boss must have gotten it wrong. I'll shoot her an email, in case her phone is busted or lost." I pulled up my Outlook, added Vera's private and work email addresses in the TO line, and typed up a quick message asking if she was okay. I requested she reach out to Mom or myself.

"Did you send a text?" I asked Mom.

"Of course!" she snapped as if I'd asked a stupid question.

In my defense, the question was not stupid. My mother was not of the texting generation, and she was ten times more likely to make a phone call than send a text. I rarely received texts from her; when I did, it usually told me to call her.

"If Aunt Vera hasn't been to work this week, where is she?" I murmured, immediately regretting speaking the words aloud.

"I don't know," Mom cried with a bit of a whine.

I didn't need my mother working herself into a dither. I knew I'd have to calm her down, or she'd be on the next flight from Colorado to Virginia. My parents moved out of the DC rat race a number of years ago when my mother retired from teaching. My father still did consulting for the federal government. They chose Colorado because it was in between their children. My brother lived in Seattle, whereas Jillian and I lived in the fifty-first state of Northern Virginia—a place vastly different from the rest of the state.

"I'll tell you what, if Aunt Vera doesn't contact one of us by tomorrow, I'll go down on Friday. Hasina's given the staff the afternoon off because the building is being fumigated."

"Fumigated?!" Mom exclaimed.

"The old coffee shop on the first floor wasn't cleaned properly before they closed for good, and the roaches moved in." My lip curled in disgust.

"Ew!"

"My thoughts exactly. The critters haven't made it to the upper floors, but businesses on the first and second floors have been complaining. So, we're all getting gassed. The building must be cleared out by noon." I shook my head. "Anyway, it doesn't matter; we've gone off on a tangent. I'll touch base tomorrow evening. If you haven't heard from Vera, I'll buzz down to Williamsburg to check on her."

"Do you think I should call the police for a welfare check? After all, she's sixty-two. Maybe she had a heart attack."

I hesitated. "You can always do that, but the fact she told her boss she'd be out of town leads me to believe something else is going on. Perhaps she's found a new man and flew to Vegas to elope." I slapped a hand over my mouth, regretting the statement as soon as it popped out.

"Good lord, I hope not. It would be that horrid Randy all over again," Mom moaned.

Aunt Vera's first husband, Uncle Jack, was an awesome guy. The type of uncle who would swoop a kid up on his shoulders to look over the crowd at Disney World. I remember marveling at his ability to pull quarters from my ears. Uncle Jack died from a brain aneurysm when Vera was only forty-six. Returning home from work one evening, the poor woman literally stumbled over him lying on the bathroom floor. A year later, still in mourning and on the rebound, Vera married Good Time Randy.

Good Time Randy loved to party ... and drink ... and spend money. Within eight months, Good Time Randy blew through all their savings on lavish purchases, expensive trips, and bad investments on stock tips he'd gotten from a "bar buddy." I could never confirm it, but I believed my parents lent my aunt the money for her divorce. Vera had been working for the Smithsonian. After the divorce, she moved away from DC and restarted her life in Williamsburg, Virginia, where she became a conservator at an art museum.

"I'm sure there is a perfectly sensible explanation for everything," I soothed. "Don't worry."

Later that night, I tried to take my own advice—oft easier said than done. Wandering around the senator's fundraiser, networking, and nursing a single glass of wine, I found myself distracted by thoughts of Aunt Vera. I constantly refreshed my email.

Nothing.

What's that saying about a watched pot?

With a sigh, I decided to leave my email app alone and focus on the task at hand—getting a cosponsor for our bill.

Chapter Two

Thursday

"Benny and the Jets" woke me from a stressful dream. Everyone has had it. I was back in high school. I couldn't remember my locker combination. There was a test I needed to study for. My notes and textbook were in the locker.

"Mom?" I rolled onto my back, rubbing a hand down my face. "What's wrong?"

"Have you heard from Aunt Vera yet?" she whispered.

"What? I don't know. What time is it?"

"Um, morning time?"

"Cripes," I muttered. "Just a sec, let me check." I swiped to my email app.

No response.

"No, not yet. But I sent the email in the evening. It's—" I checked the clock on my bedside table, "—six in the morning." A realization dinged in my head. "Which means it's four in Colorado. What are you doing up at this ungodly hour?"

"I woke up to go to the bathroom and figured you'd be awake."

That would explain the echoey sound I heard, and why she was whispering. "Jeez, Mom. Seriously, I think you're blowing this all out of proportion. I'm sure Aunt Vera is fine. Go back to bed."

"I thought you woke up at six."

"Not when I didn't get home from a fundraiser until

midnight," I grunted.

"Oh, sorry."

"Go back to bed. I'll call you at lunchtime." I hit the off button and tossed the phone back on the table. If I could just get another half hour of sleep...

Fifteen minutes later, the coffee machine belched out its magical dark brew as I hovered impatiently for it to finish. I poured in some pumpkin spice creamer, took the cup and phone to my velvet sofa, and surfed social media. At quarter to seven, the *Mission Impossible* theme sang out, and my boyfriend, Rick Donovan's smiling face lit up my phone.

I swiped the green answer button. "'Lo."

"Morning, beautiful," his yummy deep voice rumbled across the lines, giving me a warm, gooey feeling in the pit of my stomach ... or it might have been the coffee—tough to say this early in the morning. "Saw you on social and knew you were up. Are you coherent; have you had your coffee yet?" Rick was a veteran who did time in Afghanistan. The military discipline of rising at the ungodly hour of five in the morning stayed with him, so it didn't surprise me that he was up, coherent, and had probably already run three miles.

Rick had learned that I was not in his early morning league. Before seven in the morning, I could run as far as the bathroom. Seriously, if you saw me running at five in the morning, you'd better run too, because something was undoubtedly chasing me. "Just finishing my first cup."

"How did the fundraiser go?"

"It looks like the four of us, Rodrigo, me, Hasina and Cathy from Urban Health, were able to convince the senator to cosponsor our bill." I may have given a bit of a squeal at the end of that sentence.

"Congratulations. That's great."

"So far, so good. We've got a bill in the House and the Senate.

One step closer." I swallowed the dregs of the coffee and scrunched my nose in distaste. It'd gone cold.

"I was calling about our dinner with Mike. Should I make reservations for us somewhere? It is Friday night. The weekend before Halloween. Things might be a bit loony."

Crap. I'd forgotten about the dinner. "About that. I'm going to reschedule."

"Ok-ay. Fine by me, but why?"

I gave a put-upon grunt. "There's a possibility I'll need to go down to Williamsburg tomorrow."

"Spill. What's going on?"

"Why do you think anything is going on?" I shot back.

"I can hear it in your voice," he said evenly.

I sighed in defeat.

Rick was former military special forces, as was most of his team. Their security clearances made them perfect to run on- and off-the-books operations for CIA/DEA/FBI—add your own three-lettered government agency here. At least those were my suspicions.

Honestly, I knew stuff about Rick, like his family life and where he grew up, but whenever I asked questions about his job, I didn't get a lot of answers. That being said, I was certain Rick was trained in interrogation tactics, as well as asset development. I couldn't put much past him. Mike once said Rick new how to "handle" me. I'd resented the hell out of that remark, but, to my consternation, Mike may have hit the nail on the head.

I rolled out the Aunt Vera story, starting with my mom's phone call yesterday and ending with, "So far, Aunt Vera hasn't returned any calls or my email."

"Is that unusual?"

"To be honest, yes. Yes, it is."

He took a beat. "Do you want my opinion?"

Unlike most people, Rick was truly asking and would abide

by my answer. If I said no, he'd leave it alone. I couldn't say no. Actually, I valued his take on the situation. "Yes."

"I think you should send the cops over for a welfare check. Like your mom said, she's sixty-two, lives alone, and hasn't responded to your mom's queries, or yours, for that matter."

My mouth twisted, because I agreed with Rick's assessment. I'd been thinking the same thing as the coffee kicked in. "I'll phone the police as soon as we get off. If I go down tomorrow, would you like to join me? The leaves are at their peak; it'll be a beautiful drive down."

"What time would you go?"

"Noonish." I explained the fumigation situation.

"I'm starting a new security detail for a foreign diplomat tomorrow morning, and I'm meeting with a potential client at three, so that's a non-starter. I could come down on Saturday," he offered.

What a sweetie. This time I was sure the gooey feeling in the pit of my stomach was Rick and *not* the coffee. "No worries. Let's play it by ear. If I get down to Aunt Vera's and find she's simply lost her phone, I'll likely return sometime on Saturday."

"Will I see you tonight?"

I hesitated, bringing up my calendar app to see if we had something on the books. "You mean for self-defense practice?" I'd been taking self-defense from the Silverthorne guys on-and-off for over a year. "I don't see anything. Did I have an appointment?"

"Karina, we haven't seen each other in two weeks. Since I'm not seeing you on Friday, as planned, I thought, perhaps, we could get together before you leave for Williamsburg. You know, for dinner … or something…" he said in a wink-wink tone.

As head of Silverthorne Security, Rick worked all over the world providing security services for American businesses abroad, foreign diplomats in D.C., and various other missions that tended to remain hush-hush. In a way, dating Rick wasn't much different from dating my ex-boyfriend, Mike. The one main difference: I knew my ex, who worked in the FBI's cybercrime unit, wasn't walking into active war zones. I did my level best to put those types of worries out of my head. Otherwise, I'd go bananas.

I snuggled deeper into my robe and said in my most sensual voice, "Why, yes, Mr. Donovan, I'd love to get together for dinner ... or something."

"Pick you up at seven?"

"Let's meet at Southside in Old Town, six-thirty. We'll come back to my place afterward ... for dessert." I licked my lips.

"Can't wait," he said matter-of-factly. "It's after seven. Don't you need to get a shower?"

"Crap!" I launched off the couch, dropping the phone in the process. "I've got an eight-thirty breakfast on the Hill. See you tonight," I hollered.

His sexy laughter was the last thing I heard before hanging up.

Luckily, I'd brought home a pile of dry cleaning yesterday, which gave me abundant fresh-pressed clothes to choose from, so I left the condo with plenty of time to get to my meeting. In the car, I phoned the Williamsburg police station and requested a welfare check for Aunt Vera. They took all my information, Aunt Vera's information, and said they'd be in touch.

Later that morning, as I was driving away from Capitol Hill back to the office, a lady by the name of Madge contacted me. "Our officers obtained entry with the landlord and did not find your aunt in residence. They checked the parking area and did not find her vehicle on the premises."

"I see. Thank you, Madge. I appreciate it."

"No problem." She hung up, and I debated whether to contact Mom.

I decided to wait until lunch as we'd originally agreed. Maybe Aunt Vera would respond to my email before then.

Chapter Three

I walked through the front door of Southside 815 in Old Town Alexandria and breathed in the scent of comfort food. The restaurant specialized in Southern cuisine that included homemade buttermilk biscuits, barbecue, fish, shrimp, and a variety of fried items from chicken to green tomatoes.

Rick stood at the bar with a half-empty glass of beer in front of him. He wore a pair of black jeans, a French-blue button-down shirt, and a black leather jacket. His hair was close-cropped with an edging of gray at his temples, which complemented his unusual silvery eyes. He stood a little over six-one, which I enjoyed because, at five-nine, I could still wear high heels and not dwarf him.

He grinned.

Effortlessly, I slid into his embrace, breathing in the woodsy scent of his aftershave. His lips covered mine, and for a moment, I forgot we were in public. I plastered myself against him, circled my arms around his neck, and ran my fingers along the soft roots of his hairline. A catcall pulled me to reality, and I stepped back.

"Shall we skip dinner and head straight home for dessert?" he asked with an elevated brow.

While considering his suggestion, my stomach rumbled, and I thought better of it. "No. I haven't eaten since breakfast. If I don't fill the belly soon, the mean hungries will set in."

"Ah, got it. They aren't too busy. We should be able to get a table." Rick tossed a twenty on the bar, grabbed his drink, and escorted me to the hostess station.

She seated us immediately at a quiet table in the front window. We ordered drinks and a full meal as soon as our waiter arrived.

Then Rick placed his hands on the table. "Tell me about it."

I slouched in my chair and sighed. "They did a welfare check." My mouth twisted. "No luck. The house seems to be in a normal state, and her car wasn't in the driveway."

"No signs of a struggle?"

"Nope." I shook my head. "Nothing. All was normal. I spoke to Mom at lunch. I've got a nine o'clock meeting, and then I'm going to pack up and leave."

His lips turned down, and a crease between his brows formed as I delivered the news. "Where do you think she is?"

"I've no clue," I snapped.

Rick sipped his beer.

Realizing the situation was making me a tad edgy, I continued in a softer tone, "I know where she keeps the extra key, so I can get into her house. If I can find her computer, or a calendar, or-or something that would give me an idea of where she might be…"

He reached over, taking my cold fingers into his warm hands. I hadn't realized I'd been wringing them. "I'm sure there's a simple explanation. Perhaps she took an unexpected vacation and didn't have time to tell anyone."

"But the message she wrote to her boss…"

His brow winged up. "Maybe she figured her boss would be more understanding if she had an emergency rather than a chance at a quick trip to the beach?"

I nodded at his logic. Aunt Vera was no saint. She had a mischievous streak, which I absolutely loved, especially when we were kids. I remember my mother dropping the three of us off for a weekend at her house and distinctly asking Vera not to feed us a bunch of junk for the entire weekend. Vera, who was never able to have children of her own, spent the weekend spoiling the lot of us with homemade chocolate chip cookies, sundaes, and a trip to the candy shop.

"Perhaps you're right," I mused. "I suppose we've all exaggerated a cold or taken a 'well day.' Maybe an offer came up, and she couldn't refuse. I simply can't understand why she hasn't phoned or texted any of us back."

"Broken phone?" he suggested.

I chewed my lips. "Maybe."

Our drinks and appetizer arrived. Initially, I'd waved away the waiter's offer of an appetizer; however, my boyfriend realized I needed to eat sooner rather than later and ordered my favorite—spinach artichoke dip. Rick was a very smart man. I dove in like a shark going after a floundering baby seal. The poor fellow didn't get more than two or three bites. I scarfed it down, scraping the little crock with the last bit of French bread.

"Feeling better now?" My tablemate indicated the clean plate.

"Much. Thanks for getting an appetizer. I was about ready to start gnawing this cloth napkin."

He grinned and said with a touch of smugness, "Somehow, I had a feeling it might help."

I patted my stomach. "Not sure how much dinner I'll be able to eat."

"You can take it home."

I gazed at him with lowered lids and, leaning forward, said in sultry tones, "Don't worry, I'll be sure to save room for dessert."

Chapter Four

Friday

The following morning, Rick loaded the small suitcase I'd packed the night before into my red Jeep Wrangler. "Call me when you get there. Sorry I can't come with you today, but I'll be down tomorrow morning."

"Oh, I don't want to be a bother. I'm sure—"

Rick put a finger over my lips, silencing me. "You're not a bother. I'll be down tomorrow morning. Nod if you understand."

I nodded.

He gave me a toe-curling kiss, handed me into the Jeep, and sent me on my way.

That kiss scrambled my brain. I had no memory of driving to the office.

Shaking myself out of an autopilot stupor, I realized I'd been sitting in my parking space staring at the brick building in front of me. "Oh, he's good."

My morning meeting ended just before eleven. I rolled out of the city and got on I-95. Per usual, I hit on-and-off traffic all the way south to Fredericksburg. Once I cleared the Fredericksburg limits, it was smooth sailing. Around one-thirty, I motored off the highway at the Williamsburg exit and headed to Vera's place.

I always enjoyed visiting and learning about the rich history of Colonial Williamsburg. In the 1700s, Williamsburg was a thriving capital city, and, until 1780, the seat of government for Virginia—the most populated and influential American colony.

The Founding Fathers of the nation met in a local tavern and planted the seeds that grew into the first Continental Congress, which led to the Revolution, and eventually a new nation. Washington, Jefferson, Madison, Franklin spent their days at the Raleigh Tavern discussing freedom from the Crown. After Richmond became the state capital, the politicians left, and Williamsburg became a sleepy town, eventually falling into disrepair.

In 1926, John D. Rockefeller took an interest in reviving the historical city, purchased the land surrounding Duke of Gloucester Street, and set up the Colonial Williamsburg Foundation. Through research and archeological digs, the organization discovered the original foundations that lined Duke of Gloucester Street from the Capitol building down to Merchants Square. In between, you'll find historically accurate, reconstructed taverns and trade shops, along with the courthouse and the Royal Governor's Palace. If you attended a Virginia public school, you likely took a field trip to Williamsburg.

My aunt lived in a reconstructed house on Waller Street near the Capitol building and Christiana Campbell's Tavern. Many of the restored homes that aren't open to the public can be rented by people who work for Colonial Williamsburg—or, as the locals call it, just plain CW.

Her home was a simple Dijon mustard-colored box with maroon shutters and a white picket fence surrounding the dwelling. It had a small covered front porch and an old-fashioned sign with a bell painted on it. A gravel lot led to Aunt Vera's miniature but charming backyard. The gate to the parking pad was closed, and I got out to open it. A small, tasteful, black-and-white sign read, PRIVATE PARKING FOR RESIDENTS ONLY. This was an important sign to have, as parking could be scarce around CW, and, without it, an ignorant tourist might inadvertently take one of the spaces.

Even though I'd expected it, disappointment still flooded my system when I pulled into the empty lot. No sign of Aunt Vera's car. Hopping out, I closed the gate, located the extra key in the fake rock, and opened the front door. The house smelled stale but not overly unpleasant.

I heard a gentle meow from behind me. "Nightshade?"

Aunt Vera's black cat dropped the remnants of a bird on the porch, strolled between my legs, glanced around, and darted to the back of the house. I followed at my leisure, leaving my purse next to a pile of mail on the narrow foyer table.

In the kitchen, both of Nightshade's bowls were empty of water and kibble. The niggling concern that had been gnawing at my subconscious on the drive down turned into full-blown alarm. Even though I was certain Nightshade was well able to take care of himself, as witnessed by the charming delicacy he left on the porch, I couldn't imagine my Aunt Vera leaving her favorite pet without making arrangements for him.

I filled one bowl with water and found a can of cat food in the pantry. By the time I'd spooned the tuna into the second bowl, Nightshade had lapped up all the water. I refilled the vessel and left the cat to his meal.

Not much had changed since I'd been there over the summer. Aunt Vera's home was filled with antique furnishings and simple colonial interior design, in keeping with the time period of the community. However, modern conveniences such as new appliances in the kitchen, a fully renovated bathroom, and televisions intermingled with the past.

The main level consisted of four rooms and a half bath. Windows flanked the front door on the first level. The pair of windows on the left belonged to the parlor, which Vera used as her main living room. The two windows on the right housed a dining room with a fireplace and a mahogany table that sat eight comfortably. A wrought iron and crystal chandelier hung from the coffered ceiling. The dining room led into a good-sized kitchen at the back of the house. A well-worn farmhouse table dominated the center of the room.

I ran my hand along the scarred pine. Many wonderful memories sitting around that table were stored in the files of my brain. The most recent one took place after Aunt Vera's birthday luncheon. That evening, as Dad snoozed in front of the television, Jillian, Vera, Mom, and I sat around it consuming wine—three bottles—reminiscing about the past and getting unequivocally snookered. We laughed so hard, Jillian fell out of her chair.

A miniscule half-bath was added under the stairs sometime in the 90s. Aunt Vera recently had it painted a butter yellow and the lower beadboard a deep navy. I utilized the facilities before continuing my inspection of the home.

The doorway at the back of the parlor led into a narrow sitting room Vera used as her home office. Her laptop computer, which normally sat on the delicate Louis XV writing desk, was absent. The computer and phone chargers snaked across the dark wood, empty of their equipment.

A movement in my periphery startled me. Gulping in a breath, I swung around and placed a hand to my chest. Nightshade sat still as a statue in the doorway to the hall and, with ears cocked, watched one of the two toile-covered armchairs flanking the window.

"Jeez, Nightshade, how long have you been sitting there? Hm? Did you finish your tuna?"

The cat didn't deign to acknowledge my volley. His tail twitched, but that green cat stare didn't move. Goosebumps sprang to life along my arms, and a tingle slithered up my spine.

"You know, I'd never say this in front of Aunt Vera, but you're a weird cat."

This wasn't the first time I'd walked into one of the rooms to find Nightshade staring fixedly at nothing. I'd always thought the cat was on the hunt, waiting for a mouse or a spider to crawl out from under the furniture. About two years ago, I mentioned it to Aunt Vera.

She'd told me, "Nightshade likes to keep an eye on the ghost."

I suppose I should mention, my Aunt Vera believed the house was haunted by a Union soldier named Lieutenant Harold Cabway. She explained, a Union Army garrison occupied the town, and Lieutenant Cabway was billeted in her home. Supposedly, the officer was reprimanding a group of drunken soldiers who'd been harassing some townswomen, when one of the brash soldiers hauled off and shot him in the chest. Cabway was taken to a doctor, but the poor man never recovered from his wounds. Aunt Vera believed his ghost returned to her house. She said he'd been known to help her find lost items.

In all the times I'd visited, I'd never witnessed the ghost, only Nightshade's odd behavior.

I don't want to give the wrong impression—Aunt Vera was quite normal. She wasn't the family's kooky aunt. This ghost business was really her only oddity. Mom believed it made Aunt Vera more colorful in her community of living history.

Who am I to judge?

There are plenty of ghost tours to choose from when visiting Williamsburg. I'd even enjoyed taking one myself. Aunt Vera had been living here for over a dozen years; maybe she invented a spirit to keep her company or give the locals something to talk about.

I sniffed. *What is that? Patchouli and clove?*

It reminded me of the short period of time when my father took up pipe smoking. I snuffled my way around the room, but the smell disappeared as quickly as it arrived.

Nightshade rose, stretched, and sauntered past, brushing

against my leg as he went into the parlor.

I shivered, rubbed my arms, and murmured, "Damn cat."

The upstairs consisted of two large bedrooms and two bathrooms. They were painted in colonial colors. The master was a pale pink, and the guest room a bright color called Prussian blue. Both bathrooms were rather small and almost identical with stall showers, toilets, and single sinks. The plumbing rattled when the toilets flushed.

The guest room contained a pair of simple Shaker-style twin beds, each with a trundle pullout beneath. My aunt specifically set up the sleeping quarters to house our family. When we'd visit, Aunt Vera would sleep in one of the twin beds, sharing the room with the kids, giving my parents her queen-sized bed. Every time we came to visit as a family, my dad would offer to get a hotel, but Aunt Vera wouldn't hear of it—perhaps because she couldn't have children of her own. For the holidays, my aunt simply loved filling her house with our noisy family. The room didn't look as though it'd been touched since our last visit.

Aunt Vera's bedroom held a carved walnut four-poster bed, a high boy, and a dressing table with mirror. A seating area of wingback chairs and a drum table sat in front of the windows. A faint whiff of her Tea Rose perfume sailed past my senses. I trolled through the chamber, searching for something that would provide me with a clue of her whereabouts. Occasionally, she'd bring her laptop or phone upstairs. No sign of either could be found. The only technology was her Kindle sitting on the bedside table.

I picked it up and swiped. Nothing.

The battery was dead. I plugged in the charger and prowled the rest of the room. Her shoes tidily lined the closet floor, and her clothes hung neatly in two rows. A set of suitcases rested on the top shelf.

Except for the fact that her bed was unmade, I found nothing remarkable in the room. Aunt Vera was a bit of a stickler when it came to making her bed in the morning.

She once said, "Karina, if you want to start the day right, be sure to make your bed. If you achieve nothing throughout the day, at least you will come home to that single accomplishment."

For the most part, I'd tried to live by Aunt Vera's tenet, except when I was running late and short on coffee. Then it was, *to hell with the bed and hope for the best.*

I didn't know what I'd been expecting. A note left on the kitchen table explaining her absence? A big calendar on the refrigerator with days marked *Vegas Trip?* An appointment book?

Besides, those ideas were silly. I knew Aunt Vera kept track of her appointments using a calendar app on her phone. Out of curiosity, I pulled my cell from my back pocket, dialed Vera's number, and cocked an ear as I walked around the house in hopes of hearing the ringtone she used—her favorite Beatles song, "A Hard Day's Night."

Alas. Silence.

I unloaded my bag from the car and dropped it on one of the guest room beds. On my way back down the stairs, Rick texted,

>*Have you arrived?*

I responded,

>*Yes. Safe and sound. The house looks normal, no sign of Vera. No foul play. She left the cat to fend for itself, which is out of character. I've got nothing. My next step is to visit work and speak to her boss.*

He replied,

>*In meetings the rest of the afternoon. Keep me updated. Will talk tonight.* ♥

You could have knocked me over with a feather. I plopped down on the bottom stair and gaped at the heart on Rick's final text. Richard Donovan did not *do* emojis. I used emojis all the time—hearts, smiley faces, the SMH girl. However, Rick wasn't a big talker; it was occasionally a strike point in our relationship. He said what he meant without mincing words ... or he kept his mouth shut.

To tell the truth, we'd never said the L-word to each other. Yup, we'd been dating for months, called each other boyfriend and girlfriend, but neither one of us seemed to have the nerve to tell the other, "I love you." I imagined this was due to some deep-seated fear of commitment on his part. For my part, I wanted to wait until he was comfortable with the idea of saying the L-word. I knew *I* loved him. I was *fairly* certain *he* loved me. Pathetic, right?

My eyes narrowed at that heart emoji, and the screen went black from inactivity. Sighing, I stuck it in my back pocket. A problem to be solved at another time.

Chapter Five

I could either walk or drive over to Aunt Vera's workplace, the Colonial Williamsburg Museum of Arts and Antiquities. The museum was on the opposite end of Colonial Williamsburg from my aunt's home, and I knew they had parking at the museum. It would be quicker than walking.

The parking lot was almost full, but I found a space at the back of the lot. Once inside, I queued up behind half a dozen patrons to wait my turn. A family of four moved on, and I approached a staff member with short, perfectly coiffed white hair and bright blue eyes.

"Hello," she smiled at me, "how can I help you? I'm afraid we've sold out of tickets for the program at the Hennage Auditorium today, if that's what you've come for."

"Hi—" I read her nametag, "—Linda. My name is Karina Cardinal. I was wondering if I could speak with the Director of Conservators; I think his name is … Hedges, Hodges?" I'd met Vera's boss once, and my mind floundered trying to recall his last name.

"You mean Mr. Hedgewell?" Linda helpfully filled in the blank.

"Yes, Mr. Hedgewell, of course."

"Let me see if he's in the building." She picked up the phone and dialed. A moment later, she hung up. "He's not answering his phone. I'll check with Jeanine." Linda dialed another number. "Hi, Jeanine, I've got a lady here—her name is Karina Cardinal— to see Mr. Hedgewell." Linda covered the speaker with her hand.

"Jeanine's going to try to locate him."

I nodded, glancing at the line behind me. Luckily, there was another staff member working at the desk along with Linda. He moved the line along at a relatively quick pace.

"You're sure … Yes, I'll tell her." Linda hung up. "I'm afraid Mr. Hedgewell isn't in the building. Jeanine checked the Bruton Heights building too." Her mouth twisted. "But she couldn't locate him there either."

"I see. Can I get a number for him? Maybe leave a voicemail?"

Her gaze darted about for a moment in thought, and she finally offered up, "I can give you his email address."

"Great. Thanks."

Linda took one of the brochures and wrote down his email address. "Here you go. Is there anything else I can help you with?"

"You mentioned a Bruton Heights building. What's that? Perhaps I could go over there and speak with someone."

"The museum's satellite building. Storage for the pieces that aren't on display. It has labs for the conservators. Most of the museum's staff offices are located there." Linda frowned and shook her head. "I'm afraid it's a secure building and off-limits to tourists." She added as an afterthought, "The Foundation library is also located there."

"I didn't realize the Foundation had a library."

"Oh yes. It's one of the most extensive libraries specializing in the political and economic life of the thirteen original colonies and the colonial era," she stated proudly, her bright blue eyes flashing at me.

"I see. Is it open to the public?"

"Yes, it is. However, you'll need to make an appointment if you want to view any of the special collection."

I opened the map app on my phone. "And it's called Bruton Heights?"

"It's a small complex." Linda handily pulled out a paper map and drew directions for me, circling a building within a group of three.

"Thank you." I left with my analog map. It took five minutes to get over to the Bruton Heights complex.

All the buildings were brick; one looked quite a bit older than the rest, and I guessed it was the old high school that Colonial Williamsburg had purchased to house more staff offices. The building Linda directed me to had a sign out front that read, *John D. Rockefeller, Jr. Library*. The windows were tall and broad, allowing light to flood the interior. A modern metal roof arched over the steps and entryway. The entire building seemed to say "Welcome."

I turned away from the library to scrutinize its blocky neighbor. The Bruton Heights storage facility looked newer and much more secure. The windows were smaller and thick. I didn't know if they were bulletproof, but they looked similar to some of the blast-proof windows on federal buildings in D.C. The glass doors were locked, and there was a key card swiper to the left. I walked all the way around the storage facility and spotted cameras at every entrance. I was familiar with security measures in DC, and this structure all but screamed "Go away."

Back at the front door, I spotted a small doorbell and was about to ring, when a tall, thin woman with short brown hair and glasses strode up the walkway, her eyes glued to her phone.

"Excuse me."

Startled, she glanced up, adjusting her glasses. "Hello. If you're looking for the library, it's that building next door." She pointed and explained, "This is an office building. Staff only, unless you have an appointment."

"Thank you. Actually, I'm looking for Vera Wagner."

"Oh, I'm sorry, Vera's out of the office this week."

I blinked. "She's out?"

"Yes, she sent an email. Had to leave unexpectedly." The woman gave a half-shrug. "Something about a sick relative."

"Oh, I see. Do you work with Vera?"

"Mm-hm. I'm one of the museum's curators. I worked to acquire pieces for the ceramics collection that Vera oversees." She must have realized she was talking to a stranger, because she frowned and asked, "Who are you?"

"I'm Vera's niece, Karina Cardinal."

Her face cleared. "Felicity Benson."

We shook hands.

"I've heard Vera mention you. You live in DC. Right?"

I murmured an assent.

"She said you were pivotal in solving some sort of baseball-money-laundering crime?"

Ah, my last escapade, which almost got me shot, and scared the living hell out of Rick. I swished my hand. "It was nothing. Aunt Vera exaggerates. What day did Vera send the out-of-office email?"

"Hm." Felicity tapped her chin in thought. "Monday? No, she was here on Monday, because we had lunch together. Must have been Tuesday morning. Was she expecting you?"

"Oh, no. My trip was spur of the moment. I … uh … haven't been able to contact her. I was wondering if everything has been okay … at work."

"Oh yes. About two months ago, Vera was assigned to work on the Anne Hutchinson exhibit the museum is unveiling in December. Do you know Anne Hutchinson?"

I shook my head. "Never heard of her."

"She was a feminist from colonial times. One of the first this country has seen. In the 1630s, Anne demanded equal rights for women."

"Interesting. How did that work out for her?"

Felicity's features turned down. "Not well. She was

banished."

While these facts were interesting, they didn't help my mission. "Have there been any problems?" I prodded.

"No, nothing I can think—" her lips twisted, "—actually, now that you mention it, we were talking a few weeks ago about a piece that she found had been removed from the ceramics exhibit. She'd become quite agitated about it. Because she'd been so focused on the Anne Hutchinson exhibit, she hadn't noticed the piece go missing."

"Did she find the piece?"

"I helped her track it down. It had been logged as being out for repairs."

"Don't you clean and repair everything here?" I waved at the imposing building.

"For the most part, yes." Her head bobbed. "Our conservators are trained to handle that sort of thing. Occasionally, a piece needs a specialist. This was a fifteenth-century piece of pottery that needed paint and glaze work repaired."

I fidgeted with my earring. "Why didn't my aunt know about the repairs? Shouldn't she have been the one to send it out?"

"Yes and no. Norman, her boss, apparently found the damage and had it sent out. It's in his purview to do so." Felicity's gaze darted around, and she leaned in, replying sotto voce, "Between you and me, he overstepped. He should have told Vera about the damage and had her take responsibility. I could tell Vera was not best pleased that he'd gone around her. She's very good at her job, and, frankly, has more experience."

"Oh, I see." Having a small contretemps with her boss might have made for some juicy office gossip, but it didn't get me any closer to finding my aunt, or the reason she'd gone missing in the first place. "I can't figure out why she's not answering her phone."

"You're right, that is odd. Hm. If she touches base, I'll be sure to let her know you're in town."

"Here's my card. Please give me a call if you think of anything or happen to hear from her."

I watched her swipe her keycard and enter the building. Ruminating on my options, I realized, to get any further locating Aunt Vera, I'd need police involvement.

I returned to Aunt Vera's house and rang the police non-emergency number to report a missing person. The woman who answered my call took my information and said an officer would be over shortly.

In the meantime, I phoned Rick.

"Good timing. I just got out of a client meeting. How are things going down there?" he asked.

"Weird." I told him about the cat being left alone, the unmade bed, and her email to the staff.

"Did she stop the mail?"

An excellent question, which I'd overlooked. "As a matter of fact, she did not." I walked to the foyer and found today's mail scattered across the front hall. After picking it up, I placed it on the growing pile on the foyer table. My hands froze in the process, and I sucked in a breath. "Her mail."

"What about it?"

"She's got a mail slot in the front door. Someone has placed it on the foyer table."

"Likely the police or her landlord, when they performed the welfare check," Rick stated matter-of-factly.

"Yes, of course." I swallowed, and my heart slowed to normal. "Because she's got a mail slot, she doesn't really need to stop her mail." A thought occurred to me. "Uh-oh."

"What, uh-oh?"

"*I* forgot to have my mail stopped."

"It's only two days. It shouldn't be a problem," he said dismissively.

I played with my earring. "Well, normally, that would be true…"

I was terrible about getting the mail daily. I figured I was good if I checked it at least three times a week. Wandering into the parlor, I scrunched my eyes shut and racked my brain.

Today was Friday. When was the last time I stopped by the mail room? Mrs. Thundermuffin came in with her cat. She told me about his ear infection; that was…

The realization came to me, and my eyes popped open.

"Karina, you still there?"

"I, uh, haven't checked my mail since Tuesday."

Silence.

I envisioned Rick rubbing his temples and shaking his head. "Do you need me to go over and clean out your mail?"

"Mrs. Thundermuffin has a key to the box; we made duplicates and exchanged them this summer for just such occasions. I'll call and ask her to pick it up for me. But…"

"Yes?"

"If you're still planning to come down tomorrow—"

Nightshade sauntered in and leaned against my leg with a soft meow.

"I am."

I bent over to stroke the cat. "Could you possibly swing by to pick up the mail from Mrs. T, and bring it down with you? There should be a credit card bill in there that I need to pay."

"No problem."

"Thanks. You're the best." A heavy knock at the door startled me. I jerked upright.

The cat hissed and darted out of the room.

"The cops are here. I'll call you back."

The officer at the door was my height, stocky, with short dark hair. The card he handed me read *Louis Ortega*. "I understand you'd like to report a missing person."

I invited him into the living room, where he took my statement for the report. After giving a description of my aunt, her car, and license plate—RTIFACT—I told him what prompted our concerns.

"Is there anything else you can provide?

Though I didn't want to, I told him about the out-of-office email and the text to her boss.

At the end of my explanation, the officer eyed me with skepticism.

"You don't believe me," I declared.

He rubbed the back of his neck. "It's not that I don't believe you, but your aunt did say she was going out of town. And her car is not here. It does indicate that she's gone somewhere ... under her own steam."

"But she never told her family that she was going out of town."

"Does she normally?"

"Well ... yes ... um, sure." I played with my earring.

He glanced up from his little notepad; a dubious brow rose. "You're saying she's never gone away without telling anyone."

"Well ... once."

The last time Vera disappeared for a week without telling anyone, she returned with Good Time Randy as her new husband and a photo album full of their cheesy Vegas wedding—Vera in a red dress carrying a cheap bouquet of white silk flowers, boozy pictures of them living it up in a lavish hotel room dominated by an enormous champagne glass hot tub, and tons of photos of them gambling at assorted casino games.

The officer scribbled on his notepad.

"But that was more than fifteen years ago," I said in a rush.

"Sure, sure." He nodded as if placating me. "You said your aunt is sixty-two. Does she show any signs of dementia? Confusion?"

"No." I bristled, insulted he'd think my aunt had a loose screw. "Aunt Vera's still got it going on upstairs. She works a full-time job, for crying out loud."

He held up a palm. "I only ask because sometimes elderly people with dementia can wander off."

Sighing, I put away my claws and cocked my head. "That's not my aunt. Would you take this more seriously if she *did* have dementia?"

"Let me assure you, I *am* taking your concerns seriously."

"So, what will the police do about it?" I crossed my arms. "Will a detective be assigned to the case?"

"We'll post a BOLO with her description and one for her car." He closed the notebook and tucked it into his front pocket. "A detective will get in touch with you tomorrow morning."

"Thank you." We rose, and I escorted him to the door.

"You have my card. Be sure to call if you think of anything new, or if your aunt turns up."

Chapter Six

Jillian texted during my meeting with the police.

What's going on with Aunt Vera. Is she okay?

A headache had wrapped itself around the back of my head. I realized it was quarter to seven. I hadn't eaten lunch. Hunger and thirst gnawed at my empty stomach. I hit the call button on Jilly's text and headed into the kitchen to see what Aunt Vera had on hand.

"Hey, Rina. What's going on? Is Aunt Vera okay?"

"Aunt Vera is missing." I put her on speakerphone, stuck my head in the fridge, and checked the date on the milk. It was half full, and the expiration date was two weeks away. Luckily, Aunt Vera insisted on purchasing organic. "Why does organic milk last longer than regular?"

"What? Did you say something? Rina! Hello?"

"Sorry, yes. I'm starving and scrounging for food. Aha! Found a new box of cereal in the pantry." I pulled a bowl from the cabinet. With arms full of milk, cereal, a bowl, a bottle of water, and the phone, I lowered everything onto the table.

"Enough with the food. What the hell is going on?"

"Aunt Vera's car is gone, and she sent round an email to her office mates stating the same thing she'd texted her boss. She's gone out of town to take care of her sick niece." I settled into a chair and opened the cereal box.

"Does she have any other nieces besides us?"

"Not that I know of."

"So, you're saying she's playing hooky from work and skipped town? Do you think this is another Randy incident?"

"Lord, I hope not, but I don't know." I opened the water and glugged half of it before continuing, "She left the cat to his own devices."

"Nightshade? She just left Nightshade. That's not like her."

"Exactly." A thought occurred to me, and I stopped mid-drink. "Wait a minute."

"What?"

"I think…" I put the water down, grabbed the phone, and hurried up the stairs, taking them two at a time.

"What? What are you doing?"

"Hold on a minute." Turning left at the top of the stairs, I burst into Vera's room so hard, the door slammed against the wall. I headed straight for the closet.

"RINA! WHAT?" Jillian screeched.

I counted and counted again. "You know that pink-flowered, three-piece Betsey Johnson luggage she always uses?"

"Yes."

"It's all here. In her closet."

Jillian sucked wind. "She always travels with that luggage. And all the pieces are there? You're sure?"

"I'm sure." I pulled down the mid-sized suitcase and opened it up. Out fell the pink striped backpack she would use as a carry-on.

"Ugh, I've got a bad feeling in the pit of my stomach," she mumbled.

"Yeah, me too." Confused, I wandered out of the closet and plopped down on one of the chairs by the window. "The worst part is, I've no idea where to start. I thought about driving aimlessly around the area searching for her car. But it's dark now, and it feels like an exercise in futility."

"You're right, it is. Tell you what, I'll drive down tomorrow—"

"No need." I rubbed my forehead. "Rick is coming. I'm sure

he'll have formed some sort of plan."

She made a little grunting noise. "You always do this."

"Do what?"

"Try to fix everything on your own," she huffed. "You take the world on your shoulders, Rina. And you don't know when to ask for help."

"I know how to ask for help." Okay, there might have been a bit of whine in that rebuke. "I've already called the police, and, as I said, Rick is coming. He's very capable, you know."

"Oh, I know how capable your Batman is! But it doesn't matter; I'm coming!" Jillian barked at me.

"Okay, okay," I surrendered. "No need to get squiffy about it."

"Well … she's my aunt too, after all."

"Yes, I know." I breathed—in and out. Almost two years ago, Jillian was kidnapped by some human traffickers. Since then, I'd become exceedingly protective of her and did my best to keep her out of anything that held a whiff of uncertainty. However, I'd kind of reached an impasse, and having an extra hand would be useful.

"By all means, come. Maybe we can aimlessly drive around during the daylight searching for her car together," I quipped.

"Hmph. I'll text when I'm on the way. Stay safe."

"See you tomorrow, Sis."

Nightshade leapt onto Vera's unmade bed, curled up on her pillow, and stared at me with those unblinking eyes, as if to ask, "Where is she?"

"I'm working on it, buddy."

His tail flicked in response. The clock on the bedside table read 6:57.

"Crap!" I smacked my forehead. "I forgot to cancel dinner with Mike!"

Mike answered on the second ring. "Hi, K.C., what's up?"

"Mike, I am *sooooo* sorry. I know this is completely last minute, but I've got to cancel dinner." I winced.

"Yeah, I know," Mike replied with nonchalance. "Rick contacted me this morning."

"He did?" *What a good guy.*

"Said you had to go down to visit your aunt in Williamsburg."

"Um, yes, that's right." My head bobbed.

"Is she okay?"

I had a choice to make. I could either come clean with my ex, who happened to work for the FBI, or I could just shut up about it. On one hand, FBI help might come in handy. On the other, Mike's past experiences with my, let's call them ... adventures, carried with them heavy lectures, which I could do without.

"She's, um, kind of missing."

"What do you mean, missing?"

"Apparently, she's ... gone on a trip. Only she didn't inform the family, and you know my mother. She worries. Aunt Vera's probably laughing it up in Atlantic City, or Bali, or something. It's no big deal," I hedged.

"Well," Mike paused before continuing, "let me know if there is anything I can do to help."

"I'm sure it's nothing." I fiddled with my earring. "Don't worry. Say hello to Min for me. And we'll reschedule as soon as I return to DC."

"You take care." He hung up.

I ambled downstairs to continue foraging through the kitchen. On my way, I rang Mrs. Thundermuffin.

"Eccentric" would be the word that came to mind when I thought of my neighbor. She was somewhere in her seventies, and her normal hair color would be white, but she tended to dye it many colors of the rainbow. When I ran into her on Tuesday, it was burnt umber— "for the season," she'd said. Mrs. T wore bright, flowing outfits with fluffy, feathered mules, and walked her cat on a leash. As a retired CIA officer, she'd spent her life blending into the wallpaper. Retirement freed her from that cocoon and released her inner butterfly.

I kind of wanted to be like Mrs. T when I grew up.

Her bell-like voice answered, "Hello, Karina, how are you doing?"

"I'm fine, Mrs. T. I was wondering if you could do me a favor. I'm out of town, and I've forgotten to check the mail for a few days. Could you—"

"Get it for you?" she finished my sentence.

"If it's not too much trouble." I stuffed my hand in the box and pulled out a handful of cereal.

"No trouble a'tall. I'm about to take Mr. Tibbs for his evening walk. The ear infection has cleared, by the way. I'll get your mail on my way back up."

"S'mgoodere." The cereal got caught, and I gulped some of the water to clear it.

"I beg your pardon?"

Clearing my throat, I tried again, "It's good to hear Mr. Tibbs is better. Thanks for getting the mail. My boyfriend will be joining me, and I'd appreciate it if you could give the mail to him, so he can bring it down."

"The big blond fellow?"

"Uh, no, that's Joshua. He's not my boyfriend. Rick is a little leaner, looks Marine-ish, not quite so … imposing."

"Ah, the handsome gentleman with the brooding eyes and graying temples?"

I grinned at her description. "That's him."

"Yes, I remember. He's fine, but I'm partial to the blond. I've always had a thing for the big football type."

"Mrs. Thundermuffin! I thought you and Mr. Albert were going steady."

"Karina," she said in a serious voice, "I may be old, but I've got eyes. And that blond is a hunka-handsome all over. If I was twenty years younger…"

"Um…" Since Josh was somewhere in his thirties, I would think Mrs. T meant thirty years younger. On the other hand, she might have been quite the cougar back in the day. Who was I to deny Mrs. T her fantasies? "I'm sure if you were twenty years younger, Joshua would trot you out on his arm all day long."

"Tsk. Karina, you're more of a flatterer than the men. I look forward to seeing Richard tomorrow, and I promise not to steal him away from you."

I held in a snort. "I appreciate that."

"Have him text me, and we'll connect."

"Thanks for doing me a solid, Mrs. T. We'll have lunch soon."

I'd just shoveled another handful of cereal into my cakehole with animalistic furor when someone knocked on the door.

"Now what?!" Only it came out more like *mrowat,* and some Frosted Flakes may have shot out of my mouth.

As I opened the door, Nightshade strut past me to sit next to the dead bird I had yet to dispose of. He meowed at the man standing on the porch.

I swallowed the last of the cereal and opened my mouth to explain to the tourist that this was a private home, when he addressed the cat, "That's a fine catch, Nightshade." His long fingers stroked the cat, who responded with a purr before ambling down the steps.

The man straightened with a smile. He had black hair generously interspersed with gray, walnut skin, and an orange zip-up sweater stretched over a rounded potbelly. My presence had him stepping back and his dark eyes widening in surprise. "Why, hullo. Is, er, Vera available?"

"Who are you?"

"Vikram Gupta." He adjusted his glasses. "And you are…"

"Karina Cardinal. Vera's niece."

"Ah, yes, she speaks of your family. I did not realize you were in town," he intoned with a high-brow British accent. "That would explain it."

"Explain what?"

"Why Vera didn't arrive for dinner."

"I'm sorry." I blinked. "Aunt Vera had dinner plans with you? Tonight?"

"Ah, yes. We have a standing dinner Friday night at seven. Unless one of us has other plans, that is. Tonight, we were supposed to dine at my place. When Vera didn't show up, or answer my texts, I became concerned." As he spoke, the delicious aroma of soy sauce, onions, and ginger enveloped us.

I zeroed in on the white-bagged scent-wagon. "Is that Chinese takeout?"

He held the sack aloft. "Indeed, it is. My turn for takeaway. Obviously, Vera has other plans." He started to go.

He is leaving with the Chinese food!

I wasn't sure if it was my brain or stomach that had me jumping forward to grab his elbow. "Whoa! Hold up there, Mr. Gupta."

Uncertainty crossed his features.

"I-I mean, please, come inside. We need to talk." I unloaded the bagged burden from him. "Follow me."

Is this a good idea? This man is a total stranger, and you've just invited him into the house.

My stomach let out a rumble. *Shut-up, head. The cat obviously knows him. And we need sustenance. Besides, he looks like an Indian version of Mr. Rogers.*

The stomach won out over good sense, and Vikram followed me to the back of the house. Arriving in the kitchen, I pulled crockery and silverware from the cabinets.

Vikram glanced at the two place settings and scratched his cheek. "I'm unclear. You said Vera is…"

"Not here," I clarified.

His jaw dropped.

"I'll explain. But if I don't put something in my belly in the next ten minutes, I'm going to start eating the furniture." I gazed at him with wide, desperate eyes.

"Well, we can't have that now." He offered a bemused smile.

I dove into the bag. "Oo, spring rolls. Lovely. And dumplings!"

We spooned the Chinese food onto plates and took seats across from one another.

"Mr. Gupta, you are a life saver." I forked a dumpling and popped it in. "Mm..." My shoulders slumped, and I closed my eyes. "These are the best dumplings I have *ever* eaten."

"You must be hungry."

Over the meal, I explained my concerns about Vera. Why I'd come down to Williamsburg to investigate. Also, about filing the missing person report. "Now you're telling me you've got a regular dinner date that she didn't bother to cancel. Vera would *never* do such a thing. Everything just feels ... off."

"I must agree with your assessment." He wiped his mouth. "Vera is nothing if not considerate. And I can't imagine she'd leave Nightshade."

"The cat is familiar to you. How long have you and Vera been seeing each other?"

He scratched his chin in thought. "Close to two years."

"Two years?" I squeaked. "Why have we never met?"

Vikram shifted and finished chewing the bite in his mouth with deliberation. "Do you know all of Vera's friends?"

My face burned. "Why ... no. I-I apologize if my question seemed impertinent." I'd assumed they were dating. It would be nice for Vera to have a male friend who afforded her companionship.

"Perhaps Vera had her reasons for not telling you," he replied in soft tones.

"Yes, of course. What do you do for a living, Mr. Gupta?" Embarrassment had me asking the question in a rather formal manner.

"I'm a physics professor at the university, and please call me Vikram."

Nodding, I gulped down some water before asking, "And how did you meet Vera?"

"At a party hosted by the university. Through a mutual acquaintance." He wiped his mouth with a paper napkin.

Vikram's answers were straightforward, but I felt as though there was something cagey about his responses. Maybe it was his British upbringing. Or perhaps, I begrudgingly admitted to myself, the sting of being put in my place skewed my judgment.

"How long have you been at William and Mary?"

"Twenty-two years." After removing his glasses, he cleaned them with the tail of his sweater and said in an abrupt manner, "Enough about me. The more I think about this situation with Vera, the more worried I am becoming." He slipped his glasses back on his nose. "Last week, when Vera and I had dinner, I recalled she seemed rather … uptight. Strained. She even snapped at me when I spilled a tad bit of the wine."

I snickered and wisecracked, "Well, Vera does like her wine. Was it a particularly good vintage?"

"It wasn't like that."

Sobered, I asked, "Well, did she tell you what was wrong?"

He shook his head. "She wouldn't say. She apologized and simply told me work was on her mind. Later that night, I found her on the computer reviewing items from the ceramics collection."

"What items?"

His brow furrowed. "Some silver pieces. I don't rightly recall the exact items. She printed several pages and tucked them into a blue file folder."

I didn't recollect seeing a blue file folder in Aunt Vera's office, but I'd been looking for her computer and phone. I hadn't dug into the filing cabinet or desk and made a mental note to search her office thoroughly after Vikram left.

"When was the last time you saw Vera?"

His eyes went to the ceiling. "Let me think … last weekend…on Saturday. That morning we had coffee, then went to the farmers market, and had lunch at the deli."

"Did you two speak on the phone after Saturday?"

"Hm, oh, yes, on Sunday, I phoned to see if she wanted to see the matinee show at the Kimball Theater. She said she was catching up on work and didn't have time."

I chewed my lip in thought. "You weren't the last to see her. One of her office mates told me she was at work on Monday."

"I took an early flight on Tuesday morning, up to Boston for a conference. I returned late Thursday night and taught my Friday classes. Since I hadn't heard any different from Vera, I assumed we were still on for our Friday night dinner."

"You didn't speak to her at all during the week?"

He shook his head. "The conference events kept me busy."

I made an understanding *hm.*

"May I ask, can you provide me the name and contact information for the police officer to whom you spoke? I'd like to add my concerns to yours and be assured they are taking earnest efforts to locate her."

"Sure." *What could it hurt?*

With a shrug, I left the kitchen to retrieve the card Officer Ortega gave me. Returning to the kitchen, I found Vikram drumming his fingers absently on the table. The rhythm stopped, and he held out his hand.

"If you don't mind—" I did not pass along the business card, "—I'd like to keep this. Can you write down the information or take a photo?"

"Of course." He pulled his phone from a pocket and photographed it. "I believe we should exchange mobile numbers, so we can communicate further."

I agreed and rattled off my cell number for him.

Vikram tapped on the screen and wrinkled his nose. "Wait a bit … I think if I press here. Oh. No, that's not it…" he mumbled beneath his breath, scratched his head, and cleared his throat.

Taking pity on him, I held out my hand and asked, "Would you like me to do it?"

"If you wouldn't mind." With a discomfited chuckle, he handed the cell over. "I hate to play into the stereotype of the old man who doesn't know how to use his mobile, but I find the buttons so tiny for my fingers."

"I understand." I gave him a reassuring smile and started tapping away. "I'll put my information in your contacts. And then, I'll text myself. Just like that." A text message dinged on my phone. "There, that ought to do it."

He took the phone back, tucking it into his pants pocket. "Vera and I have mutual friends on the museum's staff. I'll reach out to them and let you know if I discover anything new."

"I appreciate it."

We gathered the dishes, put away the leftovers, and Vikram took his leave. Darkness veiled the night, and cloudy skies danced across the stars and moon. Turning on the porch light, I noticed Nightshade's dead bird. My lip curled in disgust at the poor mangled body.

"Shall I take care of it?" Vikram offered.

"Would you?"

"Vera keeps a dustpan and broom in the front hall closet for just such occasions." Vikram handily found both items, scooped the bird into the dustpan, and trotted around to the back of the house to dispose of the poor creature.

Meanwhile, Nightshade wound between my legs.

"In the future, leave your trophies where you found them," I admonished.

The cat meowed and prowled into the front parlor.

Vikram returned with the broom and empty dustpan, said his goodbyes, and departed.

Once I closed the door behind him, I made a beeline to Vera's office.

Twenty minutes later, I threw up my hands in frustration. I'd come across nothing of value and did not find the blue folder Vikram referenced. Vera's file cabinet seemed to hold only personal materials—bills, bank statements, tax materials, and I stumbled across her divorce papers. The drawers in her desk yielded nothing of interest. No work documents or other notes.

"I give up," I said to the empty room.

Chapter Seven

The vibrato trill of the *Mission Impossible* theme song filled the room, and Rick's photo flashed on my phone screen.

Crap! I was supposed to call him back.

Nightshade, who'd been contentedly curled up next to my leg, leapt to the floor and took up residence in front of the fireplace.

I muted the television and removed the computer from my lap, placing it on the coffee table. "Hello."

"You forgot about me, didn't you?"

I tapped a fist against my forehead. "Ugh. Only for a little while. You won't believe the night I've had. Jilly called for an update. I forgot to call Mike but found out you did it for me. Thanks, by the way. Vikram showed up, and we had dinner. My work email blew up." Sighing, I slouched against the sofa. "I'm sorry."

"Sounds like you've had quite an evening. Who is Vikram?"

"My aunt's ... uh ... man friend? Friend with benefits? I'm not really clear what the relationship status is, but there's definitely a toothbrush and razor for him in the bathroom, and a pair of pajamas in the drawer." After searching the office, I'd prowled around my aunt's bedroom looking for traces of Vikram, and I found them. I wasn't proud of my actions, but in an ongoing attempt to locate her, I'd stand by them. "He seems to be her weekend companion."

"Interesting. What's his name again?"

"Vikram Gupta, he's a physics professor at the college. I looked him up; he seems legit."

"I'll run a quick background check."

"Whatever. He looks like Mr. Rogers. He seems harmless."

"So did Ted Bundy..." He allowed the comment to hang before starting a new line of conversation. "By the way, I spoke with your neighbor. She acquired your mail. I swung by and picked it up about an hour ago."

"Great." I gave Rick the rundown of the evening's activities. "And I was just finishing up the last email when you rang. Anything of interest on your end?"

"I had Angus contact the local hospitals to check for your aunt, or any Jane Does. Nothing came up."

"Uh, thanks, I hadn't thought about checking the hospitals."

"S.O.P."

"What's sop?"

"Standard operating procedure. The police will likely do the same."

"Right-o." I yawned. "What's your plan for tomorrow?"

"I'll be down around eight."

My eyes popped open. "In the morning?"

"That's the plan."

I shouldn't have been surprised. It was nothing for him to get up at five to be on the road by six, whereas I had trouble getting up by seven to get to work by nine.

"Drive safe. See you tomorrow."

"Sleep tight." He hung up.

"Love you," I whispered and tossed the phone aside.

Nightshade sat in front of the empty hearth, his body stiff at attention, those green eyes staring.

"Don't judge me." I slapped the lid to my laptop closed and grumbled, "Dumb cat. What do you know about it anyway?"

The eleven o'clock news came on. I unmuted the television and watched until the first commercial break, when some woman came on selling a drug for psoriasis.

Yawning, I murmured, "Nightshade, I think that does it."

The cat didn't blink an eye but continued gazing at me.

I pressed the off button. The TV went dark. In the reflection of the blackened screen stood the figure of a man. Directly behind me.

"HOLY CRAP-OLY!" I leaped off the couch, over the coffee table, and snatched up one of the heavy brass candlesticks from the fireplace mantel. Wielding my weapon, I whipped around, ready to attack.

The man, for it was definitely a man, wore a pair of blue pants, yellow suspenders, and a collarless white shirt. He held a pipe in his left hand, and a dark patch stained the center of his shirt.

"Who are you?" I shrilled.

My heart pounded so hard, I thought it would come out of my chest. I chucked the candlestick. It went through him, striking the wall behind, crashing to the floor. The specter disappeared before my eyes, fading into nothingness. The scent of patchouli lingered in his wake.

Nightshade's head rotated, and I followed it to the window. An unseen draft rippled the curtains.

I glanced down at the cat. "Is he gone?"

Nightshade lifted a rear leg in the air and took to cleaning his private parts with nonchalance.

"I suppose that's a yes?" Shaking, I lowered myself onto the coffee table and stuck my head between my knees. "Jeezumcrow. Aunt Vera, I will never doubt you again. I need a drink."

The sturdy candlestick left a dent in the wall that I'd need to fix for Aunt Vera, but otherwise sustained no other damage.

Walking into the kitchen, I discovered a cabinet door had been left open. Luckily, it held the liquor, so I didn't have to search for the much-needed liquid anesthesia I desperately required.

Even after two shots of very fine bourbon, it still took a long time for the adrenaline to exit my system. I brought Nightshade up to the bedroom and left the hall light on—not that it mattered; apparently Vera's ghost showed up in the light or darkness.

It was past two when I finally drifted off into a fitful sleep. My dreams were anything but peaceful—most focused on searching for Aunt Vera through creepy forests while she cried out in the distance, "Find me!"

Chapter Eight

Saturday

Sunlight filtered through the slats of the blinds, creating a striped pattern across the patchwork quilt. One beam slashed across my pillow and shone directly in my eyes. "Ugh," I groaned, rolling away from it, and snuggled deeper under the counterpane. All thoughts of additional sleep were dashed when a small body jumped on top of me.

Nightshade walked across my face, plopped his butt on my cheek, and began purring and kneading my head with his tiny paws.

"All right! I'm up!" I grumbled through cat fur.

The clock on my phone read 7:41, and it had a text from Rick.

Got away later than expected. ETA 8:30.

Relieved Rick wouldn't be knocking on the door in the next twenty minutes, I followed the cat down the stairs, in my own lurching way, to search for the black gold called coffee.

The cabinet door was open.

"Again?" I shook my head. "I thought I closed you last night." Perhaps not.

The bourbon rested on the counter with the cap off. Returning it to its rightful place, I shut the cabinet and placed the dirty shot glass in the sink.

Nightshade stood by his bowl and meowed at me.

"Yes, yes, I haven't forgotten about you."

He tucked into the fresh food and water as soon as I placed

the bowls on the floor.

Aunt Vera's coffee maker was a fancy French press style. I preferred machines that spit out the brew in five minutes or less, but beggars can't be choosers. After a few minutes of bumbling around with the kettle and coffee grounds, I turned and smacked my head against the same cabinet door I'd closed a few minutes ago.

"What the hell?" Rubbing my forehead, I shut it with a sharp snap. "Thanks for the thought, but I don't drink this early in the morning, *Lieutenant.*"

I located a blueberry yogurt in the fridge and slurped it down while waiting for my caffeinated lifeblood to steep and the grounds to settle. Finally, it was ready. After gulping down half a cup of Aunt Vera's flavorful hazelnut brew, I began to feel more like myself.

The steam tickled my nose as I sipped. "Mm."

Nightshade licked his chops and stretched, sticking his fanny high into the air, then sauntered out of the kitchen.

"You're welcome!" I called after him.

His tail twitched in acknowledgment.

Sitting at the farmhouse table, I stretched my own legs in front of me, determined to spend the next ten minutes doing nothing but enjoying my java.

A rustle from the other room torpedoed that plan.

"All right, cat, what are you up to now?" I wandered across the hall to investigate and paused in the office doorway, the cup halfway to my mouth.

One of Vera's desk drawers had been pulled open, and papers littered the floor.

The cat sat at attention, his gaze riveted to the black leather desk chair. "What the hell, Nightshade?" I snapped, "Did you do this?"

He didn't deign to answer.

The desk chair slowly rotated 180 degrees. My breath caught, and I stood frozen, unable to move. The hairs on the back of my neck rose.

Patchouli filled the room.

A moment later, Nightshade walked out. His tail gave a swish-swish.

I didn't feel the lieutenant was a malevolent spirit, but clearly he had a mischievous streak.

"So far, I'm not impressed with your ghost, Aunt Vera. He's kind of an a-hole!" I grumbled, snatching up papers and cramming them back into the drawer.

Yesterday, I'd combed through the desk and found it filled with nothing more than unfiled explanation of benefits letters. The hands of the clock pointed to ten after eight by the time I'd put the room in order.

I needed to get dressed.

"I'm going to take a shower now. I'd better not find you in the bathroom, Lieutenant!" I spoke loudly.

In response, Nightshade's meow echoed through the house.

Before getting in the shower, I unlocked the back door, then texted Rick directions for where to park.

Thirty minutes later, with my hair pulled into a ponytail, wearing a pair of jeans, a polo shirt, and a red Washington Nationals sweatshirt, I trooped down to the kitchen to pour myself another cup of caffeine.

"Hello, beautiful."

"Aayeek!" I fumbled with the empty coffee mug, catching it just before it would have hit the tile floor and shattered. "Cripes."

Eyeing me with amusement, Rick sat at the table, a newspaper splayed in front of him, a Starbucks cup at his elbow. "You seem a little on edge."

"I'm fine." I waved away his concern. "Just surprised. I thought the ghost decided to start speaking to me."

He looked decidedly tasty in a pair of jeans, black work boots, and a white button-down with the sleeves rolled up to his elbows. His black leather jacket hung on the back of the chair. I slid into the seat next to him and leaned over for a kiss. The scent of sandalwood filled my olfactory senses.

Yummy.

My lids shuttered as the peck turned into something more. Rick slid his hand behind my neck, deepening the kiss into a sensuous, spine-tingling invasion that ended with his lips nipping across my jawline. I might have been panting as he pulled away.

"I missed you," he whispered, placing his forehead against mine.

"Me too."

Our breaths and heartbeats eased into a normal rhythm.

Rick kissed my nose and sat back. "Tell me about the ghost."

Sighing, I rose and poured the last of the coffee into my mug. I'd need sustenance to handle his teasing. "This house is haunted by a Civil War Union soldier."

Rick surveyed me, his face an indecipherable mask.

I explained Aunt Vera's story and told him about the run-ins from last night and this morning. He said nothing after I finished. His fingers stroked up and down the Starbucks cup.

Finally, I crossed my arms. "Okay, give it to me. You don't believe it. You think the area has gotten into my head. I'm under stress. It's a figment of my imagination," I rattled off the excuses for my mental lapse in one continuous string.

"Actually, I do believe you."

My jaw dropped.

He stared down at the scarred tabletop. "When you're out in the middle of the desert fighting insurgents, and a bullet, which should have gone through your heart, misses you because some unknown force knocks you down ... you rethink preconceived notions." His silvery gaze swooped up, spearing me. "And you begin to believe that maybe … maybe, there are angels looking out for us."

"Whoa," I whispered, "that's …"

"Fantastical?" A brow rose as he sipped.

I shook my head. "Amazing. Give me more."

"All I can tell you is this—one moment I was standing; the next, I was on the ground. The rest of the team had moved into position on a ridge ten yards away. I did not trip. A bullet, directly where I'd been standing a nanosecond before, blew through the Humvee's window." He shrugged. "If you tell me you've seen a ghost, who am I to disagree?"

I blinked, processing his confession. Rick was such a down-to-earth guy. I never would have guessed. I'd expected gentle ribbing from him about the ghost. Not a life-or-death story about angels.

Wow.

Rick's phone binged with a text message and broke the tension. After reading it, he pressed a button and put the phone to his ear. "Talk to me." His brows drew down along with his mouth. "You're sure … uh-huh … Email the file … Yes, I'll let her know."

The second cup had all my pistons firing, and I knew Rick's conversation had to do with Aunt Vera. I waited for him to hang up before asking, "What's going on?"

Rick didn't mince words. "Vikram Gupta is married."

"Married? Seriously?" My mouth O'd, and I placed my hand over it. "Aunt Vera, you naughty minx! Having an affair with a married man! Did Angus dig up that little tidbit?"

"Yes." Rick tapped on his phone, pulling up the file Angus emailed.

"That's why she didn't tell us about Mr. Gupta." I drummed my fingers and mused, "But how does his wife *not* know? They see each other during the weekends. They have dinner every

Friday night. How does that work?"

"It would seem he's been married close to thirty years, to a woman named …Prisha. Apparently, she comes from a rather wealthy family in London. They own an apartment in Chelsea. And—" he squinted at the screen, "—it looks like Vikram and Prisha own an antique store there too."

"Thirty years?" I jumped up and paced around the table. "Vikram's affair with my aunt has been going on for at least two years. How does this Prisha woman not know?"

"She spends time in London or traveling to gather the antiques for the shop?" Rick suggested.

My head bobbed as I paced to the other end of the kitchen muttering, "She must, because Vikram's a full-time professor at the university. He's keeping Aunt Vera on the side while his wife travels. I wonder what she knows."

"Maybe that's the point. Maybe this Vikram has been stringing your aunt along, telling her he was planning to divorce his wife—"

"But never planned to do so." I sucked wind. "I bet Aunt Vera gave him an ultimatum, or-or threatened to expose the affair to his wife. And he…" I placed a hand to my mouth in horror. "Do you … do you think … he-he disposed of Vera? Or … maybe it's the *wife*. She found out and took out her revenge on Vera!"

Rick shifted and put his phone aside. "That's a big leap. And the wife has been in London all week. Let's not get ahead of ourselves, but I think it would be a good idea to talk with Mr. Gupta. I'd like to get a read on him."

While Rick spoke, I pulled my mobile out of my back pocket and dialed.

Vikram answered on the second ring. "Hello."

I put it on speaker, so Rick could listen, and laid the phone between the two of us. "Mr. Gupta, it's Karina Cardinal, from last night."

"Karina, I'm glad you rang. The more I've thought about it, the more concerned I've become over Vera. I phoned the police early this morning, and they said they would have someone contact me, but I haven't heard anything yet."

"That's why I'm calling. I've discovered something … of importance and was wondering if we could get together. I'd like to get your thoughts on it."

"By all means. When and where? Shall I come over?"

Rick shook his head and mouthed "his place."

"Actually, I am about to leave. Would it be possible for me to stop by your place?"

He hesitated. "Well, I'm having renovations done, so my home is a bit topsy-turvy at the moment…"

"It won't matter. It's imperative we speak." I pressed him, "Sooner rather than later."

"Yes, yes. Very well, do come over. When can you get here?"

"How far away do you live?"

"About ten minutes. I'll text you the address. And …er … pick up the house a touch."

"See you soon." I pressed the disconnect button. "Did you hear that? He doesn't want us to come over. Do you think the wife is home?" My eyes widened. "Maybe he's coming up with an errand for her."

Rick didn't speak, and he wore his thoughtful brooding look.

I snapped my fingers to wake him from his trance. "Quick, let's get over there. I'll run upstairs and get my shoes on. Did you bring your black truck?"

He nodded.

"We'll take it. Less obvious than my red Jeep. I want to scout Vikram's house before we go in." I rushed out of the kitchen, not waiting for Rick's response.

Two minutes later, I bounded down the steps, jumped over Nightshade, who was passing through the hallway, and grabbed my purse and coat from the rack in the front foyer. "I'm ready," I sang, sailing into the kitchen, and pulled to a halt. "What are you doing?"

Rick hadn't moved from the position where I'd left him.

"C'mon." I clapped my hands. "Coat. Keys. Wallet."

Sluggishly, Rick rose from the table and drew on his leather jacket.

I realized he hadn't spoken since the call. "What's wrong? What did Vikram say on the phone that I missed?"

My boyfriend gazed at me with something akin to ... pity? "Renovations."

"He said he's having renovations done. So?" And then the lightbulb came on. "Oh ... no... you don't think he's walled up Vera or something horrid like that?"

His shoulders slumped.

"Huh-uh. No." My ponytail whipped back and forth as I shook my head in denial. "I realize you and I have seen some dreadful things, but this isn't Washington, D.C. This is Williamsburg. A pokey tourist town. Things like putting dead bodies in the walls don't happen down here. Don't look at me like that." I pointed at him. "Get your keys. We're going over there *now*."

"Did he text you the address yet?"

I checked my texts. "Not yet, but you've got it in the files Angus sent. The address was in there. Right?"

"Yes. Don't you think Vikram's going to wonder—"

"I don't give a damn *what* Vikram Gupta wonders. Get your keys!"

Chapter Nine

Vikram lived in a two-story, colonial-style home with brick siding, black shutters, and a green front door on a nice, quiet cul-de-sac. Neighbors had decorated their front porches with pumpkins and straw bales. Across the street, a pair of bedsheet ghosts hung from a large oak and fluttered in the autumn breeze. Next door to Vikram, a forgotten bike and pink scooter lay haphazardly at the end of a driveway. It all screamed typical suburban neighborhood. An overfull orange dumpster sat in Vikram's driveway next to a white SUV.

"Well, he wasn't lying about the renovations," I murmured.

Rick pulled to the side of the road, about two houses down from Vikram's. A middle-aged woman dressed in bright pink spandex leggings and a black sweatshirt speed-walked past us, cruised around the cul-de-sac, and headed back our way.

Rick smiled, waved, and said through his teeth, "We can't sit here very long without attracting attention."

The woman waved back, studying Rick's large F-150 pickup truck as she passed by. No other vehicles were parked on the street. Driveways were long and wide, providing plenty of space for multiple cars to park.

"Hm, yes, I see what you mean." My phone pinged. "Vikram just sent me the address. Wait a few minutes and then pull into his driveway. I want to see if his wife leaves."

We sat unspeaking.

The silence closed in around me. Rick probably could have done this for hours.

After two minutes, I released my seatbelt. The button made a distinct click, and the harness retracted with a zip. I crossed my legs, decided that wasn't comfortable, and uncrossed them. I scratched my neck and sniffed.

Rick continued to gaze out the front window. "Remind me never to bring you on a stakeout where it's important to maintain silence."

I didn't respond. Another minute ticked by on the dashboard clock. "Enough. Pull into his driveway."

"It's been three minutes," Rick commented dryly.

"You drove fast."

He rolled his eyes. The truck roared to life.

Vikram answered wearing brown cords and a William and Mary sweatshirt. His eyes widened, and he adjusted his glasses. "You got here fast."

"We weren't far away," I replied. "This is my boyfriend. He's come down to help me locate Aunt Vera."

"Rick Donovan." Said boyfriend held out his hand.

They shared a handshake. "Sorry about the mess; I'm renovating the kitchen. I don't recommend it. Just move; it's easier." He grinned at his little joke as we followed him to the back of the house.

Long sheets of plastic hung from ceiling to floor, surrounding the area where the kitchen should have been. Instead, the walls had been denuded of cabinets, and two of them were knocked back to the studs, revealing electrical wires and plumbing. The only appliance remaining was a stainless-steel refrigerator, which sat in the family room humming next to the couch. Dust rested atop all the wood furniture surfaces.

Vikram pushed aside a plastic sheet to give us a gander. "You see, they removed this wall and have just finished putting in the new beam." He pointed to the ceiling where an exposed wooden beam rested above our heads. "This is where the island will go with a cooktop and built-in microwave. The double oven will go there, and the fridge at the end of the cabinet run, here." Vikram walked around the empty space gesticulating as he described the new layout.

"Why did you and my aunt plan dinner at your house if your kitchen is in shambles?" I asked.

"Vera helped me design the space. She wanted to see the new beam," Vikram explained reasonably.

"What about your *wife?* Doesn't she have anything to say about it?" Rick gripped my elbow in warning, but the question was out. It hung heavily in the room, like a two-ton hippo.

Vikram stiffened, rotating deliberately, and, with a raised chin, said in haughty high-brow English tones, "I. Beg. Your. Pardon."

I pulled my elbow out of Rick's grip and stepped closer. We were eye to eye, but I didn't back down in the face of Vikram's icy irritation. "Your wife. How does she feel about Aunt Vera designing her kitchen?" I enunciated, crossing my arms.

His lips thinned. "*That* is a personal question, and *none* of *your* business."

"On the contrary, considering you and my aunt have clearly been carrying on for years—*and* the fact that we don't know her current whereabouts—leads *me* to believe that *you*, Mr. Gupta, and *your* relationship with your *wife* is *indeed my* business," my patronizing tone echoed in the empty kitchen.

"You are mistaken," Vikram declared.

"Or is she, too, missing?" I goaded.

When it came to interrogation tactics, Rick probably would have been a bit more judicious and circumspect. I wasn't known for my patience, and with Rick having my back, I may have been bolder than normal. Then again, maybe not.

Vikram's face blazed, and his expression looked as though I'd belted him one. "You are out of line. I think it's time you left." He indicated with a hand in the general direction of the front door. "Perhaps when you're calmer, we can speak further."

I didn't budge.

Vikram gazed past me and spoke directly to Rick, "Sir, if you please."

My fists clenched, and I whipped my head around.

Rick stuck his hands in his pockets, rocked back on his heels, and grinned. "It would be in your best interests to answer Karina's questions. When *I* ask them, it won't be in such a friendly manner." The genial tone belied the underlying threat.

Vikram blanched, dropping his hand.

"If you prefer, I can call the police, and you can tell them all about your philandering ways," I suggested amiably, but deepened my voice and continued in a menacing manner, "They might see it as a motive for getting rid of her."

He took a step backward, his eyes darting around the kitchen as if searching for an object to use in self-defense.

"Or, we can just have a conversation and sort this all out now," Rick said in soothing tones. He let out a low whistle and asked, "What kind of material did you choose for your countertops?"

Vikram adjusted his glasses and cleared his throat. "Perhaps you're right. I now realize how this looks, but I can *assure* you, it is *not* what you're thinking. Why don't we step into the other room, and I can explain."

My mouth pinched. "Please do."

Vikram guided us into a spacious combination formal living room-dining room, which looked as though it had been hastily dusted. As a matter of fact, a spray can of Pledge and a cleaning rag sat on the dining room table.

He removed a plastic tarp from a white brocade settee. "It helps with the dust. Have a seat."

I picked up a framed photo on the side table. Two teenage boys were on a beach, their arms slung across each other's shoulders, with the sun shimmering off their skinny bronzed bodies. They were laughing, and both had mops of curly black hair that matched their father's.

Vikram pushed aside a trash bag covering a cinnamon-colored chair and sat down with a resigned sigh. "I suppose it was inevitable that you would find out about my wife. How *did* you find out?"

Rick had waited for Vikram to take a seat before lowering himself next to me. While his expression remained impassive, I could feel the tautness of his muscles in the leg that touched mine.

Upon arrival, neither Rick nor I defined what he did for a living. I preferred to keep Vikram in the dark on that account.

Languidly, I draped myself into the corner of the couch and crossed my legs. "I live in Washington, DC. I've got friends in every intelligence community you can think of. My aunt is MIA. Did you really think I *wouldn't* have you checked out?"

He clasped his hands together. "Yes. I understand. Forgive my prickliness. I asked Vera to explain our relationship to your family a year ago. For her own reasons, she chose not to. However, the situation ... being what it is, it's clear you want some answers." He adjusted his glasses. "As you can probably tell from my accent, I grew up in England. However, I come from a very traditional Indian family background, as does my wife—"

"Prisha," I inserted.

His chin went up, but he chose not to comment on my knowledge of his wife's name. "Er, yes, she too comes from a traditional family ... where marriages ... are arranged."

I nodded. Arranged marriages in families from India were still a thing. I knew of such a couple, happily married, living in my building on the third floor. "Yes. I understand it still happens today."

"It does." He nodded. "Prisha and I worked hard to make a go of it. Initially, when the twins were young, we were happy.

Eventually, as time went on, we realized we hadn't much in common, besides the boys. Things got worse when I took the job here." He shifted uncomfortably.

"Prisha disliked living in the States—so far from her family. She spent her summers in England. When both her parents died within a year of each other, their antique store started as a burden, but eventually it became her passion. Growing up, she hated that musty store. As an adult, she could turn it into what she always envisioned. The twins were in high school, academically successful, very involved in football, or as you call it, soccer, and entrenched in the community. We didn't want to uproot them. We—" he cleared his throat, "—Prisha decided, she would commute back and forth from London until the boys graduated. Once they went off to college, we decided to live our own lives. She permanently moved into her parents' old flat in London."

"Why haven't you gotten a divorce?"

"Many reasons. The cost being one. The manner in which the business is tied up in my name. The boys. Prisha's notion that it would be disrespectful to her dead parents' memory." He shrugged and looked away sheepishly. "Laziness."

"Did Aunt Vera know?"

"Oh, yes! As a matter of fact, she claimed my separated but still married situation made our relationship more palatable. Apparently, her last marriage ended badly, and she said she had no more use for husbands." Vikram gazed out the window and added dryly, "'Don't need one, don't want one,' I believe is how she framed it."

That was the truth. Vera had stated in no uncertain terms, she would *never* remarry. She deeply valued her independence. I blamed Good Time Randy for her distaste for the married state.

While I mentally cogitated over this information, Rick asked, "Is your wife in London now?"

"Yes, of course." Vikram nodded.

"And how does she feel about your relationship with Vera?" he prodded.

"Prisha? She adores Vera." The professor placed a hand to his chest.

"Wait—" I frowned with astonishment, "—they've met?"

"Why, yes. Last year, Prisha was in the States visiting the boys. They've spoken many times on Zoom. Vera helped Prisha with some auction items for the shop. Prisha sent Vera that Royal Doulton figurine she keeps on her office desk for her birthday last year."

"Humph." Rick rubbed his chin, and his shoulders finally relaxed.

I blinked repeatedly. "Let me get this straight, your wife approves of your extramarital affair?"

"Well ... she'd be a bit of a hypocrite if she didn't," he said matter-of-factly. "When she moved to London permanently, her shop manager, Nigel, moved in with her."

I, for one, couldn't understand this bizarre relationship. It appeared to me it would have been easier to get a divorce and be done with it. Why keep a dead marriage going? Was it a cultural thing?

I rubbed my forehead. "Why didn't Vera tell us?"

"She didn't think you'd understand ... or approve of her decision. Judging by your shocked expression, I'd guess she was correct in her assessment."

Normally, I was better at controlling my emotions. Schooling my features, I sat up straighter.

"Would you like something to drink? I've got soda, water, and juice in the refrigerator." A repetitive beep interrupted Vikram. "That's Prisha now." He pulled his phone from his front pants pocket and swiped. "Hallo."

"Vikram, dah-ling! I got your message about Vera. Have you heard anything?" a soprano voice oozed.

"Not yet. Vera's niece and her boyfriend are here now. We were ... er ... just discussing it." He turned the phone around and handed it to me.

A woman in her fifties with two dark slashes of brows over tawny eyes, and a mane of shiny black hair, gazed back at us.

I waved. "Hello."

Her face creased with smile lines, and a ruby nose piercing twinkled as she greeted us. "Well, hallo. Which one are you? Karina or Jillian?"

"Karina, and this is my boyfriend, Rick." I panned over to him.

He gave a finger wave.

"It's lovely to finally meet you. I'm desperately sorry to hear Vera is missing. Have the inspectors discovered anything?" She hunkered in closer to the camera.

"No." I shook my head. "It's rather a mystery. She's left messages at work but not contacted the family. And she left the cat alone, without food or water. We've become quite concerned."

"I don't blame you. From what you've said, *I'm* concerned. She'd never leave Nightshade." Prisha twisted a piece of hair, distress etched in her features. "And the police have nothing?"

"I'm supposed to hear from a detective this morning. Maybe he'll know more. They've put a description of her and the car into the system to be on the lookout for."

"Well, I'll leave you to it. Let Vik know if there's anything I can do to help," she thoughtfully offered.

"Yes, I will do so," Vikram called.

"Thank you, that's very kind. Short of knowing my aunt's email password, I'm not sure there's anything you *can* do," I guffawed.

Prisha perked up. "Well, I don't have her email password, but I do have a password we've used to share files in Google. Would that help?"

"Yes, as a matter of fact it would." Wow. Vera and Prisha really did know each other.

Considering this woman's concern, perhaps I shouldn't be so judgy when it came to this weird threesome—or foursome if you included Nigel.

"Hold up, let me get it for you." Prisha disappeared from the screen and returned a minute later. "Here it is—" she flapped a yellow sticky note at us, "—have you a pen?"

"I'll put it in my phone." I pulled up a notes app. "Okay, go ahead."

Prisha rattled off a lot of random numbers and letters, "And the final is uppercase H."

"Thank you. I might be able to access something of importance."

"Think nothing of it. I'll leave you all to sleuthing. Nigel and I are having company tonight, and I've got to do some cooking."

We said our goodbyes. I handed the phone back to Vikram, and the session ended.

There was an awkward moment of silence, which I finally broke. Crossing my legs, I leaned forward. "Vikram, I'd like to apologize for … uh … thinking you may have … uh…"

"Done away with Vera," he finished for me.

I fixated on the photo of his two boys. "Something like that."

"I can't blame you. It is a bit of a sticky wicket … our relationship," he added at my confusion to the sticky wicket comment. "When we do find your aunt, I have a feeling I'm going to be in for quite the lecture."

"We'd best be off." Rick rose from the couch. "I'd like to visit the museum and speak to some of her coworkers."

Once Rick pulled away from Vikram's house, I turned on him. "I *told* you he didn't wall up my aunt."

Rick laughed. "You were right. He's not that type. Interesting life he leads, a wife, a lover. A wife *with* a lover."

"What do the French say? *Qué será será.* What will be will be. I suppose four middle-aged adults have figured out how to lead happy lives in their own way."

"How very open-minded of you." His shoulders bounced in silent laughter.

"What?"

"You should have seen your face when that Gupta guy explained the situation. I thought I'd have to help you pick your jaw off the floor."

"It's just … not what I expected of Aunt Vera. However, once I considered how badly her second marriage ended, I could understand why she'd soured on the concept. She's developed a fierce independent streak."

"Sounds like another woman I know." He delivered me the side-eye.

"Independence is a good thing." I crossed my arms and pouted.

"It's one of your finest qualities. Even if it does get you into trouble."

"That's what you're here for." I leaned over and kissed his cheek.

He took his right hand off the wheel and slid it up my leg. "Mind telling me where we're going?"

"Turn left at the light and continue straight until we reach—" My phone rang from an unknown caller but with a Williamsburg exchange. "Hello?"

"Hello, this is Detective Riggins. I'm calling for Karina Cardinal." His voice was gravelly and rough, like a chain-smoker's voice.

"This is Karina."

"I've been assigned to Vera Wagner's case. I've been looking over the report Officer Ortega took last night. I have a few follow-up questions," he rumbled in a forthright and official manner.

"Yes. No problem." I put the phone on speaker for Rick to hear. "The detective," I mouthed at him. "Should I come down to the station?"

"It's not necessary. It can be done over the phone," Detective Riggins replied. "To clarify, you spoke with Vera's supervisor, Norman Hedgewell, yesterday?"

"No. I have not spoken to Norman. My mother had a phone conversation with him on…" I counted the days backwards on my fingers, "… on Tuesday, four days ago. When I stopped by the museum yesterday, he was unavailable. So, I have not had a chance to speak with Norman."

"I see."

"But I did speak with one of Vera's coworkers, Felicity Benson."

"And Benson is the one who told you—" he paused as if reading something, "—Vera sent an out-of-office email on … Tuesday?"

"Correct. But none of her luggage is gone, and she left the cat to fend for himself. She'd never do that."

Rick pulled over to concentrate on the phone conversation. Also, because he probably didn't know where he needed to go.

"And you haven't found her phone or computer?" the detective asked.

"No. Are you able to track her phone?"

"I've put in a request to do so, but it will take time, and I'm going to see about getting her emails." He shifted gears, "The officer mentioned you hesitated when asked if Vera has done something like this before—disappeared without a word to family." He paused, and when I didn't respond, he nudged, "Want to tell me about it?"

With a sigh, I gave an abridged version of Vera's unfortunate marriage to Good Time Randy. I heard the clicking of computer keys as the detective typed.

"Does Vera have contact with her former husband?" he asked.

"Not that I know of." I fidgeted with my earring. I hated having to tell the police about Randy, my aunt's self-admitted worst mistake of her life. "A few years ago, I heard rumors that he was on his fourth marriage."

"Nonetheless, I'll investigate him. I understand you're staying at Vera's home."

"Correct." I nodded, even though I knew he couldn't see me.

"I'm not clear, what is your relation to Vera Wagner?"

Is that a hint of suspicion I hear? "First cousin once removed." I went on to explain the relationship and how Aunt Vera and my mom were practically sisters, and how we were Vera's only family since her parents were deceased and she had no siblings.

Even though I'd given my mother's number to Officer Ortega, I gave it to the detective again and encouraged him to get a firsthand account of her conversation with Norman Hedgewell. The detective asked me a few more questions about Aunt Vera's work life, which I couldn't answer, then he said he'd be in touch and rang off.

"Where are we going?" Rick restarted the truck.

"Follow this road basically until it ends and then turn right."

While he drove us to the museum, I saved the detective's number into my contacts and gave him the *Hawaii Five-0* theme song as a ringtone. We arrived at the museum ten minutes before it opened.

My phone sang out the theme from *Grease,* and my sister's face popped up on screen. "Hello."

"Where are you?" she asked in imperious tones.

"At Vera's museum. We're waiting for it to open so we can talk to her boss. Where are you?"

"Sitting outside her house. It's locked."

I explained where to find the rock with the key. "Rick came down this morning, so I moved my stuff into Vera's room. You can sleep in the guest room."

"I brought Tony with me."

"You did? Why?"

"He wanted to see the area. He said he hasn't been since he was a kid. Besides, I thought I might buy some of those colonial soaps for the guest bags for the wedding."

"Aunt Vera's missing, Jilly. This isn't a vacation," I chided.

"I'm *aware*, *Ka-rin-a*," she said in snotty tones. Then she lowered her voice, "I also thought … if Aunt Vera was hurt … or something, it would be a good idea to have someone with a medical background."

She had a point.

"You're right. It's good he's here."

"So, we can sleep in Vera's bed?"

"No. Rick and I were here first."

"But *we're* engaged," Jillian whined. "You and Rick are just … well, I don't know, but *not* engaged.

I loved my sister, and I was truly glad she'd found Tony Romero. However, in the past months since he put a ring on it, all I'd heard out of Jillian's mouth was wedding, wedding, wedding, and I'd done my darndest to be a supportive big sister and maid of honor with a smile. It stung that she hit the nail on the head when it came to my relationship with Rick—we were in the Zone of Unknown. On the other hand, she and Tony would be together for the rest of their lives. For a night they could lump it.

"Push two beds together. It'll be like sleeping in a king-sized bed," I said with finality.

"Fine!" she huffed.

"I've got to run. Show Tony around Duke of Gloucester

Street. Try the Tarpley-Thompson shop for the soaps. See you in an hour."

Different staffers were working the visitors' desk this morning. Gisele, a middle-aged woman with graying mousy-brown hair, informed us that Mr. Hedgewell was not on premises.

"Do you know if he will be in today?" Rick asked.

She nodded, her wispy hair fluttering around her face. "I believe so. There's a presentation in the Hennage Auditorium today at three-thirty."

"How much are the tickets for that event?" I asked.

"Five dollars."

"I'll take two, please." I pulled a twenty from my wallet and passed it over to her.

Her face twisted. "It'll take just a minute; the computer decided to reboot. This has been happening ever since the upgrade a few weeks ago."

"Yeah, computers," I sympathized.

A nattily dressed senior citizen wearing hot pink lipstick stood at the checkout next to us and started chatting. "I hope they've returned my favorite teapot to the ceramics collection."

"Which teapot is that, Barbara?" Gisele asked.

Clearly the lady was a regular at the museum if the staffers were on a first-name basis with her. "It's a white ceramic pot with Japanese fishermen on it. Rather simple, but always reminds me of a teapot I had when we were stationed in Japan. Sadly, mine was broken during one of our moves. I always visit the teapot here when I come."

"I don't think I know that one," the other receptionist replied.

"I always visit the grandfather clocks too. One of them is the same age as my own. I inherited it from my grandmother."

"You seem to know the collection quite well," I said.

"I come almost once a week." She wiggled a white badge hanging around her neck. "With this Good Neighbor pass, I get into the museum for free and discounts on ticketed events. Are you from around here?"

I shook my head. "Washington, D.C."

Her pink lips turned down. "My condolences. We did time in D.C. Six years."

Clearly, she hadn't enjoyed living in the nation's capital. It *is* a high-stress city full of geo-political maneuverings. It's not for everyone. I scrambled for a different topic.

Rick came to the rescue, "How long were you stationed in Japan?"

The friendly smile was back. "Three years. In Okinawa. My husband is retired Navy."

"Here we go; it's back up," Gisele said, and we returned our attention to her. She punched some buttons on the computer screen; it spit out two vouchers. "Would you like tickets to any other events or entry to the museum?"

"No, thank you." I tucked them into my back pocket, and we exited the building.

In the parking lot, standing in front of Rick's truck, I glanced around, a little lost. "Now what?"

"Is your computer back at Vera's?"

I nodded.

"Google password?"

I snapped my fingers. "I forgot. Yes, back to Vera's." When Rick beeped the locks open, I hopped into the cab and declared, "Drive on, Jeeves!"

That got me an eyeroll and a smirk. "It's a good thing you're so cute."

"I know." I flashed my teeth and leaned over to give him a big smackeroo.

Chapter Ten

Fortunately, I'd taken the extra housekey Aunt Vera always left hanging in the kitchen pantry, because my sister forgot to replace the one in the rock.

Nightshade greeted us with a meow as I opened the back door. Purring, he wound through and around Rick's legs.

"Hello. What's your name?" One-handed, Rick scooped up the cat, held him to his chest, and tickled Nightshade's neck with his fingers.

In response, Nightshade butted his head into Rick's palm.

"That's Nightshade." I squinted at the tableau the black cat and Rick made. "I didn't picture you as a cat man. I always figured you for a dog person."

"I *am* a dog person, but cats have excellent intuition when it comes to people. Dogs tend to be less discerning. It's harder to win over cats."

Nightshade spied something in the kitchen, and, with a hiss, tried to wriggle free of Rick's grasp. He sank down to a knee and allowed the cat his freedom. Nightshade darted into the postage stamp of a backyard and leapt on top of a white wrought iron bench with an incensed tail held high.

"What was that ab—" I spied a silver and white cat with crystal-blue eyes sitting on the kitchen table licking his paws. "Oh. I see Jillian brought Smokey. *This* should be interesting."

Smokey, in typical Siamese behavior, gave us a haughty glance and returned to his ablutions.

I opened my mouth to greet the cat, but "Benny and the

Jets" interrupted me. "Hello, Mom."

"Karina? I just got off the phone with Detective Riggins. He wanted to know about my conversation with Vera's boss. And I told him everything, about how we are supposed to go on a trip in February, and how I need to book the trip, but Vera didn't respond to my phone calls, and how unusual that is for her. Then he wanted to know about that awful Randy. Well, I'm sure I don't know about Randy. After all, he's been out of our lives for fifteen years or more. Terrible, terrible man. Practically ruined Vera. He had the temerity to imply that Vera might be off with another fellow, which I told him was impossible because she'd learned her lesson with Randy," my mother explained all of this in one long-winded, run-on sentence.

I imagined her conversation with the detective. No doubt he got quite an earful.

Mom continued speaking so loudly, I had to hold the phone away from my ear as she wound down the story. "Can you believe this? I'm so upset, I simply don't know what to do with myself."

"Well, Rick and I are here in Williamsburg, following up on some leads," I tried to sound reassuring.

"What about your sister? She told me she was heading down there."

"Yup, Jilly and Tony arrived a little while ago and are ... uh—" *shopping for the wedding,* "—checking around town. I think we're doing all we can."

I knew that wouldn't satisfy my mom, and I needed to give her a job, or she'd work herself into a pother. "The best thing for you to do is remain in touch with the detective. As a matter of fact, can you contact him every few hours and report back to Jilly and me? That way we can focus on searching the area and speaking to Vera's friends and coworkers."

During my mom's ramblings, Rick had gone to the truck to retrieve his duffel bag and had taken it upstairs, followed by

Nightshade. I assumed he'd identify my stuff and deposit his own in the same room. Meanwhile, I closed the open kitchen cabinet and wandered into the front room to stare sightlessly through the blinds.

"Absolutely," she was saying. "Someone needs to advocate for your aunt; otherwise, the police will simply put her in a pile with all the other missing persons."

"While I'm sure the detective is taking this seriously, I doubt he'll stay in touch with family about developments on the case. We need regular check-ins."

"I'm on top of it," Mom declared. "I'm going to know everything he knows."

Oh, how I pitied Detective Riggins. Sarah Cardinal, the bloodhound, was on the case. For good or bad, the man wouldn't get a moment's peace until Aunt Vera was found.

"I'll call your sister and see what she's discovered."

Probably some table decorations for the wedding. "Sounds good. I'll be in touch, Mom. Give my love to Dad."

"Yes, goodbye, dear. We'll speak in a few hours."

Joy.

My computer was still on the coffee table where I'd left it last night—after the minor heart attack from seeing the ghost. Lifting the lid, the screen came to life, and I logged in.

"Karina, I think the cats got into your aunt's stuff," Rick said from Vera's office.

Uh-oh, now what?

His tone turned grave, "Or someone's been here." He peered down at the floor swathed in paper. The same drawer from this morning had been pulled open and ransacked.

I breathed in deeply. Hints of patchouli remained in the air. "No. That would be the ghost."

Rick's head swiveled to me. "You're saying a ghost ... did this?"

"Indeed. Second time today. I'm assuming he's left by now. That seems to be his M.O. Make a mess. Scare the bejeezus out of me. Leave. Nightshade tends to watch him when he's in the house."

Rick looked at me, eyebrows to the roof, his face unbelieving. "The cat?"

I nodded, my arms akimbo.

"He watches the ghost?"

"I kid you not. Aunt Vera says he helps her find things. As you can see, all he's done while I've been here is trash the place. Maybe he's upset that she's not here?"

He studied the disorder, his head rotating back and forth.

"Listen, I've logged into my computer." I pulled up the notes app on my phone and handed it to him. "This is Aunt Vera's Gmail address, and here's the password Prisha gave us. Why don't you see what you can do with it? I'll clean up."

Rick took the phone into the parlor, and, with an irritated harumph, I sat on the floor to begin sorting the papers into some semblance of order. This time, the ghost had pulled almost everything out of the drawer. A few sheets were caught along the side. I tugged. Something shifted, and I heard the riiiip of paper.

"Dang it."

The ripped piece was wedged into a crack where the bottom of the drawer met the side.

"Wait a minute." I knocked on the wood at the bottom.

It wasn't as sturdy as the rest of the desk material. Pulling the drawer all the way out, I found a rounded indentation in the back corner. I slid my finger in and extracted the false bottom, revealing a blue folder.

"Rick..."

"Yes?"

"Didn't Vikram say he saw Vera with a blue file folder?"

"Not that I recall. I'm into your aunt's Google account.

Checking sent mail for the last week."

"Um-hm." I laid the file on the floor and opened it.

Inside, I found a list of at least a hundred items, four with checkmarks next to them. Behind the list were more sheets of paper detailing particular pieces—a candlestick, saltshaker, mug, and a ceramic teapot. Small two-by-two photographs of each item were attached by paperclip to the description.

I assumed these objects were from the collection Aunt Vera oversaw at the museum. Why would they be hidden in a false drawer? Except for a handwritten decimal number at the top of each page, there were no notes or other defining characteristics. I chucked the rest of the documents willy-nilly into the drawer and went back to the parlor, waving my treasure in the air.

"What do you make of these?" I dropped the stack of papers on the coffee table.

He shuffled through. "Items from the museum?"

"That's what I'm assuming. Why hide them in a secret compartment?"

We studied the material together. Each page listed information about the piece: age, maker, quality, detailed description, dates of cleaning, purchase price, estimated value, etc. Nothing stood out. Four of the items shared a cleaning date; two, a purchase date.

"Didn't that white-haired woman at the museum say she missed seeing the Japanese teapot?" Rick removed the photo from one of the sheets.

"Yes, she did."

We examined it together.

> *Description: Japanese, Kutani, hand-painted porcelain teapot, Edo Period (1603-1686). Rare.*
> *Maker: Fuku Ceramic*
> *Decoration: Orange, blue and black. 2 koi, 3 fishermen and rods*
> *Condition: No cracks, minor chip on foot.*

Purchase Price: Donation
Estimated Value: $12,450

"Does this mean anything to you?" Rick asked.

"Not a thing. I've no clue about ancient teapots. But I will say, that's one expensive pot."

"Wait a minute, I think—" Rick moused around the computer screen, clicking on an open internet tab. "Look, this is one of your aunt's password-protected Google files. It's the same list. Right?" He held the paper up to the computer. I leaned over his shoulder, and our eyes darted back and forth comparing the two. "Wait, there's an extra checkmark."

"I don't see it. Where?"

"Here on the computer." His thick, square finger pointed. "Item numbers sixty-five and sixty-six have checkmarks. Only number sixty-six is marked on the paper list."

"You're right."

"But what does it all mean?" he mumbled.

"It means, we need to return to the museum to take a look at the collection. Did you find anything else?" I asked.

"Nothing of value. Not even her out-of-office email."

"I imagine it was sent through the museum's email system. Not her private Gmail account."

"Most likely. There is something significant about this list." He tapped it with a finger. "Your aunt must be hiding it for a reason."

The back door slammed. "We're home!" my sister hollered. "Hello, Smokey."

"We're in the parlor," I called.

"Who keeps leaving this cabinet door open?" my sister mumbled, and I heard it snap shut.

She trooped in with two bulging brown shopping bags. Her fiancé, Tony, followed behind with three more bags. They plopped them in the corner.

"They had soaps *and* candle votives that will be perfect for table favors." She slipped off her black-checked raincoat to reveal skinny jeans with short boots and a cerulean-blue sweater that matched her eyes. Her dark hair was pulled into a ponytail at the base of her neck with a black barrette.

"Did you buy out the entire store?" I rose from the couch and bent to give her a hug.

"Pretty much." My sister moved to embrace Rick. "Hello, Batman," she said, referring to an early moniker I'd given him, due to the fact that he swooped in and out of my life—often saving it—like the dark knight. It was months before I learned Rick's last name.

"Hello, Jillian. Tony."

The boys nodded at each other.

Tony and I shared a side-hug. "It's good to see you, Tony. How have you been?"

"Busy." Tony had a soccer athlete's wiry strength with dark hair and dark eyes. He was the same height as my sister, which was a few inches shorter than me.

I laughed. "You're a paramedic for D.C. Are you ever *not* busy?"

His eyes crinkled with humor. "Never." He and Rick did a firm, masculine handshake. "Good to see you, man." Then he removed his windbreaker, revealing a white T-shirt that read, *Being a Paramedic is easy. It's like riding a bike. Except the bike is on fire. You're on fire. Everything's on fire.*

"Nice shirt." Rick clapped him on the shoulder.

"I gave it to him for his birthday," Jillian chimed in.

"It's fairly accurate." Tony tucked the shirt into his jeans. "Any word from the cops about your Aunt Vera?"

"Not yet," I replied.

"Well, Mom called about twenty minutes ago and gave me an earful. Did you tell her we went shopping?" My sister's question rang with accusation.

"I did not," I replied with complete honesty.

"Well, she's going to be all over that detective guy you spoke to. Poor man." She murmured the latter sentence with a head shake, then she did a one-eighty and said cheerfully, "I made lunch reservations for us at the King's Arms Tavern for eleven-thirty. It's eleven now, so we should leave in about twenty minutes."

"Great, I'm starving." The cup of yogurt I'd had for breakfast was long gone; my belly and brain needed a refill.

"I have to go to the bathroom and freshen up before we leave." Jillian started up the stairs. Before she got three steps, she trilled, "Honey, why don't you help me push the beds together?"

They clattered up the hardwoods, and the guest room door slammed shut.

"I'm fairly certain that was code for—follow me so we can have a quickie," I commented. My assumptions were proven correct when we heard the distinct squeaking of bed springs.

Rick simply grinned. "Give them a pass. They're young and in love."

"We're young and in love." The word popped out of my mouth without thought. Not wanting to make a big deal, I amended with a teasing, "Well, at least *I'm young.*"

Rick's face narrowed. He was eight years older than I. When we first met, I thought he was over forty because of the premature graying around the temples, the crow's feet, and, well … his entire bearing spoke of the maturity of a middle-aged man. I supposed war and carrying the load of a high-stakes security company on your back will do that to a person.

"Younger than *you,*" I taunted playfully.

"Who are you calling old?" In one swift move, he grabbed my wrist, pulled me onto the sofa into his lap, and commenced tickling.

My sides and underarms were very ticklish, which Rick found out early in our relationship. Being ten times stronger than me, he had no problems holding me in place with one hand, while tickling under my shirt with the other.

I giggled and squirmed beneath him, finally crying out, "Mercy! Mercy! I give!"

The hand along my bare side slowed its pace and increased pressure. I caught my breath. The stroking hand was replaced by his mouth as kisses rained across my midriff. Now I squirmed beneath him for entirely different reasons. My fingertips caressed his velvety hair. A warm hand covered my silky bra as he moved upward to nip beneath my jawline. I wrapped my leg around his hip.

The muffled sound of a techno mix song invaded our frolic. Rick froze mid-nip. The song ended, and he continued to my ear, where his teeth grazed the sensitive lobe.

The techno music started up again.

I dropped my leg away with a sigh. "Isn't that the ringtone for your office?"

"It'll go away," he mumbled, his breath tickling my throat.

I would have loved to ignore the bothersome phone, but … Rick *was* the head of an important security company. And I could tell he wanted to answer it. "Didn't you say your men were covering a new foreign diplomat this weekend?"

He groaned, levered himself off the couch, and retrieved the phone from the coat pocket of his leather jacket that he'd tossed onto an armchair. "Go for Rick … uh-huh…"

I rose, tucking the shirt back into my jeans.

"That's it? You're sure? You found nothing else?" He paced in front of the fireplace. "Okay, email me the report."

My sister's chirping cries drifted down the stairs. I rolled my eyes.

"Yes, that's fine… No, tell Joshua to put Hernandez on it.

That's all." The conversation ended, and he slid the phone into his back pocket.

"What's up?"

"I had Angus run your aunt's credit cards. There have been no transactions since Monday morning. She bought a coffee at Starbucks," he said grimly.

I deflated, sinking into the couch like the air being let out of a beach ball. "I guess I've been hoping all along that she'd packed up for a quick beach vacation, or something similar. I can't imagine she wouldn't have used her credit card at least once if that'd been the case. Unless—" I straightened, "—maybe she took out a bunch of money and is running on cash?"

Rick's mouth twitched, and he rubbed the back of his neck.

"You ran the records?"

"Her bank records reflect a hundred-dollar withdrawal on Saturday."

My spine withered. "Can't get far on a hundred bucks these days."

"I'm afraid not. And Angus didn't find any ticket purchases for a flight, train, or bus."

"No gas receipts either?"

Reluctantly, his head rotated back and forth.

"That is *not* good. The more we find, the less it's looking like she snuck off for a secret rendezvous or a last-minute vacay."

The noise coming from the guest bedroom was increasing in tempo, and I suggested we head outside for a walk.

Rick pulled me to my feet and closed his arms around me. "Don't lose faith. We'll figure this out and find her."

Whether we'd find her dead or alive was quickly becoming the question.

Shaking away such thoughts, I stepped back and straightened my top. "Right then. Let's head out." I packed the file folder into the black hole I called a handbag and hollered up the stairs, "We'll meet you at the restaurant," and purposefully slammed the front door upon exiting.

Chapter Eleven

This morning, I'd been so wrapped up in my aunt's disappearance, I'd failed to notice what a beautiful fall day it turned into. Halloween was just around the corner. The trees surrounding the Capitol building and lining Duke of Gloucester Street were at their peak. Leaves traversed the rainbow of autumnal colors: ochre, burnt sienna and candied yams. The ones that had already fallen and turned to umber crackled beneath our feet.

The day began with the mercury at the forty-degree mark, but it had risen to a mild sixty degrees. Warm enough, Rick left his leather coat behind, and I pushed the sleeves of my sweatshirt up to my elbows. Rick took my hand in his, and we walked in silence, observing the busy street of tourists.

My mind spun in many directions, and I was beginning to fear the worst had happened to Aunt Vera. I speculated about a number of possibilities. The first, that she'd gone off a bridge in her car in the middle of the night and drowned. Although, I'd no idea where a bridge existed that no one would notice a broken guard rail. The fact she and her car were missing led me to believe whatever had befallen her, it happened in the car.

Rick said he'd called around the hospitals to see if she'd been admitted, but I was fast coming to the conclusion that we needed to widen our search grid, and also perhaps start contacting the morgues. A dreadful thought.

Rick's fingers squeezed mine. "I can hear those gears grinding, and I don't think in a good way."

I explained my thoughts regarding contacting the county morgues.

A flush crept up his neck. "I didn't mention it, due to the morbid nature, but it's already been done. Don't look at me like that. I had Angus do it when he was contacting the hospitals."

I let that sink in for a minute. "S.O.P?"

He grimaced. "S.O.P."

"At least she hasn't been found at the morgue. I suppose that is a positive."

"I'd be willing to bet Detective Riggins will cover his bases by doing the same thing."

I paused to watch a horse and carriage, driven by a coachman dressed in brown livery and a smart black tri-corn hat, clip-clop past us. "Did you check just around here or..."

"I had Angus cover a hundred-mile radius, including the DC metro area, since she told her boss that's where she was headed. The police will likely do a deeper dive. Also, now that your aunt's information is in the system, should something arise—"

I nodded with comprehension, still staring at the empty street. "The cops will be notified."

"Precisely." He stopped walking. "Karina, look at me."

I rotated my body, aware of the distress that must have been written across my features. I was finding it hard to school them into insouciance.

Rick pinched my chin with his thumb and forefinger. "Like I said, don't lose faith. Right now, no news is just that—no news."

"You're suggesting I sit around on a little bubble of hope?"

"First of all, yes, keep your little bubble of hope. Second, knowing your penchant for digging like a hound on a fox hunt, I realize there will be no sitting around. Neither am I suggesting it. We'll follow up on the clues we've got and see where they lead. Don't get discouraged. We'll find her." He kissed me. "I promise." Rick didn't make empty promises, and I allowed the corner of my mouth the minutest uplift of hope. "That's better."

My stomach interrupted our little moment by making a sound like a cat in heat.

He chuckled. "In the meantime, it's almost eleven-thirty; let's see if we can get that table."

The waitress, dressed in colonial tavern wench garb, seated us at a table for four by the window. King's Arms Tavern is one of four taverns in Colonial Williamsburg that serves old-style dishes from the 1700s. Staff members wear traditional colonial attire— the women in dresses with aprons, knit cotton stockings, and mobcaps. The men wear long socks tucked into knickers, red waistcoats, and long brown coats with brass buttons and large cuffs. Inside, a warren of rooms with tables and spindle-backed chairs spill into each other. Knotty pine floors, painted wood paneling, and silk damask wallpaper all provide customers with an atmosphere of historical ambience.

By the time Jillian and Tony arrived, glasses of iced tea and cups of peanut soup sat in front of Rick and me.

"Did you get the bed moved?" I drawled, pinning Jillian with my gaze.

She had the grace to blush and hide behind the menu. "Yup, all sorted out. Thanks."

Rick's shoulders shook with silent mirth, and I couldn't help my own explosion of amusement. Tony grinned. Jillian simply hunkered deeper into the menu, her shoulders lifting to her ears.

Once our tavern wench had delivered their drinks, Jillian got down to brass tacks. "Okay, you two, bring us up to speed. What have you found? What did the police find? What is our post-lunch game plan?"

I wiped a drip of peanut soup off my chin and began, "The police are on it. This morning I spoke to Detective Riggins, the officer assigned to the case."

"So ... we think it's a case. Aunt Vera didn't just hop a flight to Vegas with her latest squeeze?" Jillian asked.

"Rick, you want to handle this?" I pointed at him.

He cleared his throat and explained the search he'd had his people conduct on our behalf, ending with the fact that Vera's credit cards hadn't been used since Monday.

Tony leaned in and said, "Let me get this straight, no sign at the hospitals, no tickets in her name, but the car is gone, and she's got a hundred dollars in her wallet. That's it?"

"That's what we know at this time," Rick said. "I've got my people monitoring her cards in case they pop up on the radar."

"Impressive." Tony stroked his chin. "What about her phone; have you been able to track it?"

I'd forgotten this was a skill Rick's people had in their toolbox, but he reluctantly shook his head. "We haven't been able to get anything. The last time it pinged was on Monday, off a tower not far from the museum."

"Have you been able to get her call logs?" Jillian sipped her iced tea through an anachronistic plastic straw.

"Is that legal?" Tony asked.

Rick cleared his throat. "Strictly speaking, it's not legal without her consent and without a warrant. I have not obtained her call logs. However, as relatives of your aunt, you and Karina can ask the police to obtain a court order. Whether or not they believe it's necessary at this time may be debatable."

I eyed Rick, but he wouldn't meet my gaze.

"She's missing. Why wouldn't the police pull the call logs?" Jillian asked.

"Privacy," Rick explained, rearranging the napkin in his lap. "So far, there is no evidence of foul play."

Technically speaking, I surmised Rick's company had the capability of obtaining those call logs if he really wanted them. I didn't press the issue in front of Jillian and Tony, but I made a mental note to follow up with him later. In the meantime, I sent a quick text to Detective Riggins requesting he obtain my aunt's cellphone logs.

"What about her car? Does she have GPS in it? Can that be tracked?" Tony asked.

"Oh, honey, no," Jillian said a bit condescendingly while patting his hand.

Tony gave my sister a hard look. "Why not? Most cars since the early two-thousands have some sort of GPS system in them. How old is your aunt's car?"

With a snort, I answered his question, "Aunt Vera drives a 1972 Volkswagen Karmann Ghia. The most advanced item in the car is the CD stereo player she added about twenty years ago."

Tony gave a sheepish grin. "Oh. I guess not."

"I suppose a secret elopement is out of the question. Not surprised, after the disaster of that Randy fellow," Jillian commented. "I don't think she's been involved with a man since then."

I opened my mouth to tell her about Vikram, but she grabbed my wrist and said, sotto voce, "Do you think she's gone gay? Maybe there's a girlfriend. Should we look into it?"

"Uh, no. As a matter of fact, there's a-a … man friend." In halting tones, I told her about Vikram, Prisha, and the oddball relationship the three of them had.

Tony seemed nonplussed and elbowed Jillian with eyebrows bouncing. "At least the old gal is getting some."

She delivered a side-eye. "I suppose." She tilted her head and addressed Rick, "You're sure this guy has nothing to do with her disappearance?"

He shrugged. "Karina and I couldn't find any reason for him to lie to us…"

"I hear a 'but' in that explanation," Jillian prompted.

"But—" he glanced at me, "—I may have some of my men digging a little deeper into his files."

My mouth dropped. "You didn't tell me that. You don't believe Vikram and Prisha?"

"It's just a precaution. It doesn't mean I disbelieve him. I'm just—"

"Covering all the bases," I finished for him.

He motioned with his hand, indicating agreement.

The server delivered our meals on thick white China plates with the King's Arms shield at the top. Tony helped himself to the salt cellar with a tiny pewter spoon, and the table went quiet for a few minutes as everyone tucked into their lunch.

Jillian swallowed a bite of Welsh rarebit and broke the silence. "What are the next steps?"

"Rick and I are visiting the museum. We plan to meet Aunt Vera's boss. I was hoping you and Tony could drive around town searching for Vera's car."

"Why? Aren't the police doing that?" Jillian asked.

"The police put out a BOLO," Rick said.

"In other words, they'll keep a look out for the vehicle, but they aren't actively searching for it," I clarified. "It's a fairly obvious car. I was hoping you could cruise some of the college's parking lots, the CW visitor center, and then spread further, like to the grocery stores, maybe the outlet mall?"

Tony's head bounced up and down. "We can do that."

"If you split up, you can cover more ground. One of you can take my Jeep." I dug into my handbag hanging off the back of the chair and encountered the blue folder. "Here are my keys."

Tony held out his hand, and I dropped them into his palm.

"There's one more thing I need to tell you about," I said, placing the blue folder next to my plate.

Rick and I told them about the hidden compartment in Aunt Vera's desk and the matching password-protected Google file.

Jillian scooped up the folder and thumbed through it. "Looks like stuff from the ceramics collection. I mean there are, like, a million different pieces in it. So, what makes these special?"

"That's what we need to find out. Rick and I plan to check on these items after lunch." I took the folder from Jillian and shoved it back into my purse.

During my explanation of the file, I failed to mention the way it was brought to my attention.

No need to tell Jillian and Tony about Aunt Vera's ghostly guest. Much more fun to let them find out on their own.

"What are you smiling about?" my sister asked.

"Oh, nothing." I bit into my thick ham sandwich.

Jillian lost interest. She shrugged, finished her iced tea, and said, "I can't see what a bunch of teapots have to do with our aunt gone missing. I think we'll get further if we can locate her vehicle."

"You may be right," I agreed with Jillian's assessment.

The car was an important piece of this puzzle, but something about the museum kept itching my brain, like an unrelenting mosquito bite. I had this gut feeling we'd find *something* there that would lead to a better explanation of her disappearance.

Chapter Twelve

Upon leaving the tavern, Rick and I decided to walk to the museum, while Jillian and Tony headed back to Vera's to get the cars. I tucked my hand into his elbow, and we strolled in unison—left-right, left-right.

Thoughts of Vera's whereabouts churned in my head. *Has she been abducted by a stranger taking advantage of an older woman? Is she chained in the basement of some creep's house? Is there a man making an Aunt Vera-skin purse right now?*

I shook my head and redirected my brain waves by turning to the mundane. "Did you enjoy your lunch?"

"It was delicious. I've never eaten at one of the taverns."

Before I could respond in shock that he'd never dined at one of the taverns—a must for visitors—we were interrupted by Elton John.

The song went on for a while, as I plumbed the depths of my handbag to locate the cellphone. "Hi, Mom."

"I've called that detective twice now, and he's not picking up."

"O-kay. Perhaps he's in the middle of following a lead," I proposed.

A big, breathy sigh blew across the phone lines. "I just hate it when people don't pick up their phones. What have you and Jilly found?"

A group of tourists following a guide came at us. To get out of their way and gain some privacy, Rick and I turned onto Botetourt Street.

"I found a file folder beneath a false bottom in Aunt Vera's desk."

"Oh, right. The secret drawer," she said in an unimpressed tone.

"Wait a minute." I threw my hand up in exasperation. "You knew Vera's desk had a false bottom, and you didn't think to mention it?"

"Well, I forgot about it … until now," she cried defensively. "What was in it?"

"An inventory list of items in the collection she manages."

"That's it? No note? No map? No weapon? No hidden money or passports with different names?"

"Um…" My face crunched together. "I believe you're confusing Aunt Vera with Jason Bourne."

"You never know," she said in her lecturing voice. "Middle-aged women have hidden depths to them. Maybe *I'm* a spy."

She wasn't wrong. I tapped my chin in thought. Last year, I discovered my eccentric seventy-year-old neighbor, Mrs. Thundermuffin, used to work for the CIA.

"*Are you* a spy, Mom?"

She didn't answer my question but continued with her suppositions, "You know, according to the Spy Museum, one in every seventh person in D.C. is a spy. Vera lived for years in D.C. *And,* once a woman reaches middle age, we become the invisible members of society. Daughter, one day, you'll learn this hard lesson too. Really, they should use more of us in their spy games."

Wow! I never thought of it that way. On the other hand… "You're not wrong. But I don't think Williamsburg is a hotbed of spy activity, *Mom.*"

"I don't know," she said in a sing-song tone. "Camp Peary isn't too far away."

I'd forgotten about Camp Peary. The base, also called, "The Farm," is a CIA training facility for covert operatives. It's on the

York River, only fifteen minutes from CW.

"Is there something you know about Aunt Vera that I don't? Should I be reaching out to my contacts at a certain federal agency?"

"No. I just don't think you should be quite so quick to jump to conclusions or dismissive of my suggestions. Little old ladies could run this world if we so chose," she declared.

That might be a stretch, but I understood the gist of her argument. Moreover, I had been a bit dismissive of her idea. "You're right, Mom. I'm sorry."

"What were we talking about? Oh, the papers you found in the drawer. Is there a secret message on them? You should try heating them."

"Heating them," I said, confused. "Like in the oven?"

"No! Hold it up to a candle. Or is it use lemon juice? I saw it in that *National Treasure* movie. You know the one, with that handsome Nicholas Cage fellow. I'm *obsessed* with him."

My eyes crossed. *Mom's got the hots for Nick Cage?*

"Now, I can't remember," she was saying. "Use Google to find out more."

"I'm fairly certain the papers are just plain photocopies," I stated; however, midway through my thought, I realized the need to placate her far-fetched ideas. "But, when we get back to the house, Rick and I will be sure to check for invisible ink messages. Right now, we are headed over to the museum to see if we can find out more about these pieces. Perhaps they have a special meaning."

"That's good thinking. But watch out for that Hedgewell fellow, Vera's boss," she warned. "I didn't like the vibes I got from him. He was very short with me when I called to ask about Vera. Seems … shifty."

"Let me get this straight, you got—shifty—from a phone call?"

"I don't know how else to explain it, but his voice was *definitely* shifty."

My breath whistled between my teeth. "Okay. We're planning to speak with him this afternoon. I'll keep my eye out for ... shiftiness."

"Good." Satisfied with my report, she demanded, "Now put Jilly on."

"You'll need to phone her. We've split up. She and Tony are driving the area looking for Aunt Vera's car."

"Well, since you've really nothing to report, I'll call your sister and will check back in a few hours. I expect to have a report from that detective by then." She hung up before I could form a response.

I checked my texts—nothing new— before tossing the phone back into my handbag and reaching for Rick's hand. "C'mon, we can walk down Francis Street to get to the museum."

"What was your mom saying about Camp Peary?" Rick asked.

"She was suggesting Aunt Vera was a secret agent for the CIA."

He pondered that for a moment. "*Could* she be?"

My eyes rolled so far back, I thought I saw my optic nerve.

"Don't give me the eye roll. You never pegged Mrs. T. for CIA ... until you knew better." His brows wiggled, taunting me.

"If Vera's a spook, I'll eat my hat."

"You're not wearing a hat."

"Smartass."

He grinned. "Got to keep all those extra brains somewhere."

"C'mon." I tugged his hand, and we jogged across the street. "By the way, I wanted to follow up on my sister's question."

"Which one?" he asked.

"The one about obtaining Vera's phone logs. I mean, *you can* obtain them. Right?"

"If you're asking if I can get them, yes, I imagine Angus could do so." I opened my mouth, but he held up a finger to stop me from speaking. "I can't do it legally."

My mouth closed. I ducked my head and kicked a stone in my path.

"I'm willing to go far for you, Karina. Before I cross that line, I need a little more evidence that they are required to locate your aunt. I'm also hoping your detective will do it for us."

On more than one occasion, Rick had gone above and beyond to save my hide. His constancy included a set of broken ribs, appointing various men in his employ to babysit me on US soil and abroad, and arresting an assassin who'd put me at the top of his hitlist. As much as I wanted those phone records, I didn't want Rick to put his company on the line on my behalf again. I owed him far, far more than I could ever repay. Honestly, there were days when I wondered why he wanted to date me to begin with. My life seemed to be a magnet for scrapes and bad luck. Mike used to say it was my tenacity and unfailing curiosity that got me into those predicaments.

My watch read half past one by the time we arrived. We paid the entrance fee, and I led him directly to the exhibit in question. The ceramics exhibit is a bit of misnomer. Not only did it include china and dishware, it also included a healthy collection of silver and pewter, as well as serving platters, salt and pepper shakers, beer mugs, teapots, and more.

It took us half an hour of searching to realize each piece in Aunt Vera's file was missing. Just as Barbara had said. Not only was her favorite Japanese teapot missing, so, too, were the other items marked on Vera's list. At least we were unable to locate them.

A young couple wandered into the section where we stood, and I murmured quietly to Rick, "Did you notice, each item is part of a larger grouping? And the other items have been rearranged to disguise the missing piece. See, there should be a hole in this shelf of teapots, but there isn't."

"Mm-hm." He moved aside, allowing the couple to pass by.

"What are these numbers she wrote at the top?" I pointed to the paper describing a silver saltshaker. "Twenty-five dot nine."

"They're dates. Written in the European manner. September twenty-fifth."

Doh! I gave myself a mental head slap. "Yes, of course. I wasn't thinking. What's the date on the Japanese teapot?" I licked a finger and stroked through the pages. "Here it is, October eighth."

A docent drifted into the exhibit area. She wore black slacks with flats, a white button-down shirt, and a badge hanging around her neck. She couldn't have been more than twenty years old. Possibly a college student.

Quickly, I closed the folder, returned it to my handbag, and flagged her down. "Excuse me."

She approached with a smile. "How can I help you?"

"I noticed some pieces are missing since the last time I was here. Can you tell me where they've gone?"

"Well, some of our pieces go on loan for traveling exhibits." She tucked her hands behind her back. "Others might be out for cleaning and assessment. Our conservators are constantly evaluating the condition of each piece."

"I see. Do you know if the little Japanese teapot that used to be in here—" I pointed at the glass case, "—is out for cleaning, or is it on tour?"

"I'm sorry, that's a question for one of our curators. They oversee acquiring the pieces for the museum and the loaned items."

"Are there any curators here today?" I glanced around as if one might pop up behind me.

She shook her head. "Our curators have offices over at the Bruton Heights building, where collections not on display are stored, and they tend to work Monday through Friday. I can take your name and number, if you like…"

"No, that's all right. My boyfriend and I were just wondering if the exhibits were being dismantled."

"Oh no, not that I know of," she said genially.

"Thank you." Rick took my arm and guided me out of the room into an area filled with folk art. "We need to find Hedgewell. Where is this talk being held?"

"Downstairs, in the auditorium. Follow me." I found an elevator to the lower floor. Exiting the lift, we trotted over to the double auditorium doors, one of which was slightly ajar with a doorstop wedged in between.

Rick pulled it open, and we entered a small auditorium draped in rich rust colors with neutral beige seats. The house lights were on low, and a woman was onstage organizing musical instruments on tables covered with a black felt cloth. She wore white gloves to handle the instruments.

"Excuse me. The doors don't open for another hour." A tall, thin man with glasses and a bad comb-over approached from a dim corner.

Rick took the lead. "We're looking for the director of conservators, Norman Hedgewell."

He frowned and reluctantly responded, "I'm Norman. What can I do for you?"

I stepped forward. "I'm Karina Cardinal. Vera Wagner's niece. We're very concerned about her, and we understand you may have been the last person to communicate with her."

He looked down his long beaky nose. "Yes. The police phoned me this morning. I'm sorry there's not much more I can add. As I told the detective, Vera texted me a message stating she was going out of town to take care of a sick niece. I assume you aren't the one who is ill?"

"Vera only has two nieces. Neither one of us is ill," I clarified.

"Can you tell us what Vera was working on?" Rick asked.

He watched the woman come on stage with a strange-looking rounded stringed instrument. "As a conservator, she's been assisting one of our curators in the development of a new exhibit that will go on display this December."

I played dumb and frowned with confusion. "I thought she was conservator on the ceramics exhibit."

He cleared his throat. "Yes, yes. She does that, of course, in addition to focusing on the pieces for the new display. We must be flexible, and *some* of us wear many hats at the museum," he said in distracted tones. "Joan, please move the hurdy-gurdy onto the table center stage. Yes, there is fine. And the viola, move it a little to the left. That's better." His attention returned to us. "I'm sorry, we haven't much time before the presentation, and I need to finish preparing. I wish I could tell you more, but that's all I know."

I got the distinct feeling we were being shooed away.

"We understand." Rick took my hand before I could pelt another question. At the auditorium door, he paused. "One more question, Mr. Hedgewell, how often are pieces removed from their exhibits to be cleaned?"

Norman jerked. On stage, a chair crashed to the floor.

"Whoopsie." Joan laughed nervously. "Everything's alright. It didn't hit one of the tables."

Norman breathed a sigh of relief and turned back to us. "What were you saying?"

Rick repeated the question.

"Why do you ask?"

Rick squeezed my fingers hard. I read into his silent message and allowed him to do the talking.

"There was a woman at the ticket counter who lamented one of her favorite teapots had been removed," he said it with nonchalance, but I knew my boyfriend better.

There was nothing nonchalant about the question, and, like Rick, I was interested in witnessing Norman's response.

"Normally, cleanings are scheduled." He'd stepped out from beneath the overhead can light. His beaky nose became even more pronounced as the shadows played across his features, distorting them.

I had difficulty reading his face.

"However, our staff is constantly monitoring the items on display and can have a piece removed if there is a concern."

"What might cause a piece to be removed out of schedule?" I asked.

He glanced back to the stage and replied offhandedly, "Perhaps a tarnished piece of silver. Joan, where is the bow for the violin? I don't see it sitting on the table."

"I'm not sure," she replied. "I didn't see it backstage."

"I'll find it."

We were forgotten as Norman strode down the steps to locate the missing bow.

Chapter Thirteen

The auditorium door closed behind us with a soft whump.

"Now what?" I asked.

Rick stuck a hand in his pocket and shrugged. "I'm not sure."

"*Grease is the word...*" sang in muffled tones from my handbag. I rummaged in my purse to locate my cellphone. "Hey, sis, what's up?"

"Rina! I've found her car! I found Vera's car!" she cried.

I clutched Rick's biceps.

"What?" he mouthed.

"She found Vera's car. Jilly, where are you?"

"I'm following it. On this street ... uh ... it's near the college." Jillian's voice sounded like she was in a cave, and my responses echoed back at me. She must have put me on speaker through the car's stereo system.

"You're following it? Is Vera in the car? Can you see who's driving?"

"No one's driving. It's being towed. The tow truck just pulled out of one of the William and Mary parking lots in front of me. OMG. I hope Aunt Vera's not ... like ... *in* there."

My fingers tightened. "I imagine the tow truck checks for people inside the vehicle."

"Are you *sure*?"

No. "Yes. Are you positive it is her car?"

"How many red Karmann Ghias with a black hard top are there in Williamsburg?"

I squeezed tighter, and, ignoring Jillian's sarcastic tone, I asked, "I don't know. Can you see the license plate?"

At this point, Rick began peeling my fingers, one by one, off his biceps. When I realized my nails had dug in, I released him immediately, mouthing "sorry," and paced over to a dimly lit corner.

"Not yet. We're on a two-lane road, and the tow truck is three cars in front. I'm going to follow it to the lot."

"Okay. Stay on the line. I'm going to call Detective Riggins." I pulled the cell away from my ear and held out my hand to Rick.

His brows rose, and he stared blankly.

"Phone, please." I snapped my fingers.

It came out of his back pocket, and he slapped it into my hand.

I swiped. A fingerprint request came up. "Can you open it?"

He didn't move. "Want to let me in on the plan?"

"Oh, sorry. Jillian's staying on the line." I waggled my cell at him. "I want to call that detective. Have him get Vera's car. Have forensics go over it ... and stuff."

Rick went through the fingerprint reader and seven-number passcode rigamarole to open the phone. "What's the number?"

"Hold on. Jilly, I've got to get into my phone. If I hang up by accident, I'll call you back."

I managed to retrieve the contact information without hanging up on my sister. However, the noise around us began to increase as people gathered in the waiting area for the auditorium doors to open. Rick typed in the detective's number and passed me the phone. While the line connected, we trotted down the hall searching for a quieter, more private space.

The detective didn't answer, and I left a message. "Detective Riggins, this is Karina Cardinal. My sister has located Aunt Vera's car. Please call me as soon as possible." I repeated my number twice before hanging up and passing the phone back to Rick. "Jilly, are you still there?"

"Still here."

"Did you get any closer to the tow truck?"

"Only one car between me and the truck now. Oh, wait … looks like he's turning off. Yes! I'm pulling closer. I think … yup. R-T-I-F-A-C-T. It's her car." A whooshing sound came across the lines. Jillian must have rolled down the window. A horn blared. "Hey! Pull over!" she yelled.

"Jillian."

HONK! HOOOONK!

My sister really laid into it. "Hey, tow truck man! That's my aunt's car! Pull over!"

"Jillian!" I barked. "He's not going to pull over."

A woman at the far side of the exhibit room gave me a dirty look.

"Sorry." I turned my back to her, cupped a hand around my mouth, and said directly into the speaker, "Jillian. You'll cause an accident."

The whooshing stopped as the car window shut. "I'm not going to cause an accident," she snapped. "What did the detective say?"

"He didn't answer. I left a message."

Rick had taken me by the elbow and tugged me up the stairs.

"Where are you now?" I asked.

"I'm on Route 60."

"Okay. I'm going to hang up. I want you to call Tony. Tell him what's going on. Rick and I are at the museum. We need to go back to Aunt Vera's house to get his truck. Once you arrive at the impound lot, text us your location."

"Will do." The line went dead.

By this time, Rick and I were fast-walking toward the exit. We burst out through the glass doors, startling a couple in the entryway, and dodged around them. Once I hit the pavement, I shifted into a jogging trot. Halfway to Vera's, the cellphone, which I still held in my hand, began buzzing the *Grease* song.

I slowed to a walk and put it on speakerphone. "Jillian?" I puffed.

"Okay. We've stopped at a lot off Mooretown Road."

"Great." I sucked air deep into my lungs to steady my breathing. "Rick and I are on our way to Vera's. Text me the address. Did you get in touch with Tony?"

"Yes. He's less than ten minutes away."

"Good." I didn't like the idea of my sister hanging around a sketchy impound lot by herself.
"See you soon."

Jillian hung up, and not a minute later, the *Hawaii Five-0* theme song played in my hand. I swiped the answer icon. "Detective Riggins, I presume."

"Is this Karina Cardinal?" his rocky smoker voice growled at me. "You left a message to call."

"My sister just followed a tow truck to an impound lot. It was towing my aunt's Karmann Ghia."

"Which lot?"

"I'm not sure. She's texting me the address. She said she saw it come out of one of the college parking lots. I'll forward the address to you as soon as I get it."

"What's your sister's name and number? I'll phone her directly and get someone out there."

I reeled off Jillian's information.

"I'll be in touch." He hung up.

"The detective is going to send someone to check out Vera's car."

I stepped off the curb, and Rick yanked me back on the sidewalk as a red minivan whooshed past, missing me by inches. The horn tooted.

"Pedestrians have the right of way!" I yelled at the vehicle and gave him the finger.

Rick eyeballed me.

"What? Well, they do," I mumbled with an embarrassed half shrug.

"We aren't in DC anymore. I've noticed people don't give out the finger for every slight around here," he said dryly. "You weren't in the crosswalk, nor were you watching where you were going."

Perhaps I'd been a little hasty with my rude gesture. I'd been so focused on my phone call with Jillian, I honestly could not recall how I arrived at our location on Francis Street. I was fairly certain Rick had guided me across roadways and kept me from mowing down anyone who might have been in our path.

"All right. I get it. Thanks for saving my ass from getting pancaked."

"No problem, it's such a nice one. Wouldn't want it to get injured." He patted said appendage.

My face burned with both embarrassment and pleasure. "It's a good thing you're here to keep me from losing my mind."

We negotiated the street *at the designated crosswalk*, and I picked up the pace, jogging the last bit. Up the wooden porch steps my shoes clomped, and, after the requisite rummaging through my handbag, I keyed into the house.

"I've got to hit the bathroom before we leave," I said, dropping my stuff in the front hall, hustling past the cat. "Hello, Nightshade. Any sign of our ghost?"

After taking care of business, I saw Rick standing in the kitchen staring at something out of my line of sight.

I trotted down the hall. "Everything okay?"

Without glancing at me, he held up his phone. "Jillian texted the location. GPS says it'll take about fifteen minutes to get there."

"Sounds good." I entered the room and squinted at him. "You've got a funny look on your face. What's up?"

He pointed. "The cats ... they seem to be friends now. What are they staring at?"

The two cats sat on the farm table side by side, gazing. Both were fixated on one corner of the kitchen.

Uh-oh. Sniff. Patchouli. The hairs on my arms rose to attention. "Um..."

The same damn cabinet door that we'd constantly been closing gradually creaked open, moved by an unseen hand.

Rick sucked wind.

The cats' heads rotated, their gazes going to the sink area. Ours followed.

The curtain at the window fluttered as if blown by a draft. Or was it something else?

Smokey jumped down, disappearing behind the table. Nightshade stretched out, yawned, and laid his head down for a nap.

"Damn. This guy is really starting to get under my skin," I muttered.

Rick didn't respond. His face had gone slack and white as Cool Whip.

"Yeah..." I breathed. "I think I probably looked like that when he showed up in the TV reflection. You need to sit down? Maybe put your head between your legs?"

"You said ... but I thought ..." Rick kind of shook himself, like a dog getting out of the pool. "Christ! That is creepy as hell."

"He keeps opening the same cabinet. Does he want some booze?" I speculated, "After all, it *was* safer than drinking the water."

"Has this happened when you've visited your aunt in the past?"

I frowned in thought. "Not that I can recall."

"Your aunt said this ghost ... he helps her find lost items?"

"Yeah. But I haven't lost anything." I squinted at the liquor cabinet, tapping my chin. "On the other hand, in Vera's desk drawer, I—"

"Found the list," we said in unison.

Our gazes locked, and it was as if Rick read my mind. "What's in the cabinet?"

"Can you look in the front hall closet? I think there is a stepladder; I'm going to need it to reach the top shelf."

While Rick went to fetch the ladder, I began removing the liquor bottles from the bottom shelf, lining them up on the farm table. A dozen bottles in all.

"I don't see anything special about this booze. Do you?"

"Not especially." He picked up a half-empty bottle of Jack Daniels whiskey and surveyed it. He suggested, tongue-in-cheek, "Perhaps your ghost has a drinking problem."

"Ha, ha."

The second level was full of fancy glassware—triangular martini glasses, elongated champagne flutes, German-style beer mugs, and bulbous margarita glasses. One by one, I handed them to Rick, who laid them next to the liquor bottles. We identified nothing special about the stemware. I required the stepladder to reach the top shelf, which housed odds and ends. Items rarely used—an ice bucket, a fondue pot, a janky old waffle iron, two glass vases.

"There's one last thing; it's in a Ziploc bag." I reached deep into the back recesses of the cabinet and pulled out... "It's a silver creamer."

I handed the creamer to Rick and stepped down from the ladder. The piece had a fluted body, with an S-curved handle that rested on a square pedestal. Flowers were engraved on either side of the creamer.

"Does this look familiar?" His brows drew together, and he turned it over before handing it back to me.

Puzzled, I shook my head. "I've never seen it before. It's a beautiful piece. I'm surprised it's not in Aunt Vera's china cabinet." I went to pull open the baggie, but he halted me mid-rip.

"Don't touch it."

"Why?"

"I'm beginning to formulate a hypothesis."

My mouth twisted. "What kind of hypothesis?"

"What if this isn't your aunt's creamer?"

Unhappy, my lips rolled in, and lids drooped. "What do you mean?"

"What if this is one of the items on the list?"

"You mean the secret list we found in her desk?"

"Yes. Let's say the ghost led you to the list. Why that cabinet? Is there anything here," he indicated the items on the table, "that you haven't seen, or seems out of place?"

My gaze scanned the objects one by one. The booze was booze—gin, vodka, whiskey, grenadine, etc. Nothing out of the ordinary. I'd seen or used the glassware over holidays or during visits. Margarita glasses in the summer, champagne flutes at New Year's; my father poured his beer in a mug every time he visited.

The top shelf items were random. I'd never seen the creamer; on the other hand, I'd never seen the vases either. However, the vases were cheap glass, the kind you get from a florist delivery. The only piece out of place was the heavy silver creamer. I couldn't figure out why it wasn't in the dining room with the rest of Vera's formal dishware.

With a defeated sigh, I put a hand on my hip. "You're right, that creamer *is* out of place. So, lay it on me. What are you thinking?"

"What if the items on your aunt's list are not actually being cleaned but have been taken?"

The moment he referenced "the list," I had a feeling that was where he was going, because I'd begun thinking something similar. "You think the items went missing on the dates she lists at the top?"

"Perhaps."

"If this is one of the pieces—" I held the creamer aloft, "—then what's it doing buried in her kitchen? Unless you're suggesting *she* is the thief."

His mouth puckered.

My gaze narrowed. "I don't like what you're insinuating."

"Just … humor me. Occam's razor says the simplest—"

"Answer is the correct answer." I placed the silver piece on the table and paced around it to get away from Rick.

Calmly, he asked, "What is the simplest answer?"

I didn't like where this was going, but with the information we had on hand, I played his game. "Okay, the simplest answer—my aunt has been stealing. And what? You think she's selling the loot on the black market? But now she's decided to skedaddle. Why now?"

My Irish ancestry was coming out—pitchy voice and big hand waving ensued. "It's been going on for months. And why leave your car in a lot where she knows it will eventually be towed? If you're going to ditch a car, leave it in a big parking lot, like long-term parking at the airport. Or leave it here at the house. She could have walked to a bus stop and got away. Also, why leave one of the pieces here in the house? A police search will easily locate it." By the time I got to the end of my questions, I'd controlled the hand-waving by placing them on my hips, nails digging tight into the flesh on either side.

"You're correct on all points." He pulled out a chair, sat down, and indicated the chair next to him.

Refusing with a head shake, I remained standing, stiff and tense, across the table from him.

"Let's *now* assume your aunt is *not* the thief. Instead, *she's* noticed items go missing."

My hands relaxed but remained on my hips.

Rick continued, "What if Vera has been trying to solve the case on her own? What if she caught the thief red-handed, and this—" he tapped the pot, and the baggie wrinkled, "—is her proof?"

"How is it proof, if it's in *her* kitchen?" Up went my hands in frustration. While I liked this theory better than the "Aunt Vera's a thief" theory, it didn't explain why she had this silver creamer in her house. "Why is the proof hidden in the back of her cabinet?" I gestured at said cabinet.

"Why would she put it in a plastic bag?" His subdued, serene tones contrasted with my own.

My brain took a moment to catch up to what Rick was suggesting. When it did, I drew in a breath. "You're suggesting fingerprints?"

"It's what I would do."

I picked up the creamer, turning it over to look at it from all sides.

"Check the maker's mark at the bottom."

I flipped it over, pressing the plastic against the bottom to get a better view. Now it was my turn to suck wind. "It's stamped REVERE." Gently, I laid the silver piece down and rubbed my temples. "You saw this?"

He gave a sharp nod.

"If it's not a fake, this is a genuine Paul Revere piece of silver. It could be worth thousands of dollars. The history alone makes it priceless."

"Where's the blue folder?"

"In my handbag. Let me fetch it." I scooped up all my belongings from the hallway and dumped them onto the counter, since the kitchen table was still covered with the items we'd removed from the cabinet. After drawing out the blue folder, I placed it in Rick's lap. "I-I can't. You do it."

My already knotted stomach tightened even more.

He opened the folder and quickly thumbed through the pages with attached photos. "It's not any of these." He pulled out the list and ran his finger down it. "But it could be this one, here. It's on the list but not accounted for with a dossier."

I peered over his shoulder to see where he pointed. It read, **Pre-Revolutionary Revere Silver: Fluted Cream Pot made for Lucretia Chandler.**

"Lucretia was a lucky woman," I commented. "It could be this piece. It is fluted, and the etchings on it are old."

My phone buzzed with a text from Jillian.

Detective is here getting car out of impound. Where are you?

I chewed my bottom lip. "Jilly's wondering where we are. Do we go? Do we tell the cops about this creamer?"

"Call your sister. See if she can handle the situation on her own."

I hit the little telephone icon next to Jillian's text and put it on speaker.

"Rina? Where are you?" she asked.

"We're at Aunt Vera's. Did the detective get there? What does he have to say?"

"He's spoken with the impound lot guy. I guess this outfit has permission to cruise the college's lots and tow anything that doesn't have a parking sticker. So, that's why her car got towed. Jerry, that's the tow truck guy, said the lot usually calls the police at the end of the day to provide a list of all the cars towed in. I guess, when people call to report a stolen vehicle, the police can check the list to see if it's been towed away," she explained.

"So, Aunt Vera's car would have come up on their radar tonight?"

"I suppose. Either case, the detective is going to have the car moved into police custody and have it checked for prints." She went quiet for a moment and then whispered, "And for bodily fluids."

I made an icky face. "That's an ewwie thought."

"I know. They're bringing it up to the front now. The detective said he wants to check the trunk before the police tow it to their own lot."

"She's not in there," I stated firmly.

"How do you know?"

"She'd never fit. The trunk is too small."

The "trunk" in a Karmann Ghia is this tiny space under the front hood—the engine being located at the back of the car. Not only is it petite in length and width, it's shallow.

"But ... what if she's been chopped to bits and stuffed in there?" she whispered in horror.

Rick rubbed a hand down his face.

My eyes goggled, and I bellowed, "Good gawd, Jilly! A bit morbid, aren't we?

"C'mon, you haven't thought about it? The fact that Aunt Vera may be ... dead," again she whispered the last word.

"No!" My ponytail flapped side to side as I shook my head. "I refuse to think it. Besides, if there was a body in the trunk, it would be days old and probably smell. Does it smell?"

"Hold on, let me check." She must have pulled the phone away. We heard talking in the background but couldn't make out the words. "No smell. The detective is jimmying open the front end now. Do you see anything? No? Whew. It looks clean. You were right. No chopped-up auntie."

I took a beat to press my fingers against my temple.

"Jillian," Rick leaned forward to speak, "what lot did they pull Vera's car from?"

"Uh, I don't know the area well enough. Hold on, I'll ask Jerry." The line went silent. Jillian must have muted us. A minute later, she came back on. "He said he towed it from the rear Sadler lot, behind the stadium."

"Okay, once you're done there, you and Tony need to get back to Vera's house. We need to, uh, meet to reconnoiter. And discuss the new evidence," I said.

"You're not coming?"

"The detective seems to have things under control. I don't see a need. Do you?"

"I guess not, but I thought you said you were coming." Disappointment laced her comment.

"We've ... discovered something here at the house that we're looking into."

"Oh. Should I tell the detective?"

"NO!" Rick and I snapped as one.

I continued, "Not yet. It's still ... formulating. We wouldn't want to waste his time."

"Fine. Tony and I will be home in a bit."

The line went dead, and I looked to my boyfriend for our next move.

"Let's call Vikram."

My brows winged upward. "Are you reconsidering your recent assessment that he might be involved with her disappearance? The car *was* located at the school."

"Not necessarily, although I'm not ruling it out. I think he knows more than he realizes."

Chapter Fourteen

"I'm telling you, Vera played things very close to her chest when it comes to her job. We don't discuss the collection she manages," Vikram repeated firmly.

"What about her coworkers, colleagues?" Rick pressed. "Did she ever complain about them?"

"Well …" He paused.

Spit it out, I wanted to yell. Instead, I reeled in my impatience and tried to emulate my Sphinx-like boyfriend, who could outwait a sloth running a marathon.

Finally, Vikram spoke, "I believe she hasn't much respect for her boss."

"Norman?" Rick clarified.

"Tall, balding fellow."

"Uh-huh." My head bounced up and down. "That's the guy. What did she say?"

"It's not what she said. Vera spent far too long in the confines of Washington politics—she wasn't one to speak ill of another person. However, I know she had the most experience of anyone at the museum, yet she was passed over, and Norman got the job two years ago."

I wonder why she never mentioned it. "Well, that sucks. I know these types of jobs are scarce and highly competitive. However, it wasn't Norman's fault the museum muckety-mucks chose him over her."

"Perhaps not, but a few months ago, she invited me to attend a fundraising gala at the museum. She introduced me to Norman, because he hadn't recalled our meeting at a prior event. He seemed like a perfectly fine person to me. After the usual small talk, a colleague pulled him away." Vikram stopped speaking.

"And, what? Did she make a snarky comment about Norman?" I prompted.

"Not a comment. It was more ... something in her face. As if she'd just seen a particularly nasty bug crawling across her shoe," Vikram explained. "The expression was fleeting. A donor came up to us. She smiled and was her usual charming self."

"Vera has never mentioned any other colleagues to you?" Rick continued to dig.

"Sure, she's *talked* about other colleagues. Felicity, one of the curators, is a good friend. They have lunch regularly. There are a handful of conservators working at the museum she's mentioned a time or two. Some woman named Elaine," Vikram explained.

Nightshade jumped up on the table, and Rick scratched behind his ears. "But none of them in a negative or suspicious light?"

"Not that I can recall. And like I said, she never uttered a word against her boss. It was just ... I don't know. But I could sense the underlying disdain she had for him."

The cat tiptoed over to me to get some love, and I ran my hand along his silky fur. "Did you ever ask her about it?"

"No. I forgot to ask her about it after the party. Why? Do you think Norman has something to do with her disappearance?"

Rick answered Vikram's question with one of his own, "What is Norman's role at the museum?"

"My understanding, he is Director of Conservators. He oversees his staff and probably has his fingers in everything that museum owns."

"So, he'd have access to all of the collections." Rick drummed his fingers against the table.

"Undoubtedly," Vikram stated.

Smokey decided to get in on the petting action. He leapt onto the table, plopped down in front of Rick and butted his shoulder.

"Anything else you know about him?" Rick asked, absently stroking the cat's head.

Vikram sighed and paused in thought before saying, "He's an advisor for the art history internship program that's run through the university."

"Interesting, but I don't see how it has any bearing on the case," I commented.

"Have you heard anything from the police?" Vikram asked.

"Not much," I replied. "Vera's car was located, and it's now in police possession. I suspect they will be checking it over."

"Dear heavens. Vera, my love, where have you gone?" Vikram asked in fadeaway tones.

Nightshade curled next to me and gave Smokey the evil eye.

"Don't lose faith. We'll find her," I replied in my most determined voice. "Thank you, Vikram. You've been a great help."

"Let me know if there is anything I can do."

"Of course, we'll be in touch." Rick ended the call and mulled. "Norman..." He pulled out his cell and started tapping.

"What are you doing?"

"Calling the office. I want Angus to run a background check on Norman Hedgewell."

I stroked Nightshade as Rick made his call.

Right now, I just wanted answers. I debated bringing up Vera's phone logs with him. Instead, I opted to nudge Detective Riggins. He'd never responded to my initial text, and I had a feeling he would continue to ignore me. It was time to sic my mom on him. Texting her, I suggested she speak to Riggins about Vera's phone logs.

A moment later she responded with,

Good idea! Anything new to report?

With an evil grin, I told her Jillian had some new information. Then I tucked the phone in my back pocket and turned my attention to Rick's conversation.

"Do a surface scan," he said to Angus.

"I want to know what Norman had for Christmas dinner when he was twelve," I joked loud enough for Angus to overhear.

Rick rolled his eyes. "Past ten years. Look into his prior employment too. Get back to me as soon as you can. This is a priority." He hung up without a farewell and scrutinized the silver creamer.

Since Smokey wasn't getting any rubbing from Rick, and Nightshade had made it clear the cat was unwelcome on this side of the table, the Siamese lightly jumped off and stalked out of the room.

"What's cookin' in your noggin?"

"It's—" he shook his head and returned his attention to me, "—nothing. Let's wait and see what Angus and the police find."

"In the meantime, we should probably put Aunt Vera's cabinet back in order."

Chapter Fifteen

An hour later, Jillian and Tony came in through the back door. She dropped her handbag on the counter, pulled out a kitchen chair, and plopped down with dramatic flair.

"That was insane. I'm still reeling," she whooshed.

Tony, with less drama, headed directly to the fridge. "I'm thirsty. What's there to drink?"

"Water bottles are on the bottom shelf, lemonade and iced tea on the door," I supplied.

Both the cats entered the kitchen from different entryways.

"Honey, you want anything?" He stuck his head into the cool fridge.

"Just a bottle of water. Thanks. Hello, Smokes," she cooed, "howyabeen?"

Smokey preened directly over to his favorite person and stropped against her leg.

Tony tossed a bottle at my sister, which she handily caught. "Anyone else want something?" he asked.

Rick and I both demurred; we had drinks in front of us.

"Mom phoned me. I told her what happened, and she spoke with Detective Riggins about getting those phone logs of Vera's." Jillian twisted off the top and gulped down half the bottle before leaning down to pet her cat. "Someone from forensics showed up. The detective wanted the car dusted for prints before it went anywhere."

"That's good." Rick nodded. "Maybe they'll find something."

Tony joined us, taking the seat next to Jillian, across from me.

"What's that?" He pointed to the plastic-wrapped creamer.

"*That* is a pre-revolutionary fluted cream pot made for Lucretia Chandler," I stated.

Jillian laughed. "Who in the hell is Lucretia Chandler? Is she one of our ancestors? A bit of a mouthful, that name. What's it doing out on the counter?"

"I have no idea who Lucretia Chandler is. Aunt Vera's ghost directed us to it," I dropped that little bomb and waited.

Jillian stopped mid-drink. Inch by inch, she lowered the bottle back down to the table. "You saw her ghost? That-that—" she snapped her fingers, "—Civil War Union soldier she told us about."

"The very one. His name is Lieutenant Cabway."

Nightshade seemed to have taken a shine to me. He strolled over, stared up with big kitty eyes, much like Puss in Boots from *Shrek*, and patted my leg with his little paw. Then the cat launched himself into my lap.

Her mouth O'd. "You're joking."

"Scout's honor." I held up three fingers with my right hand.

"I can't believe you saw him," she said with a bit of whine. Her shoulders slumped in disappointment. "I've never seen him."

Tony, whose head had ping-ponged back and forth between the two of us, chimed in, "Wait, you're saying this house has a poltergeist?"

"Aunt Vera says he's more of a polter-guest. Because he's a friendly spirit." Jillian replied.

"Indeed," I confirmed.

"That's so dope." Tony's eyes lit up. "Halloween is in three days, and we're staying at a haunted house."

"I can't believe it. All the times we've stayed here, *I've* never seen the ghost," Jillian pouted. "And *I've* actually searched for it. Remember that time Tyler and I snuck the Ouija board into Mom's suitcase, so we could use it to contact the ghost? Only we forgot to get it out when we arrived, and Mom found it. Boy, was she steamed. You know how she hates those things." Jillian pealed into laughter. "She said it invited demons."

"I don't rightly recall that incident," I commented dryly.

"No?" My sister's smile dissipated. "You might have been on a Model UN trip that time."

"Probably."

"So, what's with Lucretia's cream pot?" Jillian finally got back on track. "Why did the ghost direct you to a creamer?"

"Ah, the question of the hour," I mused.

Tony finished his water, and the plastic bottle made an awful crackling noise as he crunched it in his fist. "That's a mighty fancy coffee creamer."

"It was made by Paul Revere," Rick said.

The crackling noise ceased. "You mean the guy who rode his horse through Boston yelling, 'The British are coming! The British are coming!'" Tony demonstrated by bouncing up and down in his chair, pretending to ride a horse. "That guy?"

My boyfriend nodded. "The very man."

"Excellent." Satisfied, Tony sat back in his chair.

On the other hand, my sister began to clue in on the situation. Her face transformed from mild interest into concern, and she asked in low tones, "Where did you find this?"

"In the back of the cabinet," I answered.

"The one that kept getting left open?"

"The one the ghost kept opening," I corrected.

With a head shake, she moved past the ghost comment. "This looks like something from the collection at the museum."

My sister was much quicker than I'd been.

Without a word, I passed the blue file folder to Rick. He pulled the list out, placing it between Tony and Jillian, and pointed to number 127. The pair leaned forward to peer at the paper.

"Pre-Revolutionary Revere Silver: Fluted Cream Pot made

for Lucretia Chandler," Jillian read. Her eyes blinked up at me. "Rina, what is Aunt Vera doing with this ... *in her home?*"

That sick knot tightened in my stomach again. "Your guess is as good as mine." The warm bundle of fur in my lap began purring as I absently stroked him.

"Did she steal it?" Jillian asked in a pitchy voice.

"Maybe," I shrugged and then hooked a thumb at my boyfriend, "although Rick has a different theory."

"Enlighten us, please," Jillian begged.

Smokey, having been ignored since the announcement of the ghost, gave a guttural meow, akin to "screw you" in cat language. He trooped out of the kitchen in a snooty manner, as only a Siamese can achieve.

Rick gave an abbreviated version of his hypothesis. "Your aunt found it in someone else's possession. Assumed the real thief left prints. Bagged it for the purpose of preserving fingerprints."

"How does she know the thief didn't use gloves?"

I shrugged. "It's only a theory. The one I prefer over the alternative."

"Maybe the ghost knows," Tony threw in.

"You're right, babe." She slung her arm around Tony's shoulders. "Maybe he *does* know. Call him, Rina."

I shifted Nightshade into a more comfortable position on my lap. "It doesn't seem to work that way. He shows up when he feels like it."

"*Lieutenant Cabway!*" Jillian hollered, cupping her hands around her mouth. "Come out, come out, wherever you are? You-hoo!"

Nightshade gave my sister an inscrutable look, jumped off my lap and exited the kitchen.

"That cat thinks I'm nuts," she commented.

"Actually, both the cats seem to know when the ghost is present. Perhaps you should follow them around," I encouraged.

"Especially Nightshade."

Jillian didn't seem interested in my suggestion. "I know!" She snapped her fingers, and her eyes widened to the size of baseballs. "Let's hold a séance. With so many of those ghost tours about, I bet there's a medium in the area. I'm sure someone knows what to do." Enamored with her new idea, she whipped out her phone. "Siri, psychic mediums near me."

Rick looked perplexed. Tony watched my sister with a "humor her" smile on his face.

I rolled my eyes. "Jillian, I don't think—"

Jillian shushed and flapped a hand at me. "Excellent, look, there's a top ten list." She turned her phone to show us.

"Great." My comment dripped with sarcasm.

"Oo, this one sounds good. It says she's licensed. I'm going to call her." Dialing, Jillian rose from the table and headed toward Vera's office. "Hello, is this Madame Seraphina?" The rest of the conversation was muffled as she closed the door.

An awkward pall of silence fell upon us, and we exchanged uncomfortable glances.

Finally, Tony, looking over his shoulder, said, "Maybe this isn't a good idea. Do you want me to see if I can stop her?"

"If she's got the same Cardinal stubbornness her sister has, there'll be no stopping her," Rick commented.

I shoved hard enough to knock him off his chair. He fell off with a chuckle.

Tony, oblivious to our antics, continued looking at the door to Vera's office. "I don't know, these psychics can be charlatans…"

"Leave her. Unfortunately, Rick is right." I turned a palm toward the ceiling. "Who knows, maybe this psychic will be able to draw out our Union soldier."

Tony shifted back to us. His lip quirked. "You didn't *really* see a ghost. Did you?"

I blew air through my lips, making a b-b-b-b noise. "Tony, as God is my witness—" I held up my right hand, "—that damn ghost has been turning up *all over* this house. Rick and I watched as he opened—" I stomped over to the liquor cabinet and rapped my knuckles against it, "—this cabinet. Right here. Plain as day. This cabinet creaked open by itself." I looked to Rick for confirmation.

Reluctantly, he nodded. "It's true, man."

"I swear, the cats can *see* him. And I can *smell* him." I pointed to my nose.

Confusion crossed Tony's features, and he fidgeted with Jillian's bottle top. "What do you mean, you can smell him?"

"Any time he's in a room, I smell pipe smoke. Patchouli and clove. You know, there was a lot of smoking back then."

Tony delivered a side-eye, unsure if I was putting him on. "They do say … animals can sense things humans cannot."

"There you have it." I rapped the cabinet door one more time.

My sister burst out of the office, startling Tony. He jerked involuntarily.

"I've booked her! Madame Seraphina will be here in half an hour!" she cried triumphantly.

"Half an hour!" Tony exclaimed. "I thought séances happened at nighttime."

"Apparently, she's got a gig tonight at eight. I explained the nature of the situation, and she said she'd fit us in immediately."

I dreaded to ask, but I had to know. "And … how much will Madame Seraphina charge for her services?"

"Three hundred! And she'll give us the entire hour." Jillian's arms spread expansively in front of her as if she'd scored a bargain.

I blinked. "She charges three hundred bucks an hour?" My sister was a middle school teacher. It wasn't as though she had money to burn. "Can you afford that, Jilly?"

Her face fell. "I thought we'd split the cost. C'mon, you spent more than that on the shoes you're wearing."

I hadn't, but there were plenty of other shoes in my closet that had cost me more than $150, so I didn't argue with her on that point.

Tony tried to reason with her. "Um, babe, do you think this is the best idea…?"

My sister shot daggers at her fiancé. "Can't you just support me?"

Tony turned to me and scratched his head. "Maybe this woman is the real deal, and she'll be able to give us some sort of clue.

Perhaps pigs can fly. "Jillian—" I started, but the *Hawaii Five-O* theme song interrupted my attempt to reason with her, and I let it go. "Hello, Detective Riggins. Did you find anything interesting in my aunt's car?"

"That's what I'd like to discuss." He got directly to the point, "Would it be possible for me to meet you at your aunt's house?"

I zoned in on the silver creamer. "By all means, Detective; when were you thinking of stopping by?"

"Soon. Are you there now?"

"Y-yes."

"I'm fifteen minutes away," he said curtly and hung up.

Rick and I locked gazes, my eyes practically popping out of my head. "He's coming over in fifteen minutes!"

"You should probably put that away until we know more about it," he casually suggested.

I tilted my head. "Ya think?"

"Oh dear," Jillian murmured. "I hope he leaves before Madame Seraphina arrives. I'd rather not have those two cross paths. I don't want him thinking we're a bunch of crackpots."

I rubbed my temples. "Rick, can you find someplace safe for Lucretia's cream pot?"

"I'd better wipe down the baggie too," he replied.

I nodded in agreement. "Jilly, can you and Tony clean off the dining room table? It's got about an inch of dust on it. I imagine the medium will want to host her séance there. Meanwhile, I'll clean up the front parlor and bring the detective to that room when he arrives. If our psychic shows up while he's still here, you and Tony can take her into the dining room and close the pocket doors."

Everyone scattered to do their respective jobs. True to his word, fifteen minutes later, Detective Riggins knocked on Aunt Vera's front door.

"Hello," I greeted, pulling the door wide.

"Detective Riggins." He passed me a business card. "You must be Karina Cardinal."

"Won't you come in, Detective?"

The man was a barrel-chested fellow, with sandy gray hair, a bulbous nose, and a deeply lined face. It was the craggy face of a man who'd seen some shit in his day. He wore a pair of jeans, a blue button-down shirt with a striped tie, and a brown sport coat. The scent of cigarettes overwhelmed me as he entered the tiny foyer. He must have been a heavy smoker; the smell encircled him like the character Pig Pen in the Charlie Brown comics. His dark hooded eyes darted around, assessing the house the moment he set foot inside.

I indicated to my right. "Why don't we go into the parlor?"

Once he passed me, I raised the same hand to my nose. The smell of the jasmine hand lotion I recently rubbed on before he arrived aided in masking the stink.

Rick rose from the sofa, and I introduced the two gentlemen. Meanwhile, Jillian and Tony waited in the kitchen for the arrival of Madame Seraphina.

"Have a seat, Detective." I indicated one of the armchairs and took my own place next to Rick.

He put his arm around my shoulder and asked, "What can you tell us about Vera's car?"

The detective's knees creaked and popped as he lowered himself into the seat. When he landed, his breath wheezed in a drawn-out puff. "Preliminary reports revealed no bodily fluids or fingerprints in the vehicle."

"Besides Vera's you mean," I added.

"Could you repeat that?" He turned his left profile to me and held a hand to his ear. "I'm hard of hearing in my right ear."

I raised my voice, "You're saying you didn't find any fingerprints in the car beside Vera's. Correct?"

"No," his tone was abrupt. "I'm saying we didn't find any fingerprints inside the car."

Rick squeezed my shoulder. I glanced at him, then back to the detective. "I'm not sure I understand. How can there be no prints?"

"The interior of the car had been wiped down. Completely. No prints whatsoever." He had a way of speaking that reminded me of the actor Wilford Brimley—sharp, gravelly, and direct.

"That seems … odd." I crossed my legs.

"To say the least."

"What about the exterior? Door handles? Trunk?" Rick suggested.

"We were able to lift some prints from the driver's side window. We'll run those through the AFIS system. See if anything comes up."

"Do you have my aunt's fingerprints for comparison?" I asked. "And what about security cameras in the area? The college must be littered with them."

"Yes. She'd been printed when she worked for the Smithsonian. I'm getting the camera footage pulled as we speak." His stout fingers reached into an inner coat pocket and drew out a pad and pen. "This case with your aunt has me scratching my head."

"In what way?" I made a concerted effort to keep my tone even.

"Were you aware she was dating a married man by the name of Vikram Gupta?"

I nodded. "I've only recently learned about their relationship. Is Mr. Gupta under suspicion?"

"At this time, I'm not ruling anyone out." Riggins' gaze explored the room as he continued, "However, after speaking with Mr. Gupta, I tend to doubt he's got anything to do with Vera Wagner's disappearance. He was out of town on the day she disappeared."

"Did you check his alibi?" Rick piped in.

"I confirmed he checked into the hotel on Tuesday and out on Thursday," Riggins rumbled.

"What's your working theory, Detective Riggins?" Rick crossed his legs.

"According to her boss—" he flipped through his notebook until he found what he was looking for, "—Norman Hedgewell, your aunt stole from the museum. He believes she's skipped town with her ill-gotten gains."

Rick squeezed my shoulder, but I wouldn't be silenced. "Where on earth did he come up with such an idea?"

Riggins' attention alighted on me. "The parking lot from which Mrs. Wagner's car was towed was only a few blocks' walk to the train station."

I sputtered, "Why, that's the most preposterous accusation I've ever heard!"

"Hedgewell told me he recently noticed a piece missing from one of the collections she manages."

"I see." I caught myself fidgeting with my earring and tucked an errant curl behind my ear to mask my unease. "And he's reported this missing piece to the proper authorities?"

"Apparently not."

I did my best to display shock. "Why not? Theft from a museum is quite a crime. Why didn't he report it?"

An itty-bitty grin finally broke through those craggy features, and his cheeks filled with deep craters that once would have been dimples. On the other hand, that might have been a grimace. It was difficult to determine. "I asked him the same question."

I didn't need the pressure of Rick's hand to hold my tongue. Instead, I tilted my head and waited for Riggins to continue.

The detective looked down at his notes. His next comment seemed to come out of left field. "Do you know if Mrs. Wagner liked to gamble?"

I blinked a few times before responding, "No. She absolutely did not."

I knew for a fact, after Vera's marriage to Good Time Randy, she'd sworn off gambling. She even refused to purchase a lottery ticket.

"Did you know your aunt filed for bankruptcy about fifteen years ago?"

I hadn't known for sure, but the fact didn't surprise me. The detective was clearly trying to throw me off-balance, to get some sort of response out of me or dirt on my aunt.

I ground my teeth with irritation and strove to answer in neutral tones, "After her first husband unexpectedly died, my aunt went through a rocky period in her life. She made a poor choice marrying her second husband, who was a liar, spendthrift, and inveterate gambler. It was that man and his debts that forced Vera to file for bankruptcy. Before Randy came into her life, my aunt was fiscally solvent, which she strove to become again after their divorce."

"Yes, it seems she was—" he gave a phlegmy smoker's cough, "—fiscally solvent, as you say."

With composure, I said, "You didn't answer my earlier

question, Detective. Why didn't Norman Hedgewell report the theft?"

One side of his mouth rose. "Something to the effect, he was fond of your aunt and wanted to give her the benefit of the doubt. He planned to speak with her about the missing piece this week," he paused as if for dramatic effect, "before she went missing."

Rick finally spoke up, "What motive did Norman give for the theft and her subsequent disappearance?"

"He didn't."

Rick licked his lips. "How much is he claiming she stole? Monetarily, that is. What's the value of the item?"

Riggins checked his notes. "Along the lines of fifteen thousand."

"What would that item fetch on the black market?" I asked.

His mouth formed a straight line, and his gaze narrowed. "That's an interesting question."

"Obviously, my aunt couldn't steal items from the museum and sell them legally. She'd have to do it on the black market," I said in a patronizing manner, as if everyone knew about the black-market underworld.

Many people probably did not know. I knew about it because this wasn't my first rodeo with black-market artifacts. While my name wasn't in the newspapers, it was in some FBI reports surrounding an Egyptian death mask. Although I wasn't sure Detective Riggins had access to such reports. On the other hand, if he had FBI contacts…

The detective didn't seem to care for my attitude and asked in sharp tones, "And what do you know about black-market artwork, Miss Cardinal?"

"Enough to know they wouldn't go for retail or auction value," I snapped back.

He shifted in his seat. "You would be correct."

"Well…?" I waited with a raised brow for Riggins to enlighten me.

"Maybe half," he grumbled.

Or less.

I kept that thought to myself; instead, I leaned forward. "Detective, I'm sure you've been looking into my aunt's background, finances, phone records, and more," I reeled off. "Have *you* found a motive for such a paltry theft, which my aunt surely realized would put her job in danger, not to mention the possibility of jail time."

I jumped up and spun in a slow circle with my arms outstretched. "I mean, really. I've seen you looking around my aunt's home."

"It's a very nice home," he agreed.

"I can assure you, she's got more than fifteen-thousand dollars' worth of furnishings, crystal, china, jewelry, and clothing," I counted the items with my fingers, "within the confines of this house. I know she's also got a 401K with plenty in it. Why would she steal a piece worth such a paltry sum?"

When the detective didn't immediately answer, I prodded, "Moreover, why would she abandon her car, wipe it down, and skip town with hardly any money in her pockets? With an artifact worth a measly fifteen grand, no luggage, and no jewelry?" I collapsed onto the sofa, crossed my arms and legs, and sat back with a pinched mouth, waiting.

"How do you know she didn't take any luggage or jewelry?" he asked.

"Because her luggage set is still in her bedroom closet, and, as far as I can tell, none of her jewelry is missing."

"Perhaps you can show me this luggage and jewelry."

Rick straightened, but I didn't need his warning hand on my knee to know instinctively what my answer should be. "Not without a warrant."

The pressure on my knee relaxed, and Rick said, "You didn't

answer Karina's initial question. Why would she perpetrate a theft such as the one you're describing?"

He cleared his throat. "I don't have an answer for you."

"What if my aunt has been abducted? Are you following any leads with that theory in mind?" I pressed.

"Of course, your aunt might have run into foul play trying to fence the items," Riggins threw back at me. "We haven't ruled it out."

My gaze narrowed, but I didn't respond.

"Detective, what if, instead of *being* the thief, Vera *discovered* the thief?" Rick tossed into the fray. "And he's ... doing what he can to cover up his crimes?"

The bing-bong of the doorbell interrupted the detective's response.

I stiffened. *Damn! I'd prayed we'd be done with the detective before Madame Seraphina arrived.*

None of us moved.

"Do you need to get that?" the detective asked.

Jillian's hurried footsteps pounded down the hall, answering his question.

"No," I responded for good measure.

The door opened, and high-pitched dramatic tones greeted my sister. "Hel-lo! You must be Jill-ee-anne! And *who* is *this* handsome kitty?"

"That's Nightshade," my sister said in hushed tones. "If you'll follow me."

"Oh, my! You've got *such* a strong pink aura! You must be a very kind and giving person. Ohhh, I feel so much *energy* coming from this house."

There began a humming sound.

Jillian cleared her throat. "If you'll just come this way."

"In a moment, dear. I'm *getting* something. It's coming from ... *this* di-rection."

"Oh, I don't think—"

It didn't matter what my sister thought, because in flowed Madame Seraphina. Her caftan-style dress full of colorful swirls straight out of the seventies fluttered around her ankles where a pair of hot pink Chuck Taylor sneakers peeked out from beneath the dress. She couldn't have been more than five-two. Her hair was bright, big, and curly, and must have been dyed because the color was too unnaturally orange.

"Well, hello!" She waved with both hands. Rings of all sizes encircled her fingers. They blinked in the sunlight as she pointed at each one of us. "Red, violet, and, oh, a little muddled brown."

"I beg your pardon," I said, making no effort to rise.

"Your aura, dear. Lots of red. You must be quite strong-willed. *You're* obviously her lo-ver." The woman squinted at Rick for a moment, then her eyes widened, and she licked her lips. "Oh, honey," she directed at me, "you're a lucky one ... *if* you can keep a hold of him."

My eyes narrowed. Rick grinned. The detective gawked at the woman.

"Hello, Detective Riggins." Her fingers wiggled at him like worms.

"Have we met?" He hacked one of his phlegmy coughs.

Madame Seraphina smiled and gave a droll look. "Why, I helped the police on the Blackstone case. You remember, three years ago, the little five-year-old boy who went missing? They found him in the crawlspace beneath the neighbor's house. I helped point the police search in the right direction," she said the last as an aside to Rick and me.

"I recall the case. I don't remember you. You a P.I. or something?"

"Psychic." Hiking up the enormous tote bag she had slung over her shoulder, Madame Seraphina smiled angelically at the detective. "Perhaps you remember me by my legal name, Sara

Frogmore."

"Nope," the detective replied without compunction, "doesn't ring a bell."

Jillian tried to reel in her wayward guest. "Madame Seraphina, if you don't mind. We've set up in the dining room, over here. Across the hall."

Nonplussed, the psychic shrugged the unencumbered shoulder and allowed my sister to lead her away. "Yes, of course."

The pair departed, and to my relief, I heard the pocket doors to the dining room slide shut.

"What the hell was that?" the detective asked rather rudely.

"My—" I began to say.

But Rick cut me off, "No one of importance."

I snapped my trap and allowed him to continue, "As I was saying before we were interrupted—what if Vera was onto the real thief, and he found out?"

"You're assuming Norman's accusations are genuine?" The detective continued to watch the empty doorway the two ladies had exited.

"Apologies, I must have misunderstood." Rick asked for clarification, "You mean, you *don't* believe Norman about the theft?"

That gaze riveted on my boyfriend. "Do you?"

Rick didn't respond, instead allowing the question to hang in the air. This was a game Rick was very good at. It took every ounce of my own willpower to continue holding my tongue and wait out the detective.

Finally, he replied grumpily, "As you said, why didn't he file a report?"

I couldn't help it; the question popped out: "So, you *don't* believe there's been a theft?"

"I'm waiting to see the evidence," he replied.

"Okay, let's assume, for just one moment—" I held up a

finger, "—there was a theft. And my aunt stumbled across the thief, maybe caught him red-handed."

"Lady, I think ... *if* that's the case, your aunt is either dead, or in some very, very bad trouble." He tucked the notepad and pencil back into the pocket.

Unhappy with that response, I continued to probe, "But are you going to look into the theory?"

"I'm exploring many theories. Do you have anything further you can provide? Something based in fact or evidence? Something I should know?"

You mean like a hidden list of missing items? Or perhaps a silver creamer made by Paul Revere?

I didn't need the pressure of Rick's fingers on my shoulder to warn me to stay silent on that topic.

Instead, I tilted my head. "Something you should *know*?"

"About your aunt. Her job? Missing museum pieces? The boyfriend?" the detective prompted.

"Not that I can think of." I tapped a finger against my chin. "I just met Mr. Gupta last night. As for her job—" I gave an innocent shrug, "—all I know, she's a conservator at the museum. She cleans and preserves artifacts. That's the extent of my knowledge about her job." I paused to allow that to sink in before asking, "Did you find anything interesting in her phone records?"

"I'm still waiting. We probably won't get them until Monday or Tuesday."

Ah, so he *did* ask to have the phone records pulled.

A crash came from the dining room.

Rick placed his hands on his knees, straightened his spine, and prepared to rise. "Well then, Detective. If there isn't anything else you'd like to discuss..."

The detective took the hint. Ponderously, with a groan and cracking knees, Riggins stood up. "If I have any more questions, I'll contact you," he grumbled.

"Yes. Me too." I gave him a wide smile, letting him know I expected the information to flow both ways. "Thank you for stopping by, Detective. We'll be in touch." I spoke loudly in hopes of covering up the strange moans coming from the dining room.

The detective was no dummy. I'm certain he heard the noise. He was shaking his head on the way out the door.

The latch snicked shut. I leaned against the wood, and my breath escaped in a rush. "I don't like that Norman guy. Why didn't he say something to us when we asked about Vera?"

Rick pulled me into his arms. "Maybe he didn't want to cause a scene. He was in the middle of preparing for a presentation and fairly dismissive. Also, he may sense Vera's antagonism toward him, since he got the job she obviously wanted ... maybe even deserved."

"I suppose you're right." I gave him a kiss and stepped out of his embrace. "Any news from Angus?"

"Not yet." Rick jammed his hands in his pockets and hunched his shoulders. "Listen, something came up, and I had to re-task him for one of my clients. I don't expect him to get back to me until tomorrow."

That wasn't great news, and I could tell Rick felt bad about taking Angus off the case even for a little bit of time. However, he did have a business to run. I wasn't foolish enough to believe Rick's company assets were available to me twenty-four-seven.

"I appreciate any help he can give, but I don't want him staying up half the night over this. He's got a job to do for Silverthorne. Obviously, *your* clients are his priority."

Rick tipped his head in the direction of the dining room. "Shall we see about the shit show in there?"

"Lieutenant, please join us." Madame Seraphina's voice warbled through the walls in octaves much too low for her sunny high-pitched voice.

I ran a hand down my face. "Cripes. I suppose so."

Chapter Sixteen

As unobtrusively as possible, I slid open one of the pocket doors. I'd been expecting strange, but this was almost comical.

The plantation shutters had been closed, darkening the room. The table was covered in a purple cloth with a giant white hand pattern embroidered on it. Strange symbols were printed on the fingers—runes or zodiac symbols perhaps. In the center of the palm was an eye with a triangle around it. I'd once heard the symbol referred to as the magic eye. On each corner of the triangle, a white candle burned. The flickering flames threw eerie shadows on the ceiling. At the tip of the middle finger, someone had poured sugar or salt in a circle about the size of a dinner plate. A small brass bell of my aunt's rested inside the circle.

Madame Seraphina sat at the head of the table. Her eyes were closed, and her lips moved, but I couldn't understand what she whispered. It sounded as if she spoke in tongues. Her beringed fingers moved in a circular motion above three different-colored stones that had been polished to a shine.

My sister hunched forward, her hands tucked beneath her legs, watching the medium with rapt attention. Tony appeared less impressed with the psychic's machinations. He leaned as far back as the shield-back chair would allow, with his arms crossed, barely hiding the abject confusion he must have felt. But it wasn't the human beings in the room that amused me.

In the center of the triangle, sitting directly over the pupil of the eye, was Smokey giving a look of disgust as only a Siamese cat can. He'd been watching Madame Seraphina's show, but his head turned when I opened the door. I swore that cat spoke telepathically to me, along the lines of, "What the devil is this wingnut going on about?"

Full of attitude, Nightshade stalked past me into the hallway. Obviously, he'd had enough of the tomfoolery.

I was about to close the door and leave Jillian to it when Madame Seraphina's eyes popped open. "Kanga-langa-coo."

"Sorry," I whispered. "I didn't mean to interrupt."

Jillian gazed at me with irritation writ across her features. Incensed that I'd interrupted, she hissed, "*Karina!*"

I stepped back.

"Wait!" the medium's voice rang out, and she pointed at me, her arm stiff. "Don't go. Has the detective left?"

I nodded.

"Good. He was blocking my energy. His aura is very muddy today. *You* must join us. I can use the red aura to harness the spirits. Sit there, next to the young man."

I glanced at my boyfriend, who'd remained hidden behind the other door, shaking in silent laughter. An evil grin crossed my features. I grabbed him by the elbow and dragged him into the room. "How about some violet aura too?"

"Yes, marvelous. You must sit there," she directed, pointing to the empty chair next to my sister. "Jillian, dah-ling, I need something personal from your aunt."

"This entire house is personal to my aunt. It's all her stuff," I drawled.

The springy orange hair flopped around her shoulders as she shook her head. "Something even more personal. Something she touches every day. Like a phone, or computer."

"They're missing," Rick supplied.

"Like a piece of clothing?" my sister asked.

"Not unless she's worn it in the past forty-eight hours." The psychic tapped a finger against her lips in contemplation.

"How about Aunt Vera's favorite wine glass?" I may have accidentally added a snort to my comment.

Jillian slit her eyes at me, but Madame Seraphina perked up. "Is it dirty?"

"No. It's been through the dishwasher."

"Then no. Perhaps a hairbrush?" she suggested hopefully.

"I'll run up and get it," Jillian volunteered and went banging upstairs, leaving the three of us with Madame Seraphina.

While the medium was no longer making strange noises, she had again closed her eyes and started rotating her head back and forth. I was afraid it might spin around on its axis, like the possessed girl in *The Exorcist* movie.

Smokey yawned, turned round in a circle three times, and lay down over the eye.

The silence stretched. Madame Seraphina moved into full head rolls.

"You sure you don't want the wine glass?" I half rose. "Aunt Vera *did* drink out of it every night."

The medium didn't bother to open her eyes. "All of her energies will have been cleansed by the detergent."

I tucked that little piece of information into my brain box. Perhaps the next time the ghost turned up, I would try to lure him into the dishwasher. Wash away his energy so he'd quit bugging me.

Finally, Jillian whisked into the room holding a round hairbrush. "There were a couple to choose from. I brought the one with the most hair in it."

Ew.

The head rolling stopped, and Madame's eyes opened. "Wonderful."

Jillian passed it into her open palm.

"Everyone, place your hands flat on the table," the medium demonstrated, "and open your minds to allow the spirits in."

Madame began stroking the circular brush in a slightly erotic manner. "Mm, yes, I can feeeeel her." The psychic's lids drooped. "Yes. Come to me. Talk to me. If there is a ghost here who can tell me where Vera Wagner is, please come forward." Up and down, she stroked the brush.

Tony watched, wide-eyed, in fascinated horror. The cat squinted over his shoulder with a Siamese glare. I glanced at Rick, whose silvery gaze met mine, dancing in merriment. Biting my lip, I swiveled away for fear I'd embarrass myself and burst into giggles. Even Jillian's face was pulled down into a confused frown.

"Speak through me. Vera Wagner, where are you?" The brush stroking increased in speed. "Your loved ones wish to find you." She let out a moan that sounded like the mating call of a wild animal.

I slapped a hand over my mouth to keep the mirth from exploding out. Rick, my supremely controlled boyfriend, even rolled his lips inward.

The moaning increased, and her head began rocking side to side.

A visual of Meg Ryan having her fake orgasm at the restaurant in the movie *When Harry Met Sally* popped into my head. If this woman started yelling, "YES! YES! YES!" I would've undoubtedly lost it.

As it was, someone kicked me under the table. Hard. My merriment instantly disappeared, to be replaced by pinpricks of tears as pain shot up my left shin.

"Ouch!" I leaned down to rub the injury.

Across the table, I found Jillian's gaze shooting daggers my way.

Our contretemps failed to arouse Madame Seraphina from whatever trance she was in. The stroking continued, as did the random moans. "My third eye is open; I can see. Yes. More.

Deeper. Allow me to see."

I didn't believe the brush stroking and weird noises would materialize our lieutenant or bring forth Vera. Furthermore, in pain and no longer entertained by our guest, I was about to pull the plug on this spectacle when the hairbrush went flying across the table, whacking hard against the pocket door. One of the triangle candles extinguished.

Everything went silent.

Madame Seraphina slumped forward.

Suddenly, the room broke into exclamations.

"For chrissake!" hissed Rick.

"What in the hell?" came from me.

"Madame Seraphina! Are you alright?" That from my sister.

Tony jumped up and pressed his fingers against the psychic's neck.

The overhead chandelier flickered on, momentarily blinding me.

Smokey meowed and jumped off the table, elegantly missing both still burning candles.

Rick, standing by the light switch, asked, "Is she okay?"

"She's got a pulse. It's steady and strong," Tony replied. "Madame?" He thrust her shoulders back against the chair. Her orange hair draped in front of her face.

"Madame Seraphina! Can you hear me?" He pushed a swath of hair aside.

Madame's eyes fluttered open. "I saw her," she whispered. "Up and down."

Yeah, you really got off on that hairbrush.

Jillian knelt on the ground next to the psychic and gripped her hand. "Is she alive? Is Vera alive?"

"Yes," Madame replied hoarsely, looking deep into my sister's eyes. "But her corporeal body is waning. Her spirit is hovering between two worlds. I see the color red everywhere. And blue," she added.

Tony held Madame Seraphina's wrist with two fingers and checked his watch. Meanwhile, Rick opened the shutters. The softened, fading daylight filtered through the slats.

"Anything else? A location? Is she inside or outside?" my sister pressed.

"I didn't see a location. I think. ... she's inside. It's up and down," Madame said, her voice fading on the last syllable.

"Like, on an airplane," Jillian said. "Is she on a private jet?"

"I don't ... it's ... it's unclear," the medium whispered, slumping in her seat. A coughing fit ensued.

Jillian patted her back. "Are you okay, Madame?"

The psychic cleared her throat. "Water."

Jillian's eyes widened with comprehension. "You see water? She's on a boat. You said up and down. Karina!" She looked at me with excitement. "Aunt Vera's on a boat."

"Your pulse is in the normal range." Tony dropped her wrist but continued to hover nearby.

Jillian gripped the psychic's hand so hard, Madame Seraphina cringed. "Where? Where is the boat?"

"I-I don't know, dear." She extricated herself from Jillian's death grip. "May I have a drink?"

"I'll get it," Rick volunteered. "Water, coffee, or something stronger?"

"Just water," she rasped.

This lady is full of it.

I strained to hold back the uncharitable thought from bursting out of my mouth. I rubbed my shin, which was still smarting from my sister's kick. "Can you grab an ice pack from the freezer, please?" I hollered.

Rick returned with a full glass of water in one hand and a blue gel pack in the other.

Madame Seraphina gulped down the entire contents of the

glass, like she'd not had a drink in days. A rivulet of water snaked down the side of her mouth as she chugged.

Rick sat down in the chair vacated by Tony, lifted my injured leg, and laid it across his lap. "Where does it hurt?"

I pointed, and he placed the cold pack over top of my jeans. Jillian rose, rolling her eyes at me as if I was making a big deal over nothing. She'd nailed me right on the shinbone with the point of her boot. There would certainly be bruising. Meanwhile, Tony blew out the other two candles.

Once Madame finished her water, she wiped her chin and let out a satisfied, "Ah. That's better."

The water perked her up like a plant reviving from a long dry spell. She announced, "I believe I told you my fee was three hundred. I take cash, credit, or Venmo."

"I can Venmo one-fifty," Jillian said. "Rina, how would you like to pay for your half?"

I desperately wanted to tell Jillian where she could stick "my half," but I took the high road and kept my thoughts to myself. Besides, for entertainment value, Madame Seraphina certainly put on a good show.

"I'll pay with a credit card. My purse is in the front hall. Can you fetch it?" I smiled sweetly at my sister.

Jillian childishly stuck her tongue out at me as she left the dining room. A moment later, my handbag unceremoniously dropped into my lap, barely missing my head.

Madame gathered her things from the table, stuffing them back into the ginormous tote bag, and collected her fee. As she walked her out, I heard Jillian profusely thanking the medium for giving us her time.

"It's no problem, dear. Happy to do it. Sometimes flashes of insight come to me afterwards. I have your number if that happens," Madame Seraphina trilled.

On her way back into the room, Jillian picked up the

forgotten hairbrush.

"I'd be careful with that brush," I drawled.

Jillian rotated it around. "Why, what's wrong with it?"

"It's been violated by Madame Seraphina. It was so upset by her manhandling, it flew across the room in protest," I deadpanned.

Rick and Tony both broke into laughter.

Jillian put a hand on her hip and directed her ire at her boyfriend, "Oh, you think this is funny?" She brandished the hairbrush.

"C'mon, babe, you've got to admit, she gave that brush a solid hand job," Tony replied gleefully.

Even though she fought against it, a smile broke through, and the tension I'd felt since I walked into the room finally abated.

Jillian laid the brush on the table and good-naturedly gave in. "Okay, you're right, the hairbrush thing was kind of weird."

I guffawed. "Kind of?"

She pulled out the chair at the foot of the table and collapsed. "Well, at least we know Aunt Vera is still alive, and she's on a boat."

I glanced at the faces of the two men, who made it clear they weren't willing to tackle that one. I considered leaving Jillian in her cloud of relief, but ... something in my DNA simply wouldn't allow it. "Uh, Jilly, I'm not sure we can take Madame Seraphina's assertions at face value."

"What? You don't believe her? You think Aunt Vera's dead?"

"Well, what did she really give us? She's inside. The colors red and blue. And I'm not so sure she meant boat." I shrugged. "She coughed and said 'water.' *You* jumped immediately to a boat. *She* didn't say the word boat; *you* did. I think she was asking for a drink. You saw how she gulped it down as if she were a camel preparing for a trek across the desert."

I expected one of the men to back me up. When neither did,

I continued, "Her assertions are all rather nebulous, much like a horoscope. Easy to interpret and bend to your own mind, depending on how your day goes."

"Do all of you agree?" My sister's gaze scanned the room, landing on both men in turn.

Tony chickened out and shrugged. "I don't know, babe. None of it made much sense to me."

She pinned Rick. "What about you, Mr. I'm-so-serious-I-only-deal-in-the-facts?"

"Although I found Madame Seraphina rather unorthodox, at this time, I'm not ruling anything out," Rick replied diplomatically.

"Were you a politician in a former life?" my sister scoffed.

He checked his watch. "It'll be dark soon. We need to start thinking about dinner. Shall we eat in or go out?"

"A clever way of changing the subject," Jillian harrumphed.

"We had a pricey lunch." *And I blew a hundred and fifty bucks on a wacko who just jacked off a hairbrush.* "My vote is to eat in," I suggested.

"I'm with Karina." Tony raised his hand in the air.

"All in favor, say aye." I raised my hand along with Tony.

Both Rick and Tony said, "Aye."

Everyone turned to Jillian, who reluctantly raised her hand. "Fine."

"The ayes have it. Motion passes." I slapped my palm on the dining table. "The only problem is we are limited on food in the fridge."

"I can make a grocery run," Rick suggested.

"I'll go with you," Tony offered. "What do you girls want?"

I pulled my leg off Rick's lap, and the gel pack slid to the floor. I dived under the table to retrieve it. "I'm up for anything, as long as it includes a salad."

My sister agreed with me. "While you're gone, I'm going to

make a list of marinas in the area and start calling around. Maybe someone has spotted Aunt Vera."

It couldn't hurt and would keep Jillian busy, so I left it alone.

An enormous yawn snuck out, and I announced, "I'm going upstairs to lie down for a bit. I didn't get much sleep last night. Wake me when you get back, and I'll help make dinner."

Chapter Seventeen

Nightshade stood in the center of the bed, his hackles raised, his gaze riveted on the chair in the front window. My senses heightened, and goosebumps littered my arms.

"Are you here?" I said aloud.

Nothing.

"Show yourself!"

The lamp beside the chair flicked on.

Even though I'd been waiting ... no, expecting something to happen ... the fact that it *did*, had me gasping. My heartbeat sped up like a galloping gazelle. "Do-do you know where V-vera is?"

Silence. Nothing moved.

Clearing my throat, I tried again, "Turn the light off if you know where she is."

The light remained burning.

"Did Vera steal the creamer from the museum?"

The light snapped off.

I realized I didn't know if that meant yes or no, so I decided it would be best to clarify the situation. "Um, I didn't quite get that. Turn the light on if she stole the creamer. Leave it off if she did not steal it."

The light remained off.

Frustrated, I gripped my head and flopped onto the bed. "I don't know where to look for her."

A book on the bedside table fell to the floor, jerking me from my thoughts.

"What the hell does that mean?"

Patchouli.

Nightshade settled, curling himself into a black ball of fur, his green eyes glittering like bright emeralds in the night sky.

"I guess he's gone." I kicked off my shoes, pulled up a silky microfiber throw Aunt Vera left at the end of her bed, and watched the sunset through the windows. Oranges and pinks streaked across the skies.

The tints reminded me of our recent guest. She was certainly colorful. Should I follow Madame Seraphina's lead like Jillian? I wasn't one to go for all that psychic mumbo-jumbo, and the show she put on didn't inspire my confidence in her prediction. I feared we'd waste precious time and resources running around town searching the marinas. On the other hand, I didn't have any other ideas or places to search.

Detective Riggins didn't provide new information or have anything encouraging to report. He seemed to be waiting on a number of items that could give us clues—Aunt Vera's phone and text logs, fingerprints on her car, DNA from her car, camera footage, etc.

Angus found us interesting information, but nothing actionable. Vikram seemed to be the person he claimed, and I could identify no motive to abduct or snuff Vera out. His wife seemed to like Aunt Vera as much as Vikram did.

The fact that Aunt Vera's trail ended on Monday was most alarming. I knew we should have been widening the search for her. However, something deep in my gut, call it women's intuition, kept telling me there were clues here in Williamsburg. The fact that her car was located not far away cemented that hunch.

Chapter Eighteen

I woke to someone shaking my foot.

"Rina, wake up. Dinner's ready."

Groaning, I rubbed my eyes. "What time is it?"

"Half past seven." Jillian turned on the bedside light and bent to pick up the book that our friendly ghost had knocked to the floor. "*The Art Museums at Colonial Williamsburg*," she read, making a face. "I can see why this put you to sleep."

Sitting forward, I blinked away the cobwebs. "What's for dinner?"

"The boys are grilling steaks. I think I saw some potatoes and salad from a bag."

"Any luck with the marinas?"

"No. Only one place I called answered the phone. I left messages for six other dockmasters." Jillian sank onto the edge of the bed and gripped the coverlet in her fist. "Is this a wild goose chase?"

My mouth had gone dry and cottony, and I smacked my lips, trying to work up some saliva. "I don't know, but it can't hurt."

Gloomily, she looked at me. "Yeah, that's what Rick said."

"Cheer up. You'll feel better after we eat." My shin still ached, and I pulled the pant leg up to my knee to get a gander at the damage. Purply lump with a hard knot in the middle. "Nice work."

Jillian cringed. "Sorry. I didn't mean to kick so hard."

"Yes, you did." I shoved the pants down. "Do you think they picked up any wine?"

"I saw a bottle of red sitting on the counter. Tony probably picked it out. We hit a bunch of wine festivals this summer, and now he fancies himself an amateur sommelier."

"Good, because Rick's more of a beer or scotch man. I don't think he knows the difference between pinot noir and pinot grigio. I've learned, when in doubt, he buys the most expensive thing he can find and expects it to be good." I scooted to the end of the bed, put my feet on the floor, and stretched my arms high above my head. Lacing my fingers together, I pushed them out; my joints snapped and cracked.

"Jeez, you sound like Rice Krispies. Snap, crackle, pop. You're getting old."

"Hey, I'm not that far ahead of you." I gave her a shove.

"But I will always be younger," she said with an evil grin. "After all, I'm still in my twenties."

"True, but those extra years have given me great wisdom."

"Ha! Keep telling yourself those lies."

"C'mon, brat. I can smell dinner, and I'm in desperate need of a glass of wine." I pulled Jillian to her feet.

"You and me both, sister." She grabbed my hand. "I am sorry about your leg."

I slung my arm around her shoulders. "I know."

Someone had found Aunt Vera's toile placemats with the matching napkins and laid them out on the farmhouse table. A wine and water glass rested at each place, and the wine bottle sat uncorked on the counter. The salad bowl was in the center of the table. A soft breeze blew in the scent of grilling meat through the open back door.

Tony pulled baked potatoes from the oven and laid them on my aunt's plain white dishes. "The potatoes are done. How's the meat coming?" he called.

The screen door slammed, and Rick walked in carrying a platter full of T-bone steaks. "All set." He smiled at me. "Did you get some rest?"

My belly fluttered, and the return smile spread reflexively across my lips. "Yeah, took a nap. Thanks for getting dinner together, boys. It smells fantastic." I chose a seat at random. "Nobody woke me. I would've helped."

"You don't think two men can put together a decent meal?" Tony asked, faux offended.

"Not at all. If it tastes as good as it smells, I think this should become a regular ritual." I rubbed my hands together in anticipation. "What do you think, Jilly?"

"I'm with Rina." Jillian took the chair across from me.

I waited for Tony and Rick to start protesting. Neither of them did.

Rick simply said, "I'm fine with that."

Tony placed the plates with potatoes on the table, screwing up his face in thought. "We'll have to work around my shifts. We can rotate where to cook."

Rick started plopping T-bones on each plate. "I'm happy to do it when I'm in town."

Jillian and I shared stunned glances, but I wasn't one to let a good thing slip away. "Great. Jillian and I can check everyone's calendar and arrange a schedule."

Tony poured the wine, then took the chair next to Jillian. Rick sat next to me. We passed the salad around, filling our plates with fresh greens.

"This would be a forty-dollar meal at a restaurant," I commented, biting into a perfectly seasoned, medium-rare piece of steak, which practically melted in my mouth. The beef slid down my throat, and I sipped the deep black currant-flavored wine. Closing my eyes, I sighed, "Mm, this is perfection. I think I just had a mini orgasm."

"If you keep talking dirty at the table, I'm going to have to throw you over my knee," Rick threatened.

Leaning into his shoulder, I whispered, "And do what?"

"Get a room, you two," my sister moaned.

"I have one. And not all of us got our afternoon delight," I shot back.

My sister turned chili-pepper red. Tony simply snickered and gave Jillian a lascivious grin.

"Alright, children," Rick tutted in fatherly tones. "Let's remember this is the dinner table."

I would argue there wasn't anything father-like about Rick. Even though he was the oldest among us, there was no Dad Bod beneath the shirt he wore. I could attest to the fact his abs were rock hard. If I kept thinking about it, the rest of the meal might become quite uncomfortable.

Lucky for me, Jillian changed the subject. "So, what did the detective have to say? Anything of value?"

Rick and I gave them the rundown of our interview with the detective. Further discussion led Jillian to conclude the best lead we had was Madame Seraphina's vague innuendo that Vera was on a boat, floating between life and death.

I feared Madame might be right about Aunt Vera's current state; although, I wasn't sure I believed she was on a boat. However, as a group, we resolved to follow the psychic's tip in the morning.

After that, the meal got quiet. The silence went on for so long, it turned a little awkward.

Tony broke the uneasy lull by asking, "Jilly, why don't you and Karina tell us a funny story about your aunt?"

My sister's dancing eyes looked across the table at me. "Do you remember the Christmas with the snake?"

"Oh, lord! I do!" I burst with laughter.

"Wait, there was a snake? Was it poisonous?" Tony asked.

I set the stage. "Okay, this goes way, *way* back, to the days when we were kids. When Uncle Jack was still alive. Over

Christmas break, Tyler had volunteered to bring home the classroom snake—much to my parents' dismay. It came home in a ten-gallon aquarium."

Jillian took over the storytelling, "I can remember him carrying it so carefully off the bus and down the street to our house. Proud as a peacock. My brother was so excited to take care of Salazar the snake. My parents, Rina, and me … not so much."

"Mom told Tyler he had to keep it in his bedroom during the holidays." I sipped my wine.

"On Christmas Eve, we were invited over to Aunt Vera's and Uncle Jack's house for dinner," Jillian said.

I inserted for clarity, "And we were all going to go to the nine o'clock candlelight service. So, everyone came dressed in their church finery."

Jillian nodded. "Right. That Presbyterian church on King Street." She diverted for a moment, explaining exactly where the church was in Alexandria. "Anyway, Tyler wanted to bring Salazar to show Uncle Jack. But Mom told him no. Uncle Jack could see the snake when they came over on Christmas Day."

"But—" I held up a finger, "—that did not deter my brother."

"Let me guess," Rick said, "he snuck the snake over to your aunt's house."

"Of course, like any boy would do," I confirmed, waggling my head. "However, he did *not* bring it in the aquarium. He just slid it into his backpack."

Jillian continued the tale, "Once we arrived, Uncle Jack told the three of us there was twenty-five dollars hidden around the house."

"Oh, goodness!" I put a hand to my heart. "I'd forgotten all about Uncle Jack's scavenger hunts. He was always hiding stuff for us to find."

"Sweet. An uncle, hiding cash for you," Tony commented.

"Well, it wasn't actually cash," Jillian clarified. "It was those chocolate coins you get around the holidays. But we didn't care. It was candy, and we wanted it!"

"My bother dropped his backpack off in the front hall." I closed my eyes, watching the memory play out in my head. "And he chased after Jilly and me, in search of our golden coins."

"Meanwhile, Tyler, in all his ten-year-old wisdom, never bothered to zip up the backpack." She made a zipping motion.

Tony slapped a hand over his wide-open mouth and shook his head. Rick grinned in anticipation.

"You see where we're going with this." I wiggled my brows.

"Yes," Jillian said, "Salazar, a ball python, slithered out."

"Oh, no," Tony moaned.

"Oh, yes!" My head bobbed. "About half an hour later, Tyler remembers the snake, and decides it's a good time to show Uncle Jack. But, when he goes to get the backpack, he realizes it's unzipped and…" I held out my hand, gesturing to Jillian.

"No snake," she supplied for our cringing audience. "Consequently, he comes to find us."

"Actually," I correct, "he came to find me, because I'm the older sister, and less likely to tattle on him."

"*Hey! I* didn't tattle." Jillian threw her napkin at me.

"Not on this occasion, but you have to admit—" I pointed at her with my fork, "—you were the worst tattletale when we were kids. We kept all sorts of secrets from you."

"Well, I was the youngest. You two always ganged up on me." She crossed her arms and gave a pretend pout.

I dismissed her pout with a flick of my wrist. "Anyway, Tyler told *me*, and we both started sneaking around the house, crawling on all fours, trying to find the snake. Under the couch, under the chair, beneath the Christmas tree—"

"But they never found it," Jillian interrupted. "Rina was called away to set the table, so Tyler decides to enlist *me* to help him search for the snake."

"You know," I mused, spinning my wine glass around by the stem, "it was lucky Vera did not have a cat or dog at that time, or else I think Salazar would have been eaten."

"Or vice versa," Rick supplied.

Jillian winced. "Fast forward twenty minutes—dinner is ready. It's time to bring the food to the table."

"Mm, I remember, Aunt Vera had cooked a ham and mashed potatoes, green beans, corn, and biscuits. Mom was helping her put everything onto the serving dishes and giving them to me to carry into the dining room," I explained.

"Then we hear The. Most. Blood. Curdling. Scream." Jillian threw her hands over her eyes. "It was like something from a horror film."

Tony crunched his own eyes shut. "I'm afraid to ask."

"The snake ... curled up ... inside..." I paused for dramatic effect. "The gravy boat!"

"You're kidding." Tony shook his head and laughed.

Jillian's palms slammed onto the table. "No, she is not."

"*And* ... Salazar wasn't too happy when Aunt Vera started to pour hot gravy over him." I mimed a demonstration. "Vera freaked. She dropped the pot of gravy all over the floor."

Rick had his head in his hands, shaking it back and forth.

Jillian whistled. "Mom flipped out and started screaming for Tyler. Dad and Uncle Jack came running in to see what the hubbub was about. Everyone was shouting. Gravy all over the floor."

"Dad slips and falls in the gravy puddle. *Splat!* In his best suit," I cried with glee.

By this time, both Jillian and I were laughing so hard, we couldn't continue the story.

"What happened to the snake?" Rick asked after we'd settled down.

"Wait. Wait." I drew in some deep breaths and explained,

"Uncle Jack placed a pot lid over the gravy boat, dumped the snake into a cardboard box, and told Tyler he could take it out when he got home."

"Sounds like something out of one of those *Home Alone* movies," Tony suggested.

"But that's not the end of the story," Jillian countered. "The following year, Uncle Jack got it into his head that it would be a funny joke to play on Aunt Vera. He bought a rubber snake and stuffed it into the gravy boat."

"That's diabolical!" Tony exclaimed.

"The scream was no less piercing the second time," I assured the audience.

"Mom started yelling ... at-at Tyler again ...only-only he said ... it-it wasn't his snake!" Jillian was laughing so hard, she could barely get the words out.

"Yeah, Uncle Jack, who'd been hiding around the corner watching the entire thing, finally came clean after mom chewed Tyler's ass for five minutes," I whooped.

"Remember, Aunt Vera was so mad, she threw the gravy ladle at Uncle Jack." Jillian mimed the spoon-throwing. "It beaned off his forehead and left a welt, which was in all the Christmas pictures that year."

"Oh yeah," I confirmed. "After that, it became a thing. Every year, somewhere that rubber snake would turn up around Christmastime. And every year Aunt Vera saw it, she would scream her head off. Until she realized it was just a rubber snake."

Jillian gripped her gut, and laughter huffed out like a collapsing accordion. "She took to scooping it up and throwing it at Uncle Jack."

"Ah, good times." I wiped tears out of the corners of my eyes.

"Whatever happened to the rubber snake?" Tony asked.

Jillian shrugged. "I don't know. We never saw it after Uncle Jack died."

"Aunt Vera gave it to Tyler, the first Christmas after his death," I murmured somberly.

The merriment fizzled like a balloon that lost its air, and the room fell into a contemplative silence.

"Where do you think Aunt Vera is?"

"I wish I knew, Jilly." I reached across the table to grip her hand. "I wish I knew."

She turned her palm into mine and squeezed.

"Don't fret, ladies. We'll find her," Tony said with assurance, hugging Jillian to his side.

But I knew better, and when I glanced at Rick, his stolid features did not reassure me.

Chapter Nineteen

The cars in front of me refused to move. Traffic blocked me in on all sides—a large semi to my right, a gas company van on my left, and a black SUV in front and behind. I could not see ahead of the SUV, but I could see behind, where the traffic backed up for miles. Rain sluiced against the windshield in pounding waves. My wipers, at full throttle, whipped back and forth. People honked their horns. We crept forward an inch and came to another stop. All I could see were red brake lights in front of me. The SUVs reminded me of the one used to kidnap Jillian.

This wasn't unusual for a rainy day in Washington, D.C. Traffic was always bad at rush hour, worse in the rain, but something was different.

Something was off; only I couldn't figure out what it was.

A horn honked. The semi next to me blared his oversized trumpet. More drivers joined the fray, blending their noise into a cacophony. I was alone in the car, but I felt as though someone should have been with me. Someone I was supposed to pick up.

Who was missing? My sister? My mom? No, they weren't supposed to be here. Who?

I squinted through the driving rain, anxiously trying to remember who should have been sitting next to me. Suddenly, the traffic began moving forward, and the blaring horns subsided. At first it was just a creep, and then we picked up speed until we were moving about fifteen miles per hour.

I realized I wasn't driving my new Jeep. I was sitting in my old car.

Where was the Jeep?

My eyes darted frantically back and forth and caught sight of a figure sitting in the back seat.

I did a double take. "Aunt Vera?"

"Hurry, Karina. You must hurry," she urged. "I haven't much time. It's important. Don't be late. Please hurry."

"I'm sorry, Aunt Vera. I can't move any faster," I tried to explain. "The traffic…"

"Go around. Go around those in your way."

"What? I can't go around." The SUV's brake lights flashed, and we slowed. "There's nowhere for me to go around."

"HURRY!" she cried.

I turned fully to look over my shoulder, and that was when the bang of bumper against bumper rent the air. We crashed into the SUV. It got worse when the trucks on either side of me began to close in. The shrieking high-pitched sound of steel shredding off the sides of my car pierced the air. The passenger door collapsed—

I came out of the nightmare, gasping. The tendrils of the dream tugged at my subconscious. Vera's cry, "hurry," along with my own shouts, seemed to hover above me. I opened my eyes and blinked.

Where am I?

This was not my apartment.

I blinked again, trying to orient myself. We'd forgotten to close the blinds at bedtime, and the moonlight shimmered in rows across the ceiling. In my half-awake state, I realized I was in Aunt Vera's bed.

Clearly my subconscious was as strained as my conscious, and the dream was due to Vera's unexplained absence. It had no basis in reality.

Although I imagined Madame Seraphina would argue the dream should be taken as a sign my aunt's energy was reaching out to me … or some such nonsense.

The familiar scent of patchouli entered my nostrils. I turned my head.

At the foot of the bed stood Lieutenant Cabway in his ghostly form.

Am I still dreaming?

Goosebumps shivered across my body, and I pulled the blanket closer to my chin. I watched as his figure slowly dissipated, fading from the bottom up. The impression of his young whitish-gray face was the last to disappear into the darkness. It hung, glowing eerily, detached and bodiless.

I heard the rustle of Nightshade leaving his perch on the windowsill. He jumped down and sloped out of the cracked doorway.

A wave of dizziness overcame me. Weird, because I was already lying down. What was that rasping noise?

Sleepily, Rick rolled over and snaked his hand across my stomach. His arm tensed into wakefulness. "What's wrong?" he rasped. "You're shaking, and you're breathing too fast."

That was when I realized the noise in the room was me, huffing in short little gasps.

"Karina, you need to calm down. You're hyperventilating." Slowly he rubbed my stomach, moving his warm, strong hand in circles. "In—one, two, three. Hold—one, two, three. Out—one, two, three. Just listen to my voice. In—one, two, three. Hold— one, two, three. You're in bed. Everything is fine. In—one, two, three. I'm right here for you. Everything is okay."

I listened to his calming voice and struggled to follow his directions. After a few minutes, my breathing returned to normal, and the dizziness subsided.

"What happened; did you have a nightmare?"

"Yes. The ghost was here. I think he woke me up. I'm afraid something bad has happened to Vera. And if we don't find her soon, she'll be dead," I whispered, my voice full of dread.

"That sounds like Madame Seraphina talking. Not you. Tell me about your dream," Rick's deep tones encouraged.

I concentrated, trying to remember everything, but, as my brain came to full consciousness, the dream began to slide away. I told Rick what I could remember. It came out in disjointed sentences.

"Stuck in rush hour traffic. My old car. Aunt Vera in the back seat. Rain coming down in torrents. Cars so tightly packed, I couldn't move. There were trucks on either side of me. Boxed in. Vera spoke, urging me. 'Go around,' she kept saying, 'go around, because we can't be late.' I think…" I attempted to capture the essence, but it was like straining to hold on to a cloud. The thoughts slipped through my fingers.

I began to wonder—had I dreamed up the ghost as well?

His deep tones murmured into the quiet night, "Let it go. It was a stress dream. We'll have more information about Vera in the morning, I promise."

His hand slid up beneath my pajama top, and the patting turned into a stroking. A sensual stroking. I rolled into his arms, seeking assurance and protection. Protection from my own fears.

Our legs twined. Our arms tangled around each other. He tugged off my pajama top. His lips found the hollow in my neck.

Soon the dream was pushed into the deep recesses of my mind.

Chapter Twenty

Sunday

In the morning, we were slow to start. I should amend that to say, Jilly and I were slow to start. Tony and Rick were up and dressed and had thankfully taken care of the French press ritual. I followed my nose down to the kitchen where the nutty aroma invaded my senses, making me salivate for the heart-jolting caffeine.

Rick stood at the stove cooking bacon. When he noticed my arrival, he paused his culinary efforts to pour me a cup. "You look like you could use this."

Tony sat at the kitchen table scrolling through the day's news headlines on his phone. "Didn't you sleep well?"

Rick gave me a lecherous grin and licked his lips. A jolt of desire went straight to my hoo-ha.

My eyes flared, and I forced myself to turn away. "I had stress dreams."

Tony, so focused on his phone, was oblivious to our byplay. "Yeah, Jillian said she had bad dreams too. She woke me up. Said the ghost was in the room."

This time when my eyes met Rick's, it wasn't with desire but, rather, dismay and, on my behalf, a touch of fear.

"Did she say anything else about her dreams?" I asked.

He shook his head. "Only that she felt some sort of urgency coming from your aunt. I think that psychic kinda messed with her head." He did a twirling motion with his finger around his ear.

"Yeah," I agreed. "Is she up yet?"

"I left her sleeping. When she woke me in the middle of the night, she was in a bit of a tizzy. I helped her calm down using an old-fashioned remedy … if you know what I mean." Tony winked at me.

Yikes! This house was becoming quite the bordello. The fact that Tony and my sister were probably doing the higgity-piggity at the same time Rick and I were left me discomfited. I rolled my eyes for Tony's benefit, and he went back to reading his phone with a cocky grin.

Rick removed the bacon from the pan, laying the slices on paper towels. Then he drained the fat into a can he must have found in the recycling bin. "Who is up for some eggs?"

Tony didn't bother looking up from his phone. "I'll take two, thanks. As long as they aren't runny. I like my eggs to bounce."

"I'll take one." I patted my stomach. "Maybe some toast too?"

Tony dropped his phone. "I can't read any more. It's too depressing. I'll make the toast. Where's the bread?"

"Aunt Vera keeps it in the fridge." I hooked a thumb over my shoulder.

Tony retrieved the bread and handed a carton of eggs to Rick. They must have purchased the eggs and bacon on their grocery run, because I didn't recall seeing them in the fridge when I rooted around yesterday morning.

I sat back, sipping my coffee, and watched the men prepare the meal. Rick had cooked meat on the grill at my place, but I couldn't remember an instance when he'd done more than that for dinner. In general, the meals Rick organized consisted of take-out or making reservations at a restaurant. I had cooked for the both of us on plenty of occasions. I'd always assumed Rick made the eateries choice because either he didn't know how to cook or preferred the ease and speed of having meals prepared by others.

I was watching an anomaly. I'll be honest, it was quite the turn-on.

"When did you two become so domesticated?" I teased.

Tony made an offended cry. "I cook all the time at the station house. We rotate duties throughout the week."

"Okay, yeah, I buy that. I'll clarify—my comments were primarily directed at my boyfriend."

"I have hidden depths still to plumb," he drawled, cracking eggs into a glass bowl. "Can't give away all my secrets too early in the relationship."

"Ah-ha!" I pointed my red-tipped finger at him. "You have just confirmed the moniker I gave you when we first met ... Batman."

"Does he hang from the ceiling when he sleeps?" Tony asked.

Rick delivered a secretive grin.

"Well, I'll admit, if last night's dinner was anything to go by, I'm going to want to see more of this side of you." I raised my mug to him.

"What side of him?" My sister dragged into the kitchen and plopped herself onto the chair next to me. She stared at my coffee mug. "Is ... is there more?" she asked in a pitiful voice. Laying her head on the table, she murmured, "Gawd, I had a miserable night's sleep."

Rick stopped his egg prep to pour my poor sister a cup.

"Cream and sugar," Tony told him.

Rick added the ingredients and placed it next to her nose.

Her eyes opened. "Oh, you are a savior, sir." She drank deeply, gulping down half the mug in one go. Then, raising it in the air, and, with great flourish, she quoted that well-known English bard. "I do love nothing in the world so well as you—is not that strange?"

I quirked a brow. "*As You Like It?*"

"*Much Ado About Nothing,*" she corrected. My sister was

heavily involved in the drama club at her middle school.

"I don't care if it's *Star Wars*," Tony retorted. "What's my fiancée doing giving her love to a practical stranger over a cup of coffee?"

"Clearly her love can be bought rather cheaply," I pronounced.

"They say the key to a man's heart is through his stomach. Perhaps the same goes for your fiancée," Rick joked, whisking the eggs.

Highly incensed by the nonsense banter, Jillian clarified, "I wasn't speaking to Richard, *darling*. I was speaking to the coffee. The key to *my* love is certainly *not* through my stomach."

"Isn't that coffee you proclaim to love going into your stomach?" I quipped.

Jilly was about to take a sip when my comment hit home. Her jaw dropped. She closed it, then responded with a childish, "Oh, shut it. I didn't get enough sleep for all this witty banter."

"So we've heard. Tony told us all about it," I lightly jeered.

Jillian's head whipped around, her gaze piercing her fiancé. "*Tony!*" Her palm slapped the table.

His back remained toward her, but his shoulders stiffened to his ears.

"I would appreciate it if you wouldn't bandy my name about over the breakfast table." My sister was in rare form this morning.

He came over and kissed her jawline. "They're just jealous, honey."

Jillian giggled.

I made a gagging motion with my finger. "Get a room."

Rick gave a low, rumbling laugh and gazed at me as though he saw straight through the sweatshirt I'd thrown over my pajamas before coming downstairs. My smutty brain flashed to our nighttime romp, and a lovely little tingle shivered along my spine. Maybe *we* should be the ones to get a room.

Jeez, what is wrong with me? My aunt is missing! Get a grip!

Mentally, I shook off the out-of-place desire and stood up. "I'll get the plates and pour drinks. Who wants more coffee, and who wants juice?"

The boys finished preparing the meal, I set the table, and Jillian did nothing but drink her coffee like an indolent cat.

When I accused her of such, she sat upright and asked, "Speaking of cats. Did anyone feed them?"

"Already done," said Rick, scooping eggs onto a platter. "Nightshade went out back, and last I saw, Smokey was sitting in the parlor window."

"Thanks," Jillian murmured.

Once everyone was seated, I dove into the topic at hand. "Have you heard anything from Angus?"

"He's running some searches this morning. I told him to call back with an update when they finished."

"Have you heard anything from our detective?" Jillian asked.

"Not yet. I'll call after breakfast. What about Mom? I haven't heard from her since yesterday. Have you?" I buttered my toast and took a bite.

My sister nodded, scooping a pile of eggs onto her fork. "I spoke to her last night while you were napping. She's getting antsy. I have a feeling if we don't find something soon, she'll be on a flight out here."

"That could make things a little crowded around here," Rick commented.

"Too crowded for my taste. Did you tell her about the psychic?" I asked Jillian.

Chewing, she shook her head and swallowed the bite with a drink of coffee before answering, "Knowing how much Mom hated that Ouija board, I didn't think it would be a good idea to tell her we hired a professional medium. She'd probably believe we were forced to eat raw chicken guts and sell our souls to the devil during an induced trance."

One might laugh at Jillian's description. Tony gave a chuckle, which Jillian squelched with a glance. She was right. Mom held both a fascination with and aversion to the paranormal. She often watched that show *Ghost Hunters*. When asked, she said, "I can't tear myself away when it comes on."

She once confided in me her belief that, if you weren't careful, your soul could be sucked into the "other side" by evil spirits. She also regularly watched the show *Stranger Things* and may have gotten ghost hunting confused with The Upside Down portal. I wondered what her reaction would be upon coming face-to-face with the lieutenant.

After breakfast, everyone worked together to clean up the dishes, then Jillian and I went upstairs to shower and dress. Rick said he would telephone Angus. Tony offered to start contacting the marinas from the list Jillian prepared yesterday.

Exiting the shower, I heard knocking at the front door. Plenty of people were around to answer, so I thought nothing of it and continued my preparations. I was in the bathroom in my underwear and bra, with my head turned over and a hair dryer blowing out at full force, when someone tapped my shoulder. I flipped the dryer off and turned my head to the side to see who invaded my space.

Jillian stood in front of me, an eyelash curler in hand. She wore a blue robe and had half her makeup done. "That detective is downstairs with a search warrant," she hissed.

I straightened. "A search warrant? What's he searching for?"

"I heard him say they were looking for a silver museum piece."

Our eyes collided.

Jillian's were full of trepidation.

I imagined my own mirrored her concern. "I asked Rick to hide the silver creamer. Do you know where he put it?"

The moment I mentioned the creamer, Jillian began wringing the curler between her fingers. "He got a work call. And left it sitting out on the counter. I stuffed it into the back of one of the kitchen cabinets. Do you think they'll find it?"

"Undoubtedly." Sighing, I laid the hair dryer on the counter. *So much for a nice blow out today.*

"They haven't come in yet. Rick told them we were naked and needed a moment to finish dressing. Should I move it?" The eyelash curler snapped beneath her fingers. "Oh, damn."

Smart man. Naked woman in the house was a good delaying tactic. I brushed my damp hair back, binding it into a low ponytail. "No. Leave it. I want them to find it and run prints. Rick believes Aunt Vera bagged it for a reason."

"Very well. I'd better go. I need to get dressed. You'd better hurry up too. I don't think they'll wait very long."

I'd love to say having the police knock on my door early in the morning with a search warrant had never before happened to me. Unfortunately, it had, and not too long ago.

As I dressed in jeans and a sweater, I considered simply going downstairs and retrieving the item for the detective. I knew exactly what he was looking for. Handing it over might cause a lot less mess, not to mention the time and headache it would be for me to clean up after their search. However, I doubted they'd cancel the rest of a search and decided it was best for the police to find the item.

Had Rick wiped down the plastic baggie? I thought he said he would do it. If he did, our prints wouldn't be on it.

Jillian's prints, on the other hand…

I grimaced, shaking those thoughts away. *Deal with one thing at a time.*

Besides, I had some questions for the detective today. What better way to ask him than to dog his steps around the house?

On the main level, I found the detective and two officers

searching Vera's office and the dining room. All three wore purple rubber gloves. My aunt's silver serving ware was piled up on the dining table.

I stalked over to Detective Riggins. The dining room already reeked of cigarette smoke. "Good morning, Detective Riggins. May I see the search warrant." I didn't deliver it in the form of a question.

He grunted at me and pulled a paper from his back pocket. "Here you go. If you'll step outside with the rest of your crew, we'll be about our business as quickly as possible."

"Mm." My gaze scanned the document, targeting the most important part—what the warrant covered. "I see you've included paper documents as well as ... what is this? A silver cream pot? Care to explain?"

To my surprise, the gruff detective answered my question. "I have a picture of an item Norman Hedgewell claims is missing from the collection." He pulled a photo from his tweed sport coat and held it out to me.

Prepared for something like this, I maintained a look I'd labeled back in law school—interested neutrality. We'd been trained during mock trails to "never allow a jury to see you sweat." I'd spent hours in front of the mirror schooling my features into the look. It came in handy when meeting with senators and congressmen. Unfortunately, it was becoming handy when dealing with law enforcement—an all-too-common occurrence for me.

"That's quite a pretty piece," I commented, staring at the photo of the creamer buried somewhere in Aunt Vera's kitchen.

"It's—" That hacking cough interrupted his response.

When he finished, I handed the photo back to him. "Is there anything I can do to help?"

"Nothing. I'd appreciate it if you would simply wait outside," his tone brooked no opposition, and I had a feeling, if I didn't cooperate, he'd have me bodily removed from the premises. Possibly in handcuffs.

My phone had been upstairs with me and now resided in the back pocket of my jeans. However, I couldn't find my purse. I remembered leaving it on the counter next to the refrigerator. That would be the purse that held the blue file folder I'd found in Vera's desk drawer. My gaze frantically darted around the kitchen.

The prickling on my neck let me know I was being watched.

"Looking for something?" Detective Riggins said so near, I felt his breath on my neck.

"Nope." Either they'd found it, or they soon would. Not much I could do now, and I'd no plans to lead them directly to it. "I'll just take the cat with me." I scooped up Nightshade, who'd taken up residence on the kitchen table, and headed out back to join the boys.

Birds twittered endlessly in the surrounding flame-colored trees. The sun shone bright, with only small wispy clouds occasionally blocking its rays. The temperature was set to climb into the sixties today. A light breeze toyed with my ponytail, and I zipped up my red hoodie to keep out its chill. If it hadn't been for my missing aunt, we'd be enjoying the wonderfully mild fall weather and taking in the tourist sights. The thought depressed me, and I let out a troubled sigh.

Tony peered through the window into Vera's office, while my boyfriend tapped on his phone and paced the miniature yard. I released Nightshade, who sat down and began cleaning his paws.

Sidling up to Rick, I asked, "Do you know where Jillian put the creamer?"

Rick shrugged. "No clue.

Tony murmured, "One of the lower cabinets."

"Has anyone seen my handbag? I thought I left it in the kitchen," I said in muted tones. "Do you know if they've already confiscated it?"

Rick took my arm and turned me to face away from the windows of the house. "I had Tony put your purse and Jillian's in my pickup truck while I delayed the detective and his men from entering the premises."

I nodded. "Do you think we should show the file to the detective?"

Rick squinted at the back door in thought. "Not yet. I want to see what kind of information he's willing to share with us. I'm afraid the creamer *and* the list are pretty damning evidence. I want to get a sense of the direction the detective is taking the investigation."

A few minutes later, Jillian came outside, her toilette completed. Her waterfall of silky dark hair cascaded straight down her back, while mine curled and frizzed in its ponytail. Just one mark against the detective's timing. She took Tony's arm and guided him to the sweetheart bench along the back fence line. Tony whispered in her ear, and she nodded. Then the pair of them cuddled lovey-dovey, enjoying the mild morning.

Rick and I withdrew to his pickup truck to wait.

I stared sightlessly out the front windshield at the roof line of Aunt Vera's house. "What's Angus got for us?"

Something on the phone held his attention. He didn't bother to look up to answer, "Nothing new yet."

My leg bounced, and I fidgeted with the hem of my hoodie. "I'm feeling this ... pressure ... to *do* something. Only I'm not quite sure *what*. The ghost. The dream. Stupid Madame Seraphina. It's getting to me. All these warnings. Rick," I threw up my hands in frustration, "tell me what to do."

He tossed his phone on the dash and pulled me into his embrace. "If Angus hasn't called me by the time the cops leave, I'll phone him. I've got a bad feeling about Norman Hedgewell. I can't figure out why he's waited this long to call the police over the missing museum piece."

I snuggled into Rick's neck. "Can't we just snatch him off the street and the beat the crap out of him until he tells us something?"

His chest rumbled against my ear. "I think you know the answer to that question."

"Yeah," I sighed. "But it would certainly make me feel better if we could."

****

Even though Aunt Vera had a relatively small house, it took the team over an hour to search it. Jillian let out an exclamation of dismay when we were allowed back inside. Kitchen dishes, spices, oils, glassware, and more covered the counters and table.

"Did you find what you were looking for, *Detective*?" Jillian prodded rather snidely, picking up and putting away a glass, a bottle of olive oil, and a pepper grinder.

"As a matter of fact, we did." He held up the bagged creamer.

"What else have you found?" I leaned against the counter, crossing my arms. "You left several of my questions unanswered yesterday. I'd like an update on the investigation."

"Take this to evidence lock-up." He passed the creamer to one of the police officers. A mobile began to ring, and the detective held up a finger. "Just a moment." He swiped the answer icon. "Detective Riggins."

The person on the other end spoke so loudly, we could hear his tinny voice. "Did you find it?"

"Yes, sir, we did."

"Wonderful. Where should I go to pick it up?"

At this point, I surmised the person calling Riggins was Norman Hedgewell, and I leaned in a bit closer to listen.

"I'm afraid you can't," Riggins boomed.

"What do you mean, I can't? That piece belongs to the museum!"

"Right now, it's evidence in a crime. I've sent it along with one of my men to be stored in our secure evidence room."

There was a pause. "I see. When can the museum expect to get it back?"

"Your people can fill out the proper paperwork to request its return after the trial." He ended the call and, sticking a toothpick in his mouth, returned his attention to the four of us. "What was I saying?"

"You were about to tell us what you've discovered on the case," I prompted.

"I can tell you—the fingerprints on the car door did not belong to your aunt."

Jillian paused her tidying. "Whose fingerprints were they?"

"Norman Hedgewell's." He dropped that little bomb with nary a blink.

"Did he have an answer for those fingerprints on her car?" Jillian threw back at the detective.

Riggins shifted the toothpick to the other side of his mouth. "He said he must have closed her door at some point. Claims he would walk the ladies out to their cars at night when they didn't feel comfortable going to the parking lot in the dark."

Rick stood, arms akimbo, in the doorway to the hall. "Did any of the women at the museum back up that statement?"

The detective eyed him up and down. "Not the ones we've been able to reach. One woman even laughed in my face."

"Was Norman known for harassing any of the women at the office?" Rick probed.

"Funny you should ask." Riggins removed the toothpick. "Eight years ago, a complaint was filed, and then withdrawn. Nothing since then."

"What about the camera footage from the parking lot?" I

asked.

"White male. Six feet to six-two. Wearing dark clothes. Nothing identifiable. A William and Mary hoodie and ball cap." The toothpick went back in. "Unfortunately, it was grainy, and we didn't capture a face. He kept his head down the entire time. As if he knew there were cameras in the area."

"That's something." Jillian asserted, "We know he must go to or work for the college, if he's wearing a university ballcap and knows about the cameras."

I scrunched my nose and tilted my head. "Um ... not necessarily, Jilly. Those ballcaps are available for purchase everywhere around here." I turned back to the detective. "Unless it was special. A limited edition?"

"Afraid not." The toothpick bounced between his front teeth.

"Was Vera on any of the camera footage?" Rick asked.

"She was not." He took the toothpick out again and used it to describe the scene. "The unidentified male drove the car into the parking lot. Sat in it for eight minutes. Exited. Locked the vehicle. And left on foot."

I frowned. "What was he doing for eight minutes? Wiping down the interior?"

"It's possible," the detective replied. "We couldn't see inside the vehicle. Although we saw him wipe down the door handle after exiting."

Jillian paused her tidying, glass in hand, midway to the cabinet. "You're saying he was *trying* to cover his tracks?"

"It would seem." Riggins slipped the toothpick back into his mouth.

"What is your theory, Detective?" Tony asked, taking the glass from Jillian's hand and placing it in the cabinet.

"I'm working on a few. It's possible the man in the footage was a criminal fence that your aunt went to meet," he stated in matter-of-fact tones.

I made a moue with my mouth. "You're suggesting things didn't go well with a fence."

Riggins held up a hand. "We're still in the preliminary stages of the investigation."

My gaze narrowed. "Have you got any other theories regarding the man leaving my aunt's car in a parking lot?"

"I'm waiting for more reports," the detective explained, "before I make a determination on who the man is, and what he's done with her."

"If you think she's dead, where will you begin looking?" Rick's harsh tones sliced through the room.

Jillian gasped. A wine glass slipped between her fingers, shattering on the tile floor.

Smokey darted out of the room.

Tony immediately moved to my sister's side. "Babe, are you okay? Are you cut?" He took her hands in his to inspect them.

Riggins, perhaps realizing his responses were less than sympathetic, withdrew the toothpick and cleared his throat. "Now, hold on there, I didn't say anything of the sort. You're putting words into my mouth. I've got our IT department searching for additional camera footage for the vehicle, to determine where it originated. Also, where the man went after he left the vehicle. If we can determine the origination point of the vehicle, perhaps I'll have more information for you."

"Did the man get on a train?" Rick asked.

Riggins shook his head. "He walked in the opposite direction, and none of the cameras at the train station picked him up."

"So, you *don't* think my aunt is dead?" I prodded.

"I don't have an answer either way. I'm simply gathering evidence right now," he replied.

"Uh-huh. What do you suggest we do in the meantime?" I retrieved the broom and dustpan from the pantry.

"Wait."

Tony took them from me while my sister carefully picked up the larger pieces and dropped them in the trash.

I returned my attention to the detective. "I'm not very good at waiting, Detective."

Rick snorted, which garnered a foul glare from me.

"There's nothing more you can do." With that, Riggins turned and headed to the front door.

Of course, Rick and I followed him, leaving Tony and Jillian behind in the kitchen.

"Are you sure there's nothing else you can tell us about the investigation?" I prodded.

"Nothing. And please ask your mother not to call me every hour today. When I have more information, I'll let you know. Let me do my job." He opened the door and pointed his toothpick outside. "Williamsburg is a beautiful city; there are plenty of things for tourists to do."

I blinked in confusion. *Did he suggest we visit the sites while my aunt might be a rotting corpse?*

Rick must have been on the same wavelength. He asked in a deriding tone, "You're suggesting we play tourist all day?"

"I'm suggesting you be careful what you're about." The toothpick snapped in half, and he pointed at us with two fingers. "I'm *not* a fool. I don't know what you four are playing at, but I *am* aware you've been trotting around town sticking your noses into things you don't understand. I also believe you're *hiding* something from me. I just haven't figured out what it is … *yet.*" Those two fingers jabbed at us.

"Is there anything we need to provide the detective, hon?" I looked over at Rick to see if he wanted to offer up the materials that were in my handbag.

"Nothing I can think of." Rick slipped his arm around my waist. "Why don't we go to Busch Gardens today, sweetie?"

I didn't bother to respond. He wasn't serious. For some

reason, he didn't want to give up the materials we'd found hidden in Vera's drawer.

The detective's face reddened at Rick's mocking tone, and he grumbled back at us, "This isn't a cartoon. You aren't the Scooby-Doo gang. This is real life. Your precious aunt is missing, and from where I'm standing, it could be because she got involved with some dangerous people. If you go sniffing around, you could get yourself into similar trouble."

My eyes turned to slits. "Is that a threat, Detective?"

"No. It's a warning." He stomped out the door and down the porch steps.

"Have a nice day. Y'all come back now, ya hear," I said in a sarcastic southern drawl. Closing the door with a snap, I stomped back to the kitchen, sputtering, "That-that detective just compared us to the Scooby-Doo gang."

"I get to be Velma!" my sister trilled.

"No way, I'm Velma." I pointed to my chest. "She's the smart one."

"No, *I'm Velma*," Jillian insisted, explaining as if talking to a toddler. "*You're* the redhead; that makes *you* Daphne."

Rick followed me into the kitchen and plopped a hand on my shoulder. "I guess that makes me Fred."

"Wait a minute, does that mean *I'm* Shaggy?" Tony asked with disgust.

"Well, hon, you can be Scooby if you want," my sister teased. "Do you want a Scooby snack?"

"I sure do!" He grabbed her from behind and buried his head into her neck, making a chomping noise.

Jillian went into peals of laughter. I looked back at Rick and rolled my eyes. He simply grinned watching those two fools.

With a sniff, I headed to the dining room to begin cleaning up.

Chapter Twenty-One

The giggling in the kitchen settled, and the four of us began the tedium of putting away all of Vera's belongings. Jillian and Tony took the kitchen, while I worked in the dining room, and Rick in the parlor.

Tucking a pair of crystal wine goblets into Vera's china cabinet, it occurred to me our morning was missing something. I checked my cellphone to be sure. Nope. Nothing.

"Jilly," I hollered, "have you heard from Mom today?"

"No, ma'am." She came to stand in the doorway and checked her own mobile. "Should we call her? It's almost nine, Denver time."

I chewed my lip. *Do I want to tell my mother her cousin is suspect number one in a museum theft?*

No, I do not.

"Um, let's leave it. If she doesn't call in the next hour, we'll phone."

One of the pocket doors was closed halfway. Rick pushed it open. "I'm finished in the parlor. Shall I move on to Vera's office or start upstairs?"

"It won't take long; there isn't much left in Vera's office," Jillian put in. "The police took most of her files."

My mouth twisted. "Go ahead. Once the office is straightened, you can head upstairs."

Midway through the process, Rick's phone trilled. He brought it into the dining room. "Go for Rick. You're on speakerphone."

"I've got some information on Hedgewell, sir," Angus said.

Jillian and Tony came into the dining room to listen to Angus give us the lowdown.

"Initially, he didn't show any red flags. Hedgewell's been at the museum for fifteen years and worked his way up to the director position. Before that, he worked at Carnegie Museum of Art. He lives in a three-bedroom house not far from where he works. His two girls are in their twenties. Both graduated from college—one from James Madison, the other from Mary Washington. One is living in Richmond, working for the same realty company as her mother. The other is married, in North Carolina. She's an accountant for a medical device company."

"Is Hedgewell married?" I asked.

"Divorced. He and his wife split when the girls were in college."

"He sounds as exciting as a shrimp sandwich," my sister declared.

"At first glance, it seemed Norman was a straight arrow. However, when I looked deeper into his background, I found something."

We waited with bated breath.

When Angus didn't enlighten us immediately, Tony spoke up, "Don't keep us in suspense, man!"

"His father has Alzheimer's," Angus stated triumphantly.

It was as though the entire room deflated like a bounce house when the plug gets pulled. We'd been expecting to hear something exciting, like he bred illegal exotic animals, or cooked meth in the basement.

Rick leaned toward the phone. "I fail to see the red flag, Angus."

"The man lives in a memory unit. He's at a continuing care retirement community complex called Green Dale, in Chesapeake, Virginia."

Jillian asked, "You're implying his dementia-ridden father is stealing artifacts from the museum?"

"I doubt it," Angus replied. "They lock the unit to keep the patients from wandering off. Only family can check them out of the unit. Or if a patient must go to the doctor, and then it's done under the supervision of a qualified staff member."

"What's the point of the father?" Rick prodded Angus back on track.

"Right. It's a top-of-the-line facility. Residents enjoy a luxury lifestyle with a full schedule of activities and amenities. They have on-site therapists, doctors, and nurses. The memory care unit costs close to $7900 a month."

Tony nodded. "Yeah, sounds about right. It would cost more in northern Virginia."

I whistled. "Holy mackerel, I had no idea those places were so costly."

"I hope Mom and Dad don't have to go into one of them. How would we pay for that?" Jillian lamented.

"Does Medicare pay for it?" Rick asked.

"Not much," Angus replied.

Tony shook his head. "Hardly any. It'll cover nursing care, some of the medication costs, any sort of testing or hospital supplies. If the patient is admitted to the hospital, it'll cover more," he informed us. "Does the guy have long-term disability benefits?"

Rick got down to the brass tacks. "How's he paying for it, Angus?"

"A variety of places. Some of the money is coming from his monthly Social Security income. Some of it is from the old man's paltry retirement account. Looks like that covers close to four grand of the cost."

"Where is the rest of the money coming from?" Jillian picked up Smokey, placed his front paws over her shoulder, and began stroking his back.

"Up until nine months ago, it was coming out of Norman's younger brother's account. Johnathan Hedgewell co-owned a marketing company in Chicago," Angus explained.

"Owned?" I asked, "What happened to the brother?"

"He was a victim in a mass shooting. His assets are still being sorted out, but it looks as though the wife and kids will be the beneficiaries. In the meantime, Norman has been picking up the offset of the costs for his father."

Rick put a hand on his hip. "How's that working out for Norman?"

"Not well. Norman had to take out a mortgage to buy his wife's half of the house in the divorce. He's got a hefty car loan for a Mercedes SUV. He eats out most of the week and likes to golf. He belongs to one of the more costly clubs in the Williamsburg area. Initially, he sold off some stocks, but with the market in a downturn, he's experienced losses in the sale."

"In other words, on top of his very nice lifestyle, Norman is paying four grand a month for his father's facility," Jillian said.

"Until recently, yes. Two months ago, the additional funds started coming from a numbered Capitol Cayman Bank account." Angus's statement was met with silence.

We waited for him to continue. Tony shifted his feet. Jillian continued petting her cat. Rick stood with the phone in hand, patiently waiting for his employee to fill us in.

When his dramatic pause lasted too long, I threw out, "You want to expand on that? Did Norman take a trip to the Caymans this year?"

"As far as I can tell, he's never been."

"Well, that's no help," I snapped.

Tony screwed up his features. "Who owns the account?"

"Dead brother. Or something shadier?" Jillian suggested.

"Don't know. It's a numbered account. I couldn't get past their firewall to access the information. They've got a TDES firewall; they're using a Barracuda IDS—"

"Get to the punch line, Angus," Rick growled.

"Right, Boss. Uh … yeah … where was I?" Angus stuttered, clearly rattled by Rick's irritation. I pictured him fiddling with his glasses or tugging on his mop of red hair. "The past three months, Norman made a trip to New York."

"Why is that important?" I asked.

"One thing that Capital Cayman Bank offers … is a branch in New York City. Norman goes up to visit; three days later, money from the numbered account transfers to the CCRC facility to pay for his father's care."

And there it was.

Jillian lowered Smokey to the floor.

"Do you think he fences the stuff up in New York?" I asked no one in particular.

Angus responded, "That would be my guess."

Tony scratched his chin with a contemplative demeanor. "I'm trying to figure out how he gets the items through airport security without being noticed."

"He takes the train up to New York," Angus supplied.

"Have you figured out where he's selling the items?" Rick asked.

"Not yet, Boss. I'll keep digging."

"Find out if Hedgewell owns any property beyond the house in Williamsburg. Anything—an empty lot, storage facility, RV." Rick ended the call. "I think instead of going to Busch Gardens, we need to visit Norman Hedgewell's home."

"I think we need to make a visit *inside* … while Norman's *not* home. One of us can lure him out, while the others case the joint, looking for any signs of Aunt Vera. Maybe he's locked her up inside."

I was shocked to hear my sister make this proposal, especially in front of her fiancé. While I knew Rick had a liberal moral compass, Tony's was a straight arrow. He and FBI Mike always got along well. The look on Tony's face clearly stated he wasn't keen on Jillian's idea.

Before Tony could reply to Jillian, Rick stepped in. "Karina and I can go stake out the house. Even though the idea came from the psychic, I still believe we should follow up with the marinas. Jillian, you and Tony visit the marinas with that photograph of Vera. Also, ask if anyone knows Hedgewell. You can download a picture of him from the museum website."

"Let's go now," I suggested. "Leave this mess for later." Since we had more concrete evidence about Norman, I wanted to follow up without delay.

Chapter Twenty-Two

Watching Jillian's car pull away, I placed a hand above my brow to block the sun. The brake lights lit up, and the car cruised around the corner. Once out of sight, I contemplated the two vehicles remaining in the parking area. "There's no way we can stay under the radar driving either your giant pickup truck or my red Jeep. Just like at Vikram's, we're bound to get noticed. What's your plan for the stakeout?"

"I've called in reinforcements."

"Reinforcements?"

"Last night." Rick checked his watch. "Should be here in about fifteen minutes."

I delivered a side-eye. "Okay, spill. Who's coming to town?"

"You'll see," he replied with a secretive grin.

"You know I'm not good at waiting," I huffed with a pout.

"I'm well aware. However, I'm here to keep you from haring off like your pants are on fire, with no forethought, as is your tendency."

"Hey!" I socked him in the shoulder.

He looked at me, innocence written across his features.

Trouble was, he'd hit a little too close to the bullseye with that comment. I did have a habit of, let's say, taking things into my own hands. Patience was *not* my forte. "In my defense, I generally give forethought to my actions before taking them."

His face split into a smile, but before he could form a response, a large white van with a sewer company logo along the side rolled up the street and pulled into the little parking lot. One of my favorite Silverthorne people sat in the driver's seat.

Jin shifted the van into park and grinned at me. The wicked scar that slashed down the left side his face puckered. I'd never heard the story about how it happened, but I knew it was during his time in Afghanistan. Rick claimed to owe Jin his life. He was smaller than most of the Silverthorne guys, and his body may have been narrow and lithe, but he was quick and deadly. In a back-alley fight, I'd want Jin on my side. On more than one occasion, he'd also placed his faith in my own intuition, providing me a confidence boost exactly when I needed it.

I pulled open the passenger side door and hopped in. "Hello, stranger, it's good to see you." I leaned in for a sidearm hug. "It's been a while. Where have you been?"

"I was working out of the country for two months and then took a two-week vacation to Thailand."

"Nice. How was Thailand? I've never been. Did you go to Phuket?"

"Stunning. You should go. And, yes, I saw Phuket, also Chang Mei." His somber dark eyes twinkled at me. Jin wasn't known for his sense of humor, but, somehow, I tended to bring it out in him. Much like his Silverthorne brethren, he also used brevity in his words. "What am I doing here?"

"Ah, you haven't been told. I can't answer that question. I'm not exactly sure what you're doing here."

Our gazes turned to Rick standing next to the open door. "We're going to check out Hedgewell's house. Did you bring the equipment?"

"In the back." Jin tilted his head to indicate the rear of the van. "Who's Hedgewell?"

"Norman Hedgewell is my aunt's boss and a fishy swishy guy," I supplied. "We're concerned he's played a role in my aunt's disappearance."

"The plan is to head over to his house. I'd like to see if I can get ears in there," Rick added.

My attention returned to Rick. "How are you going to get ears in there?"

Rick delivered a blank stare.

I turned back to Jin to see what he had to say. "I brought a handful of toys."

I looked behind the seat, expecting to see a vanload full of gadgets, gizmos, and electronics. To my disappointment, it was loaded with four hard silver cases. "Huh. I was expecting more." I shrugged. "Okay, let's roll."

Jin didn't make a move to start the car. He stared past my shoulder.

I followed his gaze.

"I'd like to take your Jeep. Jin will follow in the van."

Far be it from me to question Rick's methods. My gaze alighted on my fire-engine-red Jeep. On the other hand— "Uh, you want to take my Jeep? On a stakeout? Isn't it a bit … obvious?"

"It's smaller and fits in around town. Looks like a college kid's car."

"Well … if you're sure."

"I'm sure. Let's go." He held out his hand to help me climb down from the captain's chair.

Rick typed Hedgewell's address into the GPS, and I drove, with Jin following behind at a distant pace. The house was about fifteen minutes away from CW. We rolled into a lovely neighborhood with a variety of homes ranging from colonial to mid-century modern to transitional. The varied styles made it clear the community was not tract housing, but, rather, custom builds erected over decades.

"There it is." Rick pointed. "Keep driving. We'll go around the block while Jin sets up."

We approached Norman's house—a two-story colonial with

distressed white brick, a porticoed front porch, black shutters, and a green front door. Two cars were parked side by side in the driveway—a Mercedes SUV and a shimmery rose Cadillac. A pink Mary Kay logo was emblazoned across the back window of the Cadillac.

I cruised on past and continued to the end of the street. Around the bend, we were temporarily stopped as we waited for a lawn company to disgorge a large piece of equipment from its trailer. By the time we came back around, Jin's van was parked diagonally across the street from Norman's home. Jin wore an orange vest with a yellow hard hat, and he'd put up cones around the opened manhole cover in the middle of the street.

Removing my foot from the accelerator, we slowed to a crawling pace. "Should I go around again?"

"Make a U-turn at the end of the street. Park on the opposite side, right on that curve." He pointed for clarification. "See how there's an empty lot of land in between those two houses?"

I followed his directions and rolled to a stop not far behind the van.

Jin strolled over to the Jeep and laid his elbows on the window ledge. He exuded the calm of a meditating Buddha. "Thermal imaging revealed two people inside. Looks like both are in the kitchen."

I removed my sunglasses. "You've brought a thermal imaging camera?"

"Thought it might be useful." Jin grinned.

Rick, his eyes targeted on the house, murmured, "Someone's coming out."

A middle-aged blonde woman wearing a sparkly pink jacket, black skinny pants, and high heels, clopped out to the Cadillac. She tossed a large tote bag in the back seat along with her purse.

"I thought Hedgewell was divorced." Rick squinted at the blonde.

"Maybe he's secretly a drag queen, and he's getting his monthly makeup fix," I quipped.

Rick frowned.

"Kidding. Mary Kay sells products for men and women."

"Sister?" Jin suggested.

Norman came out of the house wearing jeans, flip-flops, and a flannel shirt. He thwacked down the driveway, took the blonde into his arms, and they shared a rather passionate kiss.

My glasses slid back into place. "I don't think that's his sister."

"Girlfriend," Jin and Rick said as one.

In gentlemanly form, Norman opened the door and helped her into the Caddy. The car purred to life, and Norman waved as the woman backed out of the driveway. Grinning, he tucked his hands in his pockets and briefly glanced at the work truck.

The men next to me stiffened.

To our relief, the van didn't seem to interest Norman. He turned on his heel and loped back into the house.

"Return to your station," Rick told Jin.

We watched Jin open one of the rear doors to the van and climb inside.

"Now what?" I asked.

"Let's go for a walk."

"Seriously?"

"Seriously. I want to get a better look at the rear of the house. I need to know what the exit options are."

We left the Jeep and strolled, hand in hand, down the sidewalk in front of Norman's house. At the end of the street, we turned the corner that would take us around the block.

"He's got a Ring doorbell," I commented.

"I noticed."

My lips turned south with concern. "Won't he think it's fishy if he sees us wandering around in front of his house?"

"I planned for it. Every Jack and Jill has a Ring doorbell these days. Jin's brought a jamming device. If Hedgewell checks his Ring while we're here, the only thing he'll see is a blank screen."

"Do you think he'll get suspicious if nothing's turning up?"

"That's why Jin's here. He's got a perfectly good explanation."

I waited.

Nothing.

I swear sometimes it was like dragging a toddler to the doctor's office. As Rick didn't deem it necessary to educate me, I prompted him, "And that explanation would be…"

"The equipment they use can sometimes cause interference with cell and Wi-Fi reception. If any of the neighbors start asking questions, he'll throw out a bunch of technical terms. Confuse the hell out of them. And assure any concerned citizens, once the van leaves, their reception will return to normal," he explained in indulgent tones.

By this time, we'd made it to the opposite side of the block. Rick slowed in front of a gray clapboard house with yellow shutters and a white front door. "This is the house that backs to Hedgewell's. Can you tie your shoe?"

Bending to one knee, I asked, "How long do you need?"

"Don't hurry." He held up his phone as if checking for a text and snapped several photos.

I wore a pair of lace-up boots and proceeded to remove my left one to shake out a nonexistent rock. Traffic in this part of the neighborhood was relatively light for a Sunday.

A car drove past. The driver waved. Rick waved back.

A woman walked by with her golden retriever on the opposite side of the street. She waved. I returned her wave.

The next-door neighbor backed out of the garage, down the driveway and waved at us as he drove up the street.

"People are very friendly around here," I commented.

"Yeah, it's not like D.C., where you don't wave at anyone."

His words were sad but true.

People in the D.C. metro area generally kept to themselves. There were neighbors in my building I'd never spoken to. Silent elevator rides with another person were regular occurrences.

"Okay. You can finish."

I pulled the bow tight and held up a hand. Rick hauled me to my feet, and we continued our stroll around the block.

"Karina, I wanted to mention something."

"Yeah? What?"

"There could be other reasons your aunt had that silver piece in her house."

"Such as?" I paused.

Rick tugged my hand to keep us going. "She may be Hedgewell's partner. Or she may have been blackmailing him."

With a sigh, I agreed. "Being Hedgewell's partner did cross my mind. Maybe a double-cross that's gotten her into trouble. I hadn't thought about blackmail. Maybe Hedgewell's prints *are* on that creamer."

He squeezed my hand. "I just wanted to give you a warning."

The back door to the van was closed but unlocked. We found Jin inside, sitting on a three-legged folding camp stool, looking through a camera he'd set up on a tripod. The camera was aimed at Norman's house and peeped through the curtains of the small side window. One of the silver cases had been turned on its end. Jin's laptop was on it, and the screen revealed the feed from the camera. A small drone rested atop one of the silver boxes.

"The subject is still in the house. Second floor. Showering," Jin informed us in his tranquil manner.

"Did you send the drone up already?" I asked.

"Yes. I left it out in case we need it again," he explained.

Rick pulled the door closed, and the van darkened.

"What's the plan, Sam?" I crouched next to Jin.

"For the time being, we wait." Rick unfolded a second stool

and handed it to me. "If he doesn't leave soon, we'll create a diversion to get him out of the house."

I scooched around, trying to settle my butt cheeks comfortably on the tiny green Oxford cloth seat. "Do you think my aunt is in there?"

"I doubt it. I can't imagine him keeping her in there while he's getting it on with his girlfriend. Jin, have you seen any other heat signatures in the house?"

"No. Although, I can't see below ground. Does the house have a basement?"

"Not sure, let me check." Rick tapped on his phone. "No. It's only two floors."

I shuddered. "If he's got a large chest freezer in the garage, that's the first thing I'm checking out."

Nobody replied. Probably because my suggestion wasn't off base.

I fidgeted with my earring. "What's he doing now?"

"Getting dressed," Jin said.

My leg bounced. I tapped my foot and quietly hummed a Lady Gaga song that'd been playing when I shut off the Jeep. I caught Rick staring at me, a single brow raised, and halted the foot tapping.

He sighed. "Didn't you bring your phone?"

"Oh, yeah. Here it is, in my back pocket." I checked my messages. "There's a text from Jilly. She says they struck out at the first marina and are headed to the next one."

I texted her:

We are here at Norman's. So far nothing of note. He's in the house. Hoping he leaves soon. Have you heard from Mom?

Nothing, she texted back.

Next, I checked my emails. About twenty spam and junk emails went directly into the trash. A few work emails I left to be dealt with on Monday. One, from my boss, I answered right away.

After that, I moved to my social media accounts and spent time watching silly animal videos. One with a curious emu who kept interrupting the woman posting her informational video on how to milk a cow had me laughing out loud.

Rick and Jin suffered together in silence.

Thirty boring minutes later, to my relief and that of my van mates, Jin said, "Front door is opening."

The phone returned to my pocket; I sat forward to watch the laptop feed. Norman exited the house carrying a black backpack. He got in his car and zipped out of the driveway. He didn't give a backward glance to the van.

A thought occurred to me. "Shouldn't we follow him?"

Rick's gaze shot to Jin.

Without further prompting, Jin responded to the unasked question, "Yeah. I put a tracker on him."

He gave a sharp nod. "Karina, if I asked you, do you trust me? Your answer would be…"

Is this a trap? "Yesss … I trust you. Why?"

"If I asked you to stay in the van with Jin—"

"I'd ask, 'did you hit your head?'" My eyes widened, and my head tilted. "Because you must be out of your mind if you think I'll patiently stick around in this van while *you* case Norman's house on your own."

"You'd better let her go with you, Boss. You know she'll follow you anyway," Jin said in his dulcet, Zen-like tones. "Otherwise, you'll have to bind and gag her, and cuff her to the steering wheel."

The men shared a silent conversation, clearly considering Jin's comment.

Crossing my arms, I suggested in honeyed tones, "That's not going to end well for either one of you."

Rick finally nodded in agreement. "Fine." I went to open the van door, but he stopped me. "Listen up. You know what we're doing is highly illegal."

"Yeah. It's called breaking and entering," I drawled.

His tone remained serious, "It could end your career and get your law license revoked."

My irritation with his delay evaporated immediately. I realized he was expressing his concern for me, and he wasn't wrong. I fidgeted with my earring. Of course, I trusted Rick to do a thorough job. On the other hand, would I be satisfied with his report, or would it gnaw at me? Would I feel I'd done everything in my power to find Vera?

Sensing my hesitation, Rick took my right hand in his. "I can go in alone. You can watch my progress here in the safety of the van, on the computer," he urged.

What he said made sense, but when it comes to the people we love, sometimes the head and heart don't agree.

I blinked at those serious gray eyes and said, "She is my aunt. I need to do this."

He sighed and nodded. "Okay, then. Get suited up."

"Suited up?"

Jin spun around and, reaching past me, picked up a pile of neon-yellow cloth. He shook them out to reveal a pair of reflective vests, often worn by construction road workers.

He passed one over to me. "Put this over your sweater. If I had thought to bring an extra pair of work pants, I'd have you put them on." I realized Jin was wearing a sturdy pair of navy-blue chinos. He shook his head. "Your jeans will have to do."

Rick pulled on the other vest. On the back was the sewer company logo in bright green. "It doesn't matter. She can be the supervisor; give her the cap and clipboard."

"Here, cover your head with this." Jin handed me a green ball cap and a clipboard with a pink slip that read *Work Order* and some indecipherable scribblings.

"What am I supposed to do with the clipboard?"

"Carry it around. Look official. You'd be amazed the locations you can access with a hat and clipboard," Rick explained, plopping a yellow hard hat on his head.

Moments later, my boyfriend surreptitiously keyed into Norman's front door.

Chapter Twenty-Three

We entered a small foyer. In the corner sat a coat rack practically bending from the weight of at least a dozen coats and umbrellas hanging from it. On the left was the dining room, to the right a pair of closed pocket doors. Past the doors was the stairwell leading to the second floor.

Rick handed me a pair of rubber gloves. "Put these on."

We snapped the gloves in place and started prowling the house.

Rick and I both bypassed the dining room and moved to the back of the house. I opened doors as I went, finding a coat closet and a half bath.

The kitchen was situated in the rear of the house overlooking a good-sized backyard. It had knotty pine cabinets and stainless-steel appliances. Norman seemed to be a fairly good housekeeper. The sink was empty of kitchen dishes, and the counters were recently wiped down. Perhaps it was the blonde's doing. I opened a door and found a small pantry, everything put away in an orderly manner.

No Aunt Vera.

While I took the time to open and close every door and cabinet I came upon, Rick efficiently cruised through the main level, leaving a little listening device plugged into the wall behind the couch.

"I'm heading upstairs," he said, deftly taking the steps two at a time, lightly landing on his toes as he went.

"I'll check the garage," I called.

I opened the door to the garage and found it jam-packed. Yard tools, a couple of bikes, a wagon, skates, and other random toys forgotten from childhood were scattered in the middle of the double-car garage. A wooden rack held half a dozen colorful fishing rods; rubber waders and bright orange life preservers hung on nails next to it. Metal shelving lined the far wall with various boxes stacked on each shelf. Some were marked with holidays like Christmas, Thanksgiving, and Easter. Others were simply marked "books." Since Norman didn't have a basement, he used the garage as his storage area. The HVAC system immediately to the right of the doorway roared to life as I searched through the debris. To my relief, I did not find an extra freezer or refrigerator.

My shoe hit something hard, and I looked down to find a large footlocker tucked behind one of the bikes. I rolled the bike aside and tugged the handle of the footlocker from the bottom of a shelf.

It was heavy.

Heavy enough for a body.

I wrenched it all the way onto the concrete floor, until I had enough clearance to open the lid. My heart sped up, and, swallowing, I girded myself for the worst.

"One, two, three," I whispered and shoved open the lid.

The earthy smell of decaying paper wafted up from its depths. Hardbacks of old yearbooks and faded yellow covers of *National Geographic* magazines met my eyes. I released the breath I'd been holding with a shaky laugh. It took a bit of difficult maneuvering to jam the footlocker back into place. Some of the dust dislodged during the process. However, when I rolled the bike back in place, it became unnoticeable to the untrained eye.

Dusting my hands on my jeans, I returned to the house and went through to the family room next. A pair of shoes were tucked under the coffee table, and a couple of rumpled blankets were balled into a corner of the couch. Five remotes had been scattered across the coffee table, all aimed at the television above the fireplace. I opened one of the French doors that should have led into a more formal living area. However, Norman had turned it into an exercise room.

Unfortunately, the powder-puff air freshener failed to cover the scent of sweat and a musty metallic odor coming from the equipment. A stationary bike, treadmill, and rack of free weights sat in each corner. A floor-to-ceiling mirror covered half of one wall. A second set of doors closed off the room so it could be hidden from the foyer.

Like Rick, I took the stairs two at a time. "Have you found anything?" I called out.

The first room on the right was set up as an office. A row of floor-to-ceiling bookcases filled with thick tomes lined one side of the room. A large mahogany desk ran perpendicular to the bookcases. On it was a flat-screen monitor, a desk blotter, lamp, and pencil sharpener. My boyfriend rifled through the four-drawer filing cabinet next to the desk.

"Anything of interest?" I asked again.

He shook his head. "Nothing yet. General stuff, bills, taxes, paperwork." He paused his rummaging, pulled out a manila folder, glanced through the papers, and then put it back in the filing cabinet. "What about you? I didn't hear any screaming. Everything clear?"

"Nada. Zip. Zilch. I'm going to check the master."

"Have at it." He returned to the files.

The master bedroom was painted light gray. A king-size bed with a navy-blue tufted headboard spanned the far wall. A pair of art deco side tables flanked the bed. On the opposite wall stood two closets with mirrored sliding doors. Immediately, I went to them.

The first closet held Norman's clothes—suits, dress shirts, slacks, sweaters, and shoes rested in a neat line across the floor. The second closet held a comforter and women's clothing.

Norman's girlfriend must have been more serious than a simple fling. At least a dozen skirts and dresses hung in plastic dry cleaning bags. The other side of the closet revealed shelves of folded bras, lacy panties, socks, and some sexy nighttime lingerie.

The master bathroom had a long double sink with a separate shower and toilet area. The blonde's Mary Kay cosmetics were scattered across the countertop, along with a blow dryer and a handful of curling brushes.

Since the master bedroom held nothing of interest, I checked out the last bedroom, which had been set up as a guest room. A queen-size four-poster bed overshadowed the space. It took up so much room, the miniature side tables had to be wedged in between the bed and the wall. A gold velvet armchair and lamp sat in the corner next to a small chest of drawers. I opened the walk-in closet, turned on the light, and found comforters, mattress pads, towels, and sheets on shelves. Nothing hung on the rods except for a pair of white, fluffy robes.

It was becoming clear to me that we were going to find nothing earthshattering in Norman's home. Walking into the hallway, my eye alighted on a rope hanging from the ceiling.

"Have you been up in the attic space?" I called out.

He slammed a file drawer shut. "Not yet."

"I'll check it out." I heard a grunt of acceptance and the squeak of rusty wheels as another file drawer opened.

I couldn't reach the rope and went back into the master bedroom, where I'd seen a spindle-back chair. It was piled with slacks and a jacket. I laid the clothes on the bed and took the chair into the hallway. The attic door made a hideous groaning sound as I pulled it from the ceiling and unfolded the metal ladder.

Dust floated down, and a damp dankness radiated from the attic space. It made my nose itch, and I sneezed.

"Everything okay, beautiful?"

"Yes." I scratched my nose. "I don't think I'll be so beautiful when I get done in the attic. It smells like a dust pit."

He gave an absent-minded grunt.

I reached for my phone. Turning on the flashlight app, I climbed the stairs.

Part of the attic had been floored. Moldy cardboard boxes, yellowed with age, were stacked neatly along one side of the attic, with a decent amount of walking space. I maneuvered to the edge of the plywood, pointing my flashlight as deeply into the deep crevices as possible. The ducting created bizarre shadows, but there was nothing leading me to believe a body was hidden behind them. Boxes were labeled with things such as "Jenna's Clothes," "Maureen's Toys" and "More Books." Tucked between a stack of boxes, I discovered a rocking horse, an old highchair, and a big orange tub filled with Barbie paraphernalia. Pink insulation covered the unfloored portion of the attic.

Wiping perspiration from my forehead, I glanced around the upper floor with disappointment. The day had begun to warm, and the attic already felt eight to ten degrees hotter than the lower levels. I flapped the vest like bird wings to move the air. There seemed to be plenty of junk up here. None of it gave me a clue as to the location of Aunt Vera.

With a harumph, I made my way down the creaky ladder. After folding it, I flipped the hatch back into place and returned Norman's chair to the master bedroom, replacing the clothes on it.

Rick had the bottom drawer of the filing cabinet open.

"The attic was a bust. Nothing of interest up there. Find anything in here?"

"Not yet, and I'm on the last drawer. I noticed a filing box in the closet. Why don't you take a look while I finish up here?"

I plopped on the floor and yanked the white box between my legs. The scribble on top read *"DAD'S PAPERWORK."* After five minutes, I realized half the box was full of medical paperwork. Deeper in were old bank statements, credit card bills, and communications with the Veterans Affairs department.

"Looks like Norman's father is a vet." I skimmed one of the letters. "Oh dear, looks like Norman's been writing the V.A. to get his father's benefits adjusted. There's an entire file for it." I pulled out a thick manila folder jammed full of correspondence.

Rick glanced at it. "I feel his pain. I've got one just like it at home."

"Oh?"

"My knee injury."

I recalled the scars I'd seen surrounding his right knee and frowned. "Didn't that happen while you were active duty?"

"The injury happened while I was deployed, yes. One surgery happened while I was active duty. The second after I'd gotten out." He returned to his filing cabinet.

I continued observing him. "You've never told me about it."

"Remind me when we're not in the midst of a crime."

"I'm going to hold you to that." I flipped through the rest of the files until the second to last, which gave me pause. The title read *"BOAT & TRAILER."* "Wait a minute, Daddy's got a boat."

Rick paused his search and came over to hunker down next to me.

"These are repair bills from a marina. And here's one for fixing a trailer." My mind's eye recalled something I'd seen. "There were fishing rods and life preservers in the garage." I shuffled deeper into the pile. "And these yellow sheets are slip fees!" I cried, triumphantly brandishing it in the air.

He snatched it out of my hand to scan the information. "This was for ten years ago. Do you see anything more recent?"

A nuclear meltdown alarm blared in the quiet of the room, which nearly had me jumping out of my skin.

"Yikes! What the hell is that?" I squealed.

"It's Jin." Rick tapped his Bluetooth earbud to answer. "Talk to me." He paused to listen. "How much time?" His eyes met mine, and he relayed Jin's message. "Five minutes. Tops."

We scrambled to put things back in order. I jammed the manila folder in place and held out my hand. "I need the paper."

"Wait, let me photograph it. I want to follow up with the marina." The camera clicked twice. He handed me the paper, and I shoved the box into the closet. Rick slammed the cabinet drawer shut, and we bolted from the room.

At the bottom of the stairs, Rick gripped my elbow and swung me around the balustrade. "We're leaving through the back door. Where's your clipboard?"

My stomach dropped in a moment of panic, until I remembered I'd left it on the counter. "It's in the kitchen."

"Follow me." After snatching up the clipboard, he tucked it under his arm, and we exited through the back door, making sure to lock it behind us.

I followed as he made his way through the yard to Norman's four-foot fence. Rick sprightly jumped diagonally over it into the catty-corner yard belonging to the house where we'd seen the owner leave while I was tying my shoelace. Luckily, there were several trees in all the neighbors' yards, so we weren't obviously noticeable. He handed the clipboard back to me, and we confidently trooped through the yard and down the driveway.

"Follow my lead," Rick murmured out the side of his mouth. He went directly to the manhole cover in the middle of the street, took a photograph of it, and pointed randomly at the sheet of paper on my clipboard. "It's this one right here, 6B."

I shook my head, pointed at the manhole, and then tapped my clipboard. "No, you're mistaken; it says 210MC. Let's check the next one."

He nodded, and we carried on down the street.

Halfway around the block, Jin rolled up next to us. "Need a

lift?"

We climbed in through the back door.

"Did you find anything?" Jin asked.

"Norman's father has a boat," I said, removing the reflective vest.

"Where?"

Rick tossed the yellow hard hat into the corner. "I've got a receipt for a boat slip on my phone."

A moment later, the van came to a halt next to my Jeep. Norman's white SUV was back in the driveway, and he carried a reusable sack to the front door.

A thought occurred to me. "Um, did you lock the front door?"

"Yes," he said to me, then to Jin, "Where's he been?"

"He stopped at a grocery store and the hardware store."

"I planted two bugs. Start monitoring them. We're heading to the marina."

"Sure thing, Boss."

He swung the side door open, and we clambered out.

I started the Jeep and put it into drive. "Where's this marina?"

"Right now, just get us out of the neighborhood." He pulled up his contacts and tapped on an icon. "Angus. Get me all the information you can on Hedgewell's father. He's got a boat. Find out if it's been sold."

Once out of Norman's neighborhood, I motored down one of the main roads until coming to a drugstore, where I pulled into a parking space. The radio quietly played a U2 song. My fingers drummed to the beat on the steering wheel.

A few minutes later, Angus called back. "You were right. There is a sailboat slipped at the York River Boating Club. The slip and boat are still under his father's name. Looks like Norman's brother paid the annual slip fee just before he died."

Rick snapped his fingers. "That's it. Text me the address, slip number, and name of the boat."

Chapter Twenty-Four

"Jillian, where are you?"

"We're leaving Queen's Lake Marina. It's tiny; no one knows Norman or has seen Vera," Tony said through the speakerphone.

"We found something. We're heading to the York River Boating Club. It's across the Coleman Memorial Bridge; follow the signs to Gloucester Point. Rick will text you the address. Meet us there." I hung up before Jillian could begin quizzing me about what Rick and I had been doing with our time.

GPS took me onto I-64, and I put my foot down on the accelerator. Something deep in my bones told me this boat would be the key to finding Aunt Vera, and the urgency I'd felt upon rising from bed this morning returned tenfold. The wind whistled outside the windows. Traffic was moderate, and I weaved in and around the other vehicles. The high-pitched hum of the tires against the pavement filled the cabin, and the hardtop rattled.

"Uh, Karina, if you get pulled over going ninety, the cops will arrest you on the spot," my boyfriend kindly pointed out.

The speedometer needle inched past ninety-three.

Holy crap! I didn't realize how fast I was going.

Instantly, my foot popped off the accelerator, and the Jeep slowed to a staid seventy-five. Once we exited the highway, I got caught behind a dump truck and had to slow down to a poky thirty-eight until we reached the turn for the bridge.

"That's a fabulous view."

All I summoned was a grunt in response to his comment. I was sure the view was fabulous, but I wasn't paying attention to it. My eyeballs were lasered on the road ahead and my ears attuned to the GPS lady directing me to the marina.

Rick's phone binged with a text.

"What is it?"

"Angus got a slip number. G Dock, slip seven."

We weaved through quiet neighborhood streets and turned onto Boating Club Road. The lane had seen better days, and we jounced along, dodging potholes, until a large sign with an anchor on it welcomed us to the York River Boating Club Marina.

I rolled into the sprawling parking lot and braked. Multiple docks jutted out from the peninsula shoreline, and at least a hundred crafts were moored in their slips. Cabin cruisers and bowriders bobbed side by side with sailboats. The ends of the docks housed the big sixty-foot yachts.

"Any idea where G Dock is?"

"We have to go past the pool to get to G Dock; just park over there." He motioned to an empty space, and I pulled in between a large pickup truck and sedan.

Before I could get out, Rick gripped my forearm.

My brows rose. "What?"

"I want you to prepare yourself. This could be nothing."

My head bounced twice. "I'm prepared for that."

His voice dropped. "It could also be something very bad."

I sucked wind and put a hand to my churning gut. "I'm prepared for that as well."

"Let's go."

We had to walk past the restaurant to get to the slip. Lunch customers filled the outdoor tables, enjoying the mild weather. The briny breeze from the river, combined with the scent of fried seafood, emanated from the open doors of the eatery. My stomach roiled with anxiety, and the smell did not entice me. Instead, a mild wave of nausea rippled up my gullet.

Grease trilled, distracting me from the sick feeling. "Jilly?

We've just arrived. Where are you?"

"Approaching the bridge," Tony replied. "We'll be there in less than ten minutes. I'm looking at the marina's website. It seems rather large. Did you get a slip number?"

"The boat is at G Dock, slip seven. See you in a few minutes." I tucked the phone into my pocket and jogged to catch up with Rick.

He stood in front of a thirty-foot blue and white sailboat named *Daydreaming*. Crusty barnacles had attached themselves along the hull's waterline. The sails were down and shrouded with royal blue covers. The rope dinged lightly against the mast as the boat rocked. An osprey wheeled overhead, its shadow dancing along the deck boards.

Rick glanced around. "Looks like the coast is clear. Do you see anyone?"

I did my own cursory check. A man at the end of G Dock concentrated on hosing down his large cabin cruiser, and the Boston Whaler across from Norman's sailboat motored into the channel. The slip next to Norman's was currently empty, and no one else appeared to be in the immediate vicinity. "I don't see anyone."

"Marinas tend to be like small towns. Everyone knows each other and what boat they own. If you see anyone waddling our way, tell them you're Hedgewell's niece." Rick pulled the stern line to draw the boat closer to the dock. A fender squeaked in protest as he boarded. Ignoring the hand he held out, I clambered aboard in my own blundering manner.

We navigated around ropes, pullies, and a large steering wheel. The teak wood cabin door and hatch were closed and locked with a key-style padlock from ACE Hardware.

"Can you get that lock open without breaking it?" I asked.

Rick's response was a simple side-eye, which I interpreted to mean, *are you joking?* He had the lock undone quicker than

Norman's front door. The hasp stuck, and Rick used his pocketknife to get it up.

"You're such a Boy Scout," I muttered.

"Always be prepared," he returned, pushing back the overhead hatch and swinging open the two doors.

The combined scent of dead fish and mildew had me scrunching my nose. "Pew, what is that?"

Rick didn't respond as he gradually descended into the cabin.

I had to hold myself back from pushing him out of the way. Instead, I climbed down practically on his heels.

"Watch your head. Low beam." He flicked a switch, and a tiny sidelight illuminated a round dot the size of a saucer on the ceiling.

The galley was on our right and consisted of a two-burner stove, microwave, counter, miniature sink and refrigerator. Two long overhead cabinets spanned the length of the kitchen. The counters were clear of any dishes, but a dry, crusty, towel lay in the sink. A quick sniff identified where the rotten smell emanated from.

Pinching the nasty towel with two fingers, I flicked it up through the hatch. "That should help."

Faded red curtains covered the eye-shaped windows, creating a strange amber glow inside the cabin. Forward of the galley lay a built-in L-shaped seating area with blue striped cushions. In the center of the dinette area was a metal hole in the floor, where a table leg could be fitted. The table was missing, and a jumble of dirty clothes were piled in its place.

Wait a minute.

Upon closer inspection, I realized the clothes had hair. "Oh my God!" I crouched down and touched my aunt's shoulder. "Aunt Vera?"

Rick, who had moved to the sleeping cabin in the front of the boat, beelined to my side. We rolled my aunt onto her back. Her face was drawn and slack, and she moved limply, like a ragdoll.

"Vera!" I patted her cold, crumpled cheek. "Vera? Can you hear me? Rick?" I pleaded.

"Here now, step back." My exceedingly competent boyfriend checked her vitals. "She's got a pulse and is breathing."

The flash of Rick's phone camera had me pausing. "What are you doing?"

"Photographing the crime scene. I want to lay her down on the bench. See if you can find some light to brighten us up." Rick lifted my aunt as if she weighed no more than a stone and laid her upon the worn cushions.

I swept aside the moldy curtains, allowing a smidgeon of sunlight to filter into the cabin. Finding a bank of switches, I flicked them one by one, until, finally, the larger overhead light blossomed to life.

Vera wore a pair of brown slacks with mud ringing the bottoms of the pant legs. An overly large black sweatshirt I didn't recognize covered her arms and torso. Shallow breaths exhaled from her dry, cracked lips. Pushing the hair out of her face, we found a bruised, swollen lump with a trickle of dried blood running from her temple into the hairline.

"She's been hit on the head." I took her hand in mine. "She's freezing. Do you see a blanket?" I rubbed the chilled fingers with my own.

Rick disappeared deeper into the cabin where a pair of twin bed sleeping berths were located. I heard more camera clicks before he returned with a plaid, wool blanket. "Here, lay this on her. I don't have good reception in here. I'm going topside to phone for an ambulance."

I tucked the blanket around her legs and feet, pulling the soft material up to her chin. A beach towel lay on the floor nearby, and I placed it on top of the blanket. "Here we go, Vera. Hey, time to wake up, Auntie. C'mon." I rubbed the hand that hung out from underneath the covers. "Wake up, Aunt Vera."

Glancing around, I realized Madame Seraphina's predictions were true. Red curtains, blue cushions, water all around.

"Cripes. I guess that hairbrush really did do its job," I muttered under my breath.

I thought she sighed, but I couldn't be sure. Anything I might have heard was drowned out by loud voices on deck.

"Down in the cabin," Rick directed. "Watch your head."

Seconds later, Tony's sneakers tapped down the short ladder, followed by my sister's.

"She's here? What's wrong? Is she hurt?" My sister's panicked voice trilled, filling the tiny cabin more than our bodies. She came down the steps too fast and whacked her noggin on the beam Rick warned them about. "*Ow!*" she cried.

I winced in sympathy. "That's going to leave a mark."

"Are you okay, babe?" Tony turned with concern.

"I'm fine. See to Aunt Vera." She waggled a hand in my direction.

Stepping aside, I allowed Tony access to the patient. "She's got a bump on her head. And she's breathing but nonresponsive."

With the precision of a trained healthcare provider, Tony checked the pulse at her neck, silently counting to himself. "It's sluggish but steady. Do you have a flashlight?"

I switched my phone's light on and held it out for him.

"Is she okay? What's wrong with her?" Jillian asked, rubbing her forehead.

Tony didn't respond. He inspected the bump, gently prodding the edge. Then he checked her pupils by flashing the light in her eyes. "Hm. She's dehydrated." His head swiveled to me. "Are there any other injuries to her body?"

I cleared my throat with embarrassment. "I, uh, didn't check." *Stupid move. Where's your head, Karina?* "We found her cold on the floor. Rick put her on the bench, and we covered her up." It hadn't occurred to me to check and see if she'd sustained additional injuries.

"I need to check." He started at her feet, pulling the covers away. He shoved the pants up past her knees, revealing abrasions around her ankles, as if they'd been bound. He tugged the pants back in place and moved to her midriff, lifting the sweater up above her breasts and pushing the elastic waistband of her pants down. With two hands, he checked her abdomen for distension. "Feels normal." He slid the sleeve up her arm, exposing additional abrasions and dried blood. We located matching injuries on her left wrist. "She's been bound. I don't see any ropes?"

Jillian and I scanned the area.

"Omigod! Here, under the bench." She bent down to pick up a dirty white rope. Holding both sides up, we could see it was still knotted with jagged ends, as if Aunt Vera had sawed them apart on something sharp. There were rusty stains on it. "Is that ... blood?" my sister whispered in horror.

"That sonuvabitch," I muttered beneath my breath, clenching my fists so hard, the nails dug into my palms as a wave of wrath swept through me. "When I get my hands on him..." I took a step toward the ladder, ready to hunt Norman down and rip out his throat.

Tony's firm grip on my biceps stayed my movements. "I understand your anger, but I still need your help."

My fierce gaze speared him.

Luckily, Tony was trained to work in intense situations, and he didn't flinch. "I'm not finished checking for injuries. I need you and Jilly to help me roll her on her side, so I can check her backside." His dark-eyed stare was hard as agate, but his voice calmed the red haze of fury buzzing in my head.

I recalled myself back to the needs of the moment. "Yes, of course. Sorry."

"Jillian, leave the rope on the counter for the police," Tony directed. "You take her legs and, Karina, the shoulders.

We got into position, and I slid my hand beneath her thin torso.

"On the count of three," he prompted. "Three, two, one."

We hefted Aunt Vera onto her side, so she was facing the back cushion. Jillian and I held her in position while Tony did his inspection. "I see some bruising on her back. It's starting to yellow, so I can't say how old it is." He poked and prodded until he was satisfied. "You can lay her back down. I'd like to get an icepack on that head wound, and yours too, for that matter." He indicated Jillian's reddening forehead. "Let's look around for a first aid kit."

"I'll check the sleeping berths," I offered, moving to the forward cabin.

No one spoke as doors and hatches opened and slammed closed. Jillian checked the aft sleeping cabin, while Tony went through all the galley cabinets and cubbies.

"An ambulance is on the way." Rick's head turtled down at us from the upper hatch. "What are you doing?"

"Looking for a first aid kit," Tony explained. "Can you check the upper deck for one?"

Rick's head disappeared.

One of the compartments above the beds revealed nothing but blankets and pillows. The other, a laptop computer and a cellphone. Closing it, I made a mental note to tell Rick about it and continued my search. In the corner of the foot of the bed was another ragged piece of rope. Taking a cue from Rick, I took a photograph of it but left it in place. I went to the foot of the bed and folded the thin mattress in half like a taco to find two more cubbies beneath it. The first one I opened revealed a white container the size of a tackle box with a red cross on it.

"Found it!" I triumphantly cried.

Brandishing my prize, I passed it along to Tony. He pulled

out an instant cold pack, squished it beneath his hands to crack the interior pack and start the chemical process of cooling the water. "Here, Jilly, put this on your forehead."

"No," she demurred, "Aunt Vera needs it."

"There's another one in here." He shook the pack at my sister. Once she took it, he cracked another and gently laid it on Aunt Vera's bump.

Rick's turtle head popped in, throwing a shadow across the floor. "I'm not seeing anything up here. Did you find one?"

"Yup. All good." I gave him a thumbs-up.

"Good. Karina, we need to call your detective. Want to give me his number?" Rick asked.

"I'll do it. Can you pass me my phone, Tony?"

"Take mine." Jillian reached for her mobile, which she'd tucked into her bra.

"No, I don't need it anymore." Tony handed mine back to me.

"You two okay to stay here with Aunt Vera?" It was a silly question. I knew as soon as it popped out of my mouth. Aunt Vera was in far better hands with Tony than she was with anyone else on this boat.

Neither bothered to respond. Jillian grunted, sitting at Vera's feet with the icepack to her head while Tony dug through the first aid kit, examining the supplies at hand. He would do what he could until reinforcements arrived.

I followed Rick topside and tapped my way through the contacts list until I came upon the detective's number.

The phone rang and went to voicemail. I tried again. It rang three times before he grumpily answered, "Riggins!"

"Detective, it's Karina Cardinal. I'm at the York River Yacht Club. We found my aunt unconscious in the cabin of Norman Hedgewell's boat. It looks as though she's taken a blow to the head. An ambulance is on the way. I would suggest you get over here."

"I'm on my way," he rumbled. "It's out of my jurisdiction. I need to phone a Gloucester County detective. His name is Lang in case he arrives before I do."

Then line went dead, and the phone slipped from my hand onto the hard white deck of the boat. "Damn," I muttered.

Rick bent to pick it up.

"Is the screen cracked?"

"It's fine." Laying it aside, he took my fingers. "Your hands are shaking."

"I'm angry, confused … scared." I whispered the last in a tiny voice.

"I know." His palms slid up my arms, and he encircled me into his warm chest.

I laid my cheek against his shoulder and breathed. The salty tang of the sea and Rick's spicy scent mingled to settle in the back of my throat.

"She's going to be alright." He rubbed my spine, and the heat from the friction began to flow into my shivering body.

"I hope so." The boat rocked beneath our feet. Our knees loosened to sway along with the rhythm of the sea. I asked the question I feared the most: "How long do you think she's been here?"

A gusty breath tickled my hairline. "Since Monday."

I was afraid he'd say that. It was exactly what I believed as well. But why? Was she in collusion with Norman, and he betrayed her? I recalled the rope burns on her wrists and ankles. Did she get injured in the middle of an illegal exchange, and, out of fear, Norman stashed her on the boat? Did she accuse him, and in anger or panic, he bashed her in the head? The questions swirled around my brain box like an unrelenting tornado.

"We need to tell the detective about Vera's files. Are they still in your handbag?"

I nodded against him. "In the car."

The distant whine of the ambulance siren wailed closer and closer until it came to a halt. A few minutes later, two paramedics jogged down the dock planks. One carried a backboard, the other a black duffel bag.

With reluctance, I unfolded myself from Rick's embrace and hollered down into the hold, "The ambulance has arrived."

Rick waved at them, and the pair picked up the pace. Upon arrival, he assisted them aboard, and I directed them into the cabin.

Chapter Twenty-Five

We remained out of the way, above deck while the paramedics did their thing. I heard Tony giving them a rundown of her situation. Not long afterward, they had her strapped to the backboard, her head surrounded by black padding, and lifted her out of the cabin. She looked so fragile and pale in the sunlight. A lump rose unexpectedly in my throat, and my eyes smarted with tears. Jillian and Tony followed the paramedics out of the cabin.

"Why don't Tony and I go with the ambulance to the hospital, while you and Rick wait for the police?" Jillian suggested.

It was exactly what I'd been thinking, and I didn't demur. "Thanks. Call me if you need something."

I gave her a fierce hug, which she returned, and I did my damnedest to swallow down the tightness and fear gripping me. We spoke no other words.

Rick assisted Jillian onto the dock, then followed her down to chat with some interested lookie-loos who must have seen the ambulance arrive.

Tony made to pass me, but I halted his progress, gripping his hand. "What will they do with her at the hospital? Will they X-ray the bump or get an MRI?"

He paused to place his other hand on top of mine, and he replied in low tones, "Once they get her back to the ambulance, they'll get an IV into her. That will help with the dehydration. Her pupil response was sluggish. It's likely they do a CT scan."

I swiped away a threatening tear. "Do you think it's bad?"

Just like a doctor, Tony wouldn't commit to a diagnosis

without further review. "Hard to tell; we'll have to wait for the tests."

That didn't help my state of mind. As much as I wanted to get Norman, I started questioning if I should go with Tony and Jillian. "Look, I know it's important to have an advocate at the hospital. I'll come as soon—"

"Karina, it's fine." He gave my hand a quick squeeze. "Jilly and I will make sure they are doing all they can. You and Rick need to be here. Tell the cops everything you know."

"You're right." I sniffed and cleared my throat. "Thanks for being here for my family."

"Hey, we *are* family. In a few months, it'll be official."

"Yes. I know." I allowed a shaky grin to peek through the anxiety. "I couldn't be happier for my sister."

One side hug, and he was off, jogging down the dock to catch up with the ambulance crew.

The handful of lookie-loos seemed to have followed the EMTs back to the ambulance or returned to their own devices, except for one. Rick stood with his hands on his hips talking to a gray-bearded fellow in flip-flops, jeans, polo shirt and a ballcap.

I joined them on the dock, curling my arm around Rick's waist. "Hello."

"Dennis, this is Karina."

"Nice to meet you." We shook hands. His skin was rough and mottled with age spots. Deep crevices etched across his forehead and around his eyes, which spoke to the hours he must spend in the sun.

"Which boat is yours?" I asked.

"*Trolling About.*" He pointed to a large blue and white yacht with three outboard motors and a fly bridge docked at the end of the pier.

"Dennis said he saw Hedgewell on the boat Monday, but not since then."

"Do you live on your boat?" I asked.

"Yeah." He grinned. "She got the house, and I got the boat in the divorce."

I never knew what to say when someone told me they were divorced. Was that a good thing or bad? "Uh, sorry?"

"Nothing to be sorry for." His yellowed teeth flashed at me. "We're better off without each other."

"Were you out here on Monday night?"

"Your boyfriend here asked the same question. I was telling him something woke me around one o'clock in the morning. When I came out to look, I saw a figure leaving Norman's boat. I thought it an odd time of night for him to be about, so I hailed him to ask if everything was okay. He told me he'd left his cellphone on the boat and was fetching it. He was quite abrupt with me, and I didn't probe deeper."

"Have you seen Norman since?"

Dennis tugged his beard. "Can't say I did, but I left Wednesday and headed out to the Chesapeake Bay to visit a friend who's got a place on the water. Just returned yesterday."

"Does anyone else live on their boat? Or is out here on a daily basis?" Rick asked.

Dennis glanced at the surrounding boats. "See that cabin cruiser named *Wanderlust*?" His chin jerked, indicating a faded green and white motorboat that had seen better days parked at the opposite end of the dock.

A man stood on the swim platform with a phone to his ear and a pair of binoculars trained on us.

"That's Shaw's boat. He doesn't live on it, but he comes out almost every day to putter around with the engine. Hopes to get it going one day. If you ask me, he doesn't have a clue what he's doing. But I've seen him chatting with Norman." Dennis waved.

Shaw pulled away the binoculars and didn't bother responding to Dennis's greeting.

"He's a bit of an odd duck, believes in that lizard people conspir—"

The ambulance finally pulled out of the parking lot. I didn't hear the rest of Dennis's sentence over the wail of the siren. An unmarked cop car with blue and red flashing lights passed the ambulance as it entered the parking area and pulled to the end of the lot as close as he could get to our pier.

"We'd better go talk with the police," I said. "Are you going to be around, Dennis? The police might want to ask you some questions about what you saw on Monday night."

"I've got nowhere else to be. Feel free to send them my way." He shuffled off to *Trolling About*.

Rick didn't watch Dennis's progress; instead, he squinted, his gaze riveted on Shaw's ratty boat.

"Should we talk to Shaw?" When he didn't answer, I gently jostled his arm.

"What? Sorry, I wasn't paying attention."

"Should we talk to Shaw?"

"I think we'd best deal with the police first."

The detective was on the phone when we arrived at his vehicle, and we waited patiently for him to finish his conversation and exit the car. He wore jeans and a black hoodie with a police department logo on it, and a gun holstered on his hip. I estimated he was in his mid-thirties from his lack of gray hair and minimal lining around his features.

"Hello, are you Detective Lang?" I asked.

"That's right. Who are you?" He removed a pen and pad from his back pocket and began taking notes.

I introduced myself and Rick. "We've been working with Detective Riggins regarding my missing aunt."

"Riggins informed me you've found her. I assume she was in the ambulance that just left?"

"Yes, we found her unconscious on Norman Hedgewell's

boat. Her wrists and ankles were rubbed raw. It looked as though she'd been bound."

His head popped up. "You think she was being held captive?"

"I do. I'm also concerned she's still in danger." I didn't know if Norman would be bold enough to hunt down my aunt at the hospital, but I figured it wouldn't hurt to have the police on it.

The detective took a beat to process my statement. "Hold on, I need to send an officer to the hospital." He pulled his phone out and stepped out of earshot to make his call.

Meanwhile a local squad car arrived, and a female officer stepped out to speak with Detective Lang.

"We should wait until Riggins arrives before we tell them the rest," Rick murmured quietly.

I tended to agree. The story was a wee bit convoluted. "I'll fetch the papers from the car."

As I fetched the papers, Riggins rolled into the lot.

Showtime.

"Where's the rest of the Scooby gang?" Riggins deadpanned.

Now, I could have delivered a scathing batch of sarcasm back at him, but I was simply too exhausted to muster it up, so instead I opted for the bald truth. "At the hospital with my unconscious aunt."

My reply hit our curmudgeonly detective in the solar plexus, knocking the dry unwelcome wit out of him. He cleared his throat. "Is she going to be okay?"

"I've no idea. Looks like she sustained an injury to the head, so possibly not."

"Sorry to hear that."

Lang directed the police officer to wait at the boat for forensics and came over to our group. "Virgil, good to see you."

"David." The two men shook hands. "Thanks for coming out. I know it's your day off, and normally, I wouldn't have called you in, but—"

"Yeah, I know you and Stephens don't exactly get along. When he heard your name, he was just as happy to dump this mess on my desk. Although Vicki said you owe her one. She's got to shuttle the kids to a birthday party at a trampoline park."

Riggins allowed something akin to a smile to cross his face, which made him look almost human. "Your wife is a saint. I'll be sure to make it up to her."

"Want to tell me what's going on? I was interviewing these two before you showed up. She says—" he checked his notebook, "—her Aunt Vera was abducted, assaulted, and tied up on a sailboat," he said the last sentence incredulously.

Both the men turned to us.

Rick began by handing each of the men one of his business cards. "I own a security company in D.C. When Karina first told me about her missing aunt, I had one of my techs begin a search into Vera's last known whereabouts, much like you, Detective Riggins. Unfortunately, with no information from her phone or computer, we weren't getting very far. The camera footage from the parking lot where Vera's car was located gave us a little more to go on but not much." Rick's phone rang, and he sent it to voicemail. "It wasn't until we came upon Vera's list that we had some idea of where to begin."

I passed the blue folder to Riggins. "Not only does the list identify the object you located in Vera's home, but it lists several other objects that seem to be missing from the museum. Did Norman tell you about these items?"

Riggins shook his head. "No, he didn't. Where did you find this list?"

"Uh…"

Rick covered my hesitancy in a helpfully vague manner, "Among Vera's things."

I diverted the conversation in another direction, "Tell me, Detective, were there any fingerprints on the cream pot you obtained from Vera's house this morning?"

He gave me a shrewd stare. "There were no prints."

Rick asked for clarification, "None you could identify? Or no prints at all?"

"None at all. Either it's been handled with gloves—"

I nodded. "Which would make sense as a museum piece."

Riggins gave me a frown for interrupting and continued, "Or, like the car, it was wiped."

Rick went on to explain our theory about Norman, his father's bills at the CCRC, and the missing items. "I've had my men do a deep dive into Vera's finances—"

"This is the first I'd heard that little tidbit." I frowned at my boyfriend.

"Sorry, hon, but it had to be done." He didn't look sorry. "My man could find no additional unexplained monetary expenditures in Vera's financial portfolio. Only Hedgewell's. When I requested my tech look into his family, he came across this boat, owned by Hedgewell's father. Karina and I came out to investigate. Through the window, we saw what looked like a human form, at which point Karina and I boarded the vessel to investigate. Shall we?" He led the detectives to the boat.

The police sentry stepped aside, allowing us to board.

Using his pen as a lever, Lang inspected the open deadbolt hanging crookedly on the latch. "How'd you get in? Wasn't the cabin door locked?"

"Nope," Rick replied.

Riggins glanced at the two of us, unconvinced.

Rick didn't flinch.

I allowed my face to go slack. "By the way, while we were searching for a first aid kit, I saw a laptop computer and cellphone in one of the fore cabin compartments. I think you'll find they are Vera's."

Lang crouched to survey the cabin. "Well, Virgil, it does

sound to me like your museum theft and my abduction and assault case are connected."

Chapter Twenty-Six

While we spoke with the two detectives, three more cop cars lined the parking lot, the dock was cordoned off, and Norman's boat became a classic movie crime scene, replete with yellow tape and all the trimmings. Police officers were directed to speak with the other boat owners in the area. Rick pulled aside the female officer who showed up first and pointed to Dennis's yacht to suggest she start with him.

By this time, interested bystanders had grown from a spattering to a full-on gossiping crowd, rife with cellphones recording the spectacle. Before the pier was cordoned off, a handful of people had boarded a Larson 350, put a case of beer on ice, cranked the tunes, and sat back to enjoy the entertainment. Two officers were now interviewing the party boat. Each one spoke over the other, telling the officers every single detail they could remember about Norman. Mostly trashing his reputation by telling tales about his lack of socialization at the marina. Nothing damning, and not a one of them had been on the dock Monday or Tuesday.

Meanwhile, Rick and I were shunted off the boat, told by detective Lang to "wait here," here being on the dock. I parked myself far from all the hubbub on someone's deck box and checked to see if I'd gotten a text or missed a call from Jillian.

Nothing.

I sent her one.

Any update on Vera?

She didn't respond immediately, and my phone rang. It was

Vikram. I'd completely forgotten about Aunt Vera's amore.

"Hello, Vikram."

"Karina, I have some news. I was able to reach one of Vera's coworkers, and she told me that, two months ago, she caught Norman in one of the display cases. He claimed to have been taking up a piece for cleaning. She didn't think anything of it, but now that she's had time to reflect on the incident, she feels Norman was being quite cagey."

"Vikram … Aunt Vera's been located."

"She has? Is she … okay?"

"Unfortunately, she is not. My sister is on the way to the hospital now. You can phone her to get the name of the hospital where they are taking Vera and meet them there."

"Yes, yes. Tell me her number."

I reeled it off.

"And where did you find her?"

"Being held captive on Norman's boat—"

"That-that *bloody bastard!* I knew he was up to no good. Vera knew it too. That's the last straw!"

The phone went dead.

"Vikram? Hello?" Nothing. I shrugged and tucked the phone away in my pocket.

Rick sat next to me and checked the phone call he'd sent to voicemail. "Jin called." He put the phone to his ear to listen to the message. His features darkened.

"What is it?"

"Jin said, 'Norman left the house again, went to the Bruton Heights building, stayed there for fifteen minutes, and returned home. Now he's loading his car.'"

"Do you think someone tipped him off?"

"I think it was that Shaw fellow."

I followed his gaze to the ratty boat at the end of the pier. "Is the tracker still on Norman's car?"

"I certainly hope so." Rick dialed Jin. "What have you got for me?" He didn't want to put Jin on speaker with all the hubbub going on around us.

I leaned in close to the phone, and Rick turned the volume up to maximum level.

"Norman got a phone call. I only heard his end of the conversation, which consisted of, 'What time?' 'What did she look like?' 'An ambulance.' And 'Thanks for calling, Shaw.' Now he's loading his car up like he's going camping—tent, rope, Coleman stove, couple of Rubbermaid tubs, two coolers … you get the picture," Jin explained.

He's getting ready to run.

"I agree with Karina," Rick said. "He's going to run."

Did I say that out loud?

"Where are you now? Across the street?" Rick asked.

"I began to attract attention. I've moved further down the block. Are you still at the marina?"

"Yes, I'm here with Karina. Cops are crawling all over the place, doing their thing. Vera's at the hospital. Jillian and Tony are with her."

"I wonder where Norman's planning to go?" I mused aloud. "I figured Riggins would have sent someone over to pick him up."

"I did too," Rick agreed.

"I'll go ask."

"I'm not sure—"

I didn't wait for Rick to finish voicing his concern. I wanted to know why Riggins hadn't sent a squad car over to scoop up Norman, and I wanted to know now. Riggins was speaking with one of the police officers. I sidled up to him and waited for them to finish.

"What do you need now?" he rumbled at me.

"I'm wondering if you've sent someone over to pick up

Norman Hedgewell?"

"Twenty minutes ago."

That answer didn't compute with Jin's story. "And … is Norman in custody?"

"I assume so."

I chewed my lip and finally spit out, "You might want to check on that." My suggestion put him on the defensive, which he didn't like.

His gaze narrowed, and he literally growled. "What is it that *you* know, and *I* don't?"

I searched my brain for a good answer, but all my pistons weren't functioning, Obviously, I realized I couldn't mention the phone call by Shaw—who had conveniently disappeared from the marina as soon as the calvary arrived. I simply couldn't come up with anything but the truth and decided to provide it in limited capacity. "Apparently, our perp is loading up his SUV as we speak. There's been no sign of police activity."

"And how do you know this? Did you park the Mystery Machine out in front of Hedgewell's house? Are Scooby and Shaggy keeping watch?"

I'll admit, I pictured Jin in the gas company van and lost it. I blamed the stress of the situation for my complete and utter overreaction to the sarcastic humor.

"I'm sorry," I cried, wiping my eyes. Seriously, I tried to reel it in as quickly as it had burst out, but it still took a few moments to get under control.

Riggins didn't appreciate my mirth. He scowled magnificently at me. Those bushy brows hooded over his glaring eyes, reminding me of Clint Eastwood at his most formidable.

"Sorry." I box-breathed in counts of four to get a grip. Clearing my throat, I responded, "As a matter of fact, there is a Silverthorne agent conducting surveillance outside Norman's home. According to him, there's been no police activity."

Having no more use for me, he pivoted and stormed over to where my boyfriend sat. Rick, who saw us coming, wisely ended the phone call with Jin and rose to meet the angry detective.

"You've got a man outside Hedgewell's house? Right now?" Riggins barked.

Unrattled, Rick replied in quiet tones, "I do."

"No squad cars in sight?"

"Not at this time."

Riggins chewed on that for a moment. "Obviously, someone's screwed the pooch." He pulled out his phone and stomped out of earshot.

To my surprise, there was no yelling. Instead, he spoke in a menacing voice, using tones so low we couldn't make out exactly what he was saying, but his body language gave us the gist.

"I think it's time we tell the detective that we need to get to the hospital," Rick commented.

My head swiveled back to him. "But … we're not going to the hospital. Are we?"

"I can drop you off—"

I screwed up my features in thought. "I'd like to go by way of Norman's house."

"It's in the opposite direction."

"I'd like to be there and see him get his comeuppance."

He sighed with resignation. "Let's see what the detective has to say."

Riggins walked up to us and pointed his phone at Rick. "I've sent a squad car to Hedgewell's house. Keep your man there and apprise me of any changes."

"Would you like him to make sure Hedgewell remains at his home?"

My eyes ping-ponged between the detective and Rick.

Riggins stroked his chin. "What are you suggesting?"

"Nothing too aggressive. He can easily block Hedgewell's

driveway."

The detective began shaking his head before Rick finished his sentence. "No, I don't want your man endangered. You never know how a cornered animal will react. And I warn you, when my people arrive, your man better stay out of their way."

"Of course." Rick held up his palms. "If Hedgewell *does* manage to leave before your people show up, would you like my agent to follow him?"

The Clint Eastwood look returned. "Fine. But he'd better mind his P's and Q's. I don't need some sort of Hollywood car chase tearing through the middle of my town. Am I clear?"

"Crystal."

Neither of us bothered to let the detective know that Jin had a tracker on Norman's car and could follow miles behind without losing him. After all, having a tracker on him wasn't exactly legal. As a matter of fact, it was highly illegal, and Rick's company could be accused of stalking and possibly sued.

"Keep me informed." Riggins begrudgingly ended with a mumbled "thanks."

I decided it was time blow this popsicle stand. "If you've got no further questions for us, I'd like to head to the hospital to check on my aunt."

"Yeah—" Riggins delivered a dismissive wave, "—go check on your aunt. We might have more questions for you. So don't leave the area."

"Wouldn't dream of it," I replied over my shoulder.

Chapter Twenty-Seven

My head was buzzing with too many thoughts that ran into each other, so I handed the car keys over to Rick.

Once in the Jeep, I phoned Jillian. "What's the news on Aunt Vera?"

"They've just taken her down for a CT head scan." Jillian's voice warbled.

"Is she still unconscious?"

"I'm afraid so."

That can't be good.

She drew in a deep breath and spoke a bit steadier. "Have you left the marina yet?"

"Yes, we were just about to leave." I told her about Jin watching Norman's place.

Rick started the car and backed out of the parking spot. Luckily, I'd parked far enough away from the dock, we weren't hemmed in by police vehicles.

"Are you coming to the hospital now?"

"Uh, we were going to follow up on the Norman situation." I chewed my lip. "Do you think I should come to the hospital?"

Jillian remained quiet for a moment before answering, "Yeah, I think you should come to the hospital."

I grabbed Rick's forearm, and he jerked to a stop.

What? he mouthed.

"What aren't you telling me?" I asked Jillian.

"They're concerned Vera's had a stroke."

My heart dropped, and my hand moved to my chest. "Oh,

Jilly, no."

She sniffed.

I rolled my lips inward. "Have you … spoken to Mom yet?"

"I tried, but it went straight to voicemail. Dad didn't answer his phone either," she whimpered.

"I'm on my way. Can you please text us the name of the hospital you're at? I'll try phoning Mom." My call waiting beeped, and my mother's smiling face popped up on screen. "Speak of the devil, that's Mom now. I'll let her know what's going on."

"See you soon."

"We need to go to the hospital. Jilly's texting us the information now." I switched to the other line. "Hello, Mom."

"Hello, darling. I'm here," she spoke loudly.

I heard crowd noises in the background. "You're here?" My brows furrowed in confusion. "Where? Where are you?"

"We're at the airport in Richmond. Speak up please; it's very noisy in this terminal," she spoke so loudly, I pulled the phone away from my ear.

"I don't understand."

"*What?*"

I raised my voice, "You and dad? You're here?"

"Yes. We booked a morning flight out of Denver, on United. Where are you and Jillian?"

"Uh, we found Aunt Vera—"

"*What?*"

"*We found Aunt Vera!*"

Rick winced at my yelling.

"Wonderful. How is she doing?"

"*Not good.*"

"George, she says Vera's not doing well," my mother said in an aside to my father. "Just a minute, Karina, I'm going to get someplace quieter." Her breathing came across the line, along with general crowd noises and overhead announcements for flights. "Over here. It's fine; we can both go inside."

Suddenly, it went quiet, and I heard the distinct sound of a door locking.

"Okay, we've ducked into the family bathroom. Tell me everything."

"Jillian is at the hospital with Vera. She's gone in for a CT scan. We found her unconscious on a boat. I've just finished up with the police, and I'm headed over to the hospital now."

"Oh, my lord, she said they found Vera unconscious," Mom repeated for Dad. "Well, I don't know. Dad wants to know what hospital."

"I'm not sure. Jilly's supposed to text me the address. I'll forward it to you."

"Yes, do that. We'll get a Lyft to take us directly there."

A thought occurred to me: "Um, did you make reservations at a hotel?"

"No, I thought we'd stay with you and Jilly at Aunt Vera's."

Gee, won't that be cozy? I pictured the house, still at sixes and sevens from the morning's search party. Our four travel bags and their contents strewn throughout the second floor. "We'll get everything sorted at the hospital. See you soon, Mom."

"Yes, soon. Hugs, darling."

Chapter Twenty-Eight

Jillian texted the hospital information, and I put it in my maps app so the GPS lady could direct Rick to the facility.

Rick's phone rang. He'd left it sitting in the cupholder, and I picked it up. "It's Jin."

"Answer it, please. Put it on speaker."

"Hello, Jin. Rick is driving; I've got you on speaker. What's going on? Have the cops arrived?"

"No police, yet—"

"Did Norman split?" I interrupted.

"Nope. Someone else showed up."

"Did the girlfriend return?" Rick asked.

"No. It's a fellow ... dark hair, dark skin. I think I heard an English accent."

"Vikram?"

"*Turn right onto Yorkview Drive,*" the GPS lady directed.

"What?" Jin asked.

"Nothing. It's the GPS lady telling us how to get to the hospital," I explained.

"Turn her off, please. Leave up the map," Rick said.

"What's happening now?" I asked Jin.

"Your friend is brandishing a crowbar. Hedgewell came out of the garage, saw this man, dropped his load and took off running, with the British fellow right behind. Right now, they're doing laps around the SUV."

I pressed a pair of fingers to my temple. "Wait a minute. Vikram's chasing Norman? With a crowbar?"

"Yes, and swearing up a blue streak in proper English. Oh, no, wait ... Hedgewell just headed into the yard. And this Vikram fellow is giving chase. He's gone round the big oak in the front yard. Once, twice, third time around. Oh!" Jin sucked wind through his teeth. "Oo, that must have hurt. He tripped over a root and fell. Hard."

"Who fell? Vikram or Norman?" I probed for clarification.

"The English fellow, and the crowbar went flying into the rose bushes. Annnd ... he's back up. Do you want me to put a stop to this, Boss?"

Rick opened his mouth, but I interrupted, "No way, let it play out. Vikram is Aunt Vera's lover. He's trying to get his pound of flesh. It's quite romantic. Give me the full play-by-play, so I can tell Aunt Vera all about it when she wakes up."

Rick rolled to a halt at a four-way stop, giving me the side-eye.

"What?" I shrugged.

"Has either one of them landed a punch?" Rick asked.

"No ... they're, well, I'm not sure how to explain what they're doing. They're kind of dancing in a circle, kicking at each other and throwing air punches. Oh, Vikram got ahold of Hedgewell's leg. Hedgewell is hopping around, swiping at Vikram. Now he's shaken Vikram loose and is on the run again. It reminds me..."

We waited for Jin to complete his thought, but when he didn't, I prompted, "Reminds you of what?"

"Well, have you ever seen that old movie, *Bridget Jones's Diary*?"

"No." Rick shook his head.

"Yes! I love those movies," I replied.

"Remember when the two men are fighting around the fountain, pulling each other's clothes, kicking about?" Jin explained.

"Of course, it's when Mr. Darcy fights for Bridget's honor."

"It's kind of like that. Karina, you fight better than this pair."
I preened, grinning with pride.

"I'm not sure that's a high bar," my boyfriend taunted with underlying laughter.

"I remember knocking you on your ass more than once," I replied imperiously.

"She's right, Boss. We've got it on video," Jin supplied.

Rick held up a hand in surrender. "Okay, I take it back."

I returned my attention to the phone. "Jin, what's happening now?"

"Not much. They're swiping at each other's legs. Almost like they're trying to trip each other. Oh, now wait! They've each picked up long sticks. And ... now we're having a lightsaber fight."

"No!" I exclaimed.

"Yes. I swear, I heard Hedgewell make the lightsaber noise. Wait, looks like Hedgewell might have the upper hand. He just broke Vikram's stick. Now Vikram is jabbing at Hedgewell with the sharp end. It's like watching a pair of eight-year-olds fight. Wait, Hedgewell went in for a bash to the head, and Vikram was able to sidestep it. He's jabbed Hedgewell with his little stick dagger. Looks like he's drawn blood. Hedgewell dropped the stick and is holding his hand."

I leaned closer to the phone. "Jin, are you recording this?"

"I can, if you want."

"Yes! I want to see it!"

"It's likely already being recorded by the Ring doorbell on Hedgewell's house," Rick intoned.

"Jin's footage will be better quality," I argued.

Traffic slowed as we entered the center of town. Cute shops and restaurants lined the streets.

Jin continued his play-by-play, "I think ... yes, it looks like Hedgewell is making a T with his hands. I believe he's asking for a timeout."

Just like little kids. I didn't want to miss anything Jin said, so I tried to hold in my laughter, but a giggle managed to escape.

"Now Vikram's rushed Hedgewell. They're both down now, rolling around, but wait … it looks like … yes, Vikram has got the upper hand. Oh, that was a good hit. Hedgewell's got a bloody nose."

"Jin, get out there. *Now!*" Rick barked. "Put a stop to this. Get Hedgewell cuffed for the police."

"Right away, Boss."

The line went quiet, but I could tell Jin left it open, because we could hear his breathing as he jogged up the street. I guessed he was wearing his Bluetooth earbud.

I placed us on mute and asked Rick, "Why not let Vikram have a go at him? Norman deserves it."

"Hedgewell may deserve it, but Vera's going to need Vikram by her side while she recovers. Not rotting in jail. Now that Vikram's got the upper hand, he can do some serious damage to Hedgewell. As despicable as Hedgewell is, the man needs time in the slammer, not at the ER … or the morgue."

I slumped in my seat. "Yeah, you're right."

"Okay, pal, you've gotten your hits in. Time to get off," Jin said.

It was rather surreal voyeuristically listening to the skirmish over the phone. However, I knew if anyone could soothe the unplumbed depths of Vikram's savage beast, it would be Jin's Zen-like personality.

"Help me! This man attacked me," Hedgewell whined. "I think he broke my nose."

"He was trying to escape!" Vikram cried.

"I hear you, man. But he's not worth going to jail for," Jin counseled. "Roll him over and put these zip ties on his wrists. The cops are on their way. Perp is secured, Boss."

Norman sputtered, and we couldn't hear what he said, but I was certain, whatever it was, it wasn't complimentary.

"This bastard deserves to rot in hell." Vikram made a spitting sound.

"You've got the wrong guy," Norman denied. "I don't even know who you are, pal."

"I'm Vera's significant other. And you'd better hope she wakes up, because if she doesn't, jail will be the only safe place for you," Vikram snarled.

"Oh yeah! Let me tell you—"

"Hey, hey, back it up." We didn't hear Norman finish his threat. It sounded as though Jin successfully drew Vikram away. "Listen, your lady friend needs you at the hospital. You should go."

"I want to make sure he's still here when the police arrive," Vikram explained.

"I work with Karina, and I'm not going anywhere. It'll be easier for you if you aren't here when the police arrive. I think I see a squad car coming down the street," Jin advised.

"Yes, you are correct; I must get to the hospital. Thank you, mate."

A moment later, Jin spoke directly to us. "Alright, Vikram is off to the hospital. Hedgewell is spitting fire on the front lawn, and, unfortunately, we've attracted some attention from the neighbors."

"Understood." The light up ahead turned yellow, and Rick slowed to a halt. "Get that tracker off Norman's car and clear the scene. Can you handle it from here?"

"Absolutely," Jin said in assured tones.

Occasionally, I wondered if any of Rick's men had told him no. On the other hand, I doubted Rick asked his men to do something he was unwilling to do himself.

"Rick out." He glanced at me.

"What?"

"That's your cue to hang up."

"Oh." I pressed the end icon and sort of deflated into my seat. Slithering down so low, I was almost even with the dash.

The light turned green, and Rick accelerated. "What's wrong?"

"Nothing," I replied in an Eeyore voice.

"It doesn't sound like nothing." He rubbed my knee.

With a nervous sniggle, I confessed, "I'm disappointed I didn't see it in person."

"Jin's got it all on tape." He squeezed in just the right place to tickle me.

I yelped, pulling my knee away from his fingers, and straightened into a proper sitting position. "Yes, but it's not the same."

"Bloodthirsty, aren't you?"

"I wanted to see Norman get his comeuppance." I grinned. "I'll say, I didn't expect it to come from mild-mannered Vikram. Who knew he wore a Superman suit beneath his Mr. Rogers sweater?"

Rick harumphed, "Sounds more like a *Keystone Cops* routine."

"*Keystone Cops?*"

"Nineteen-twenties silent film."

"I know what you're referring to. My mind is boggled." I tapped my forehead. "How can you know about the *Keystone Cops* but not *Bridget Jones's Diary?*"

"One of life's great mysteries." Rick pulled into the hospital parking lot. "I'm trying to figure out how Jin knows about *Bridget Jones's Diary.*"

Chapter Twenty-Nine

As soon as the doors swept aside, I wrinkled my nose. All hospitals have a certain aroma—a touch of bitterness from antiseptic and sterile packaging, with a hint of artificial fragrance from cleaning solutions, and invariably strong coffee for all the workers who function on a twenty-four-seven schedule. A gray-haired woman sat at the desk by the doors. She checked our IDs, asked if we had any COVID symptoms, and printed out visitor stickers.

The ER waiting room was less than half full, but you needed an escort to get past the locked door. I phoned Jillian, and one of the nurses came out to take us into a small treatment room. Various monitors surrounded the room, and tubes poked out of the wall. In the center was an empty gurney. We found my sister alone, sitting on a hard gray plastic chair, hunched over, staring blankly at her phone, which had gone dark from inactivity.

I wondered how long she'd been like that. "Any news on Aunt Vera?"

Her unfocused gaze lifted, revealing wan features. "Not yet, she's still getting the CT scan, somewhere—" she waved her hand in a circle, "—in the building."

I slid into the seat next to her and leaned a shoulder against hers. "Where's Tony?"

"He's gone to get us something to eat. He said I needed replenishing. Although, my stomach is tied in so many knots, I doubt I'll be able to force anything down."

The clock above the door read three-twenty. Where had the

day gone? Now that she mentioned it, I realized the low-grade headache around the back of my head may have been due not only to stress and lack of sleep but also to dehydration.

"He's right; we should all eat," Rick asserted. "When's the last time you had something to drink?"

We glanced at each other. Turning up a palm, I took a stab at it, "Breakfast?"

Rick's head bobbed. "Did Tony go to the cafeteria?"

"I'm not sure." Jillian shrugged. "He took the car keys, so maybe he went for fast food?"

"I'll give him a call. Karina needs to eat too." He pulled his phone from a pocket. "I'll be back in a bit. Karina, why don't you brief your sister on the current situation?" He ducked out, leaving me alone with Jillian.

We could hear conversations from the central nurses' station, and in the room next door, the general mumble of a medical practitioner speaking to a patient. Some sort of wheezing noise came from the air vents, and a nearby toilet flushed loud enough it made you wonder if the person flushing got sucked down along with the water.

"Gawd, I hate hospitals," Jillian murmured.

"Right there with you, girl." I took a deep breath. "Remember what Grandma used to say? 'You're never sick until you go to the doctor.'"

A tiny half grin lifted her features.

I wrapped my arm around Jillian, and she tucked her head into my neck. It reminded me of when we were kids. When she didn't get the lead in the school play, or a boyfriend broke up with her, Jillian tended to turn to me for comfort. Today, we were both gaining comfort from each other.

"You realize Madame Seraphina was right about everything," she murmured.

I knew my sister would rub that in my face. A windy sigh

escaped. "Yeah, I came to the same conclusion. I guess that three hundred bucks wasn't such a bad investment after all."

"Guess not."

"There must have been some strong juice in that old hairbrush of Vera's."

Jillian giggled, elbowing me in the side. "Ew!"

I grinned along with her.

"I haven't heard from Mom, have you?"

"Cripes, I forgot." I rubbed my eyes. "Mom and Dad flew out this morning. That's why we couldn't get ahold of them. I expect they'll be here in the next hour or two."

She sighed. "Considering Vera might have had a stroke…" her voice cracked on the last word, and she didn't complete her thought.

"Yes, I'm glad they flew out too," I finished for her. "I expect Vikram is on his way as well."

"Vikram?" She rubbed an eyebrow. "Vera's man-friend? You called him?"

"He called me."

Lifting her head off my shoulder, she glanced around the meager space. "How will we all fit?"

"I imagine they'll admit her, and she'll get a normal-sized room."

"What happened after we left with the ambulance?"

"Well…" I gave her a rundown on the situation at the marina, Norman's house, and the fight with Vikram. She stared blankly at me as I spoke, giving no reactions to the flood of information. It was unclear how much she heard and processed, but I thought it helped alleviate her dark thoughts.

After a few minutes of silence, she finally spoke, "Vikram really went to Norman's house. To beat him up?"

"Yup."

Her face scrunched in thought. "I'm not sure Tony would

have done something like that for me."

"Tony is a Boy Scout and would most definitely wait for the police to do their job." I patted her hand in reassurance.

"Your Rick, on the other hand…"

My brows rose, and I tilted my head with interest. "Yesss…"

Jillian chuckled. "Rick would have made him disappear, leaving behind no evidence."

My lips quirked. "I don't know about that, but he would have secured the prisoner."

"Karina, that man would walk through fire for you." She pointed a finger at me. "I hope you realize it."

I tsked. "He'd do that for any one of his Silverthorne guys."

Her head deliberately swiveled back and forth. "It's not the same thing."

My mind flashed to a moment in time when I'd witnessed panic and abject fear clearly written across Rick's features. It happened after my car had been shot up like Swiss cheese … while I was in it. An organized crime boss was trying to take out his former money launderer, and my car was collateral damage in the shooting. Normally, Rick was incredibly stoic, although he often showed his softer side to me. It was the first … and last time, I'd seen that type of terror in his face. It didn't fully disappear until after a doctor removed all the glass and cleaned me up.

I opened my mouth but could think of no response. Luckily, the door to the room opened, and with it came the mouthwatering scent of burgers and fries. The boys rolled in with bags of food and bottled water. We washed our hands in the little sink the doctors use, then the four of us attacked the fast food like toddlers at an Easter egg hunt. No one spoke. Contrary to Jillian's earlier concerns, neither one of us had problems eating the greasy burger.

I chased a burger bite with a fry and sighed with satisfaction.

"This is possibly the best hamburger I've ever eaten. You're a lifesaver, Tony."

"I wouldn't go that far," he guffawed, wiping a smudge of ketchup from the corner of his mouth, "but it does hit the spot."

The room remained quiet, punctuated only by the rustle of the paper bags and sounds of mastication.

Ten minutes into the silent meal, a nurse in green scrubs opened the door. We stared mid-chew like teenagers caught drinking.

"You're not supposed to eat in here," he said.

I swallowed. "Sorry, we didn't know. Have you heard anything about our aunt? She went for a CT scan almost an hour ago."

"Mrs. Wagner has been admitted and assigned Room 303."

Jillian stood up, burger in one hand, water bottle in the other. A fry slid to the floor. "She's there now?"

He checked his big, chunky watch. "They should be bringing her up there in about fifteen-twenty minutes."

"Thanks. We'll clear out and be sure to clean up our mess," Tony replied, snatching the errant fry.

"See that you do." The door shut quietly behind the nurse.

My attention turned to Tony, and I asked in no-nonsense tones, "Tony, is it good or bad that they've admitted her?"

"Neither. It's to be expected. We won't know what the CT scan revealed until we talk with the doctor."

Jillian, who'd remained standing, shoved the last bit of burger in her mouth and began scooping up her belongings. The half-eaten box of fries went into her purse. "Les mo," she mumbled.

"Jilly." I put a hand on her arm. "What are you doing? Do you want your Coach bag to smell like French fries? The nurse said it would take fifteen minutes before she's in her room. Take a breath. Finish your food. We'll go up in a few minutes."

Jillian plopped back into her chair and chewed as if her life depended on it.

Chapter Thirty

The floor nurse directed us to Room 303 and told us Vera should be arriving any minute. The chamber was like many other hospital rooms. It was painted an unattractive putty color, with a bathroom by the entry door. A rolling table for the patient sat lonely in the center of the room, waiting for its mate, the bed. The seating consisted of a worn oxblood recliner and a fawn-colored sofa in front of the window. They both looked as comfortable as concrete. A clear plastic bag of Vera's personal items sat on the sofa. As far as hospital rooms went, it wasn't the worst or the best—it was just fine.

Yellowed blinds were closed, and Jillian gave them a twist, allowing the late afternoon sunlight to brighten the room. "There, that's a little better." She dropped her handbag on the couch and followed suit. "Oof! This thing is hard as a rock. I think I broke my tailbone."

"Aw, honey, you want me to rub it for you?" Tony reached out, and Jillian grabbed his hand, pulling him down beside her. The sofa creaked. "Oof, you weren't joking."

Rick offered me the red chair, but I shook my head. I was too antsy to sit, and instead poked around the room, asking Tony what each piece of machinery was for, until the tedium was broken by a jolly young nurse in pink scrubs and ash-blond hair.

"Look who's awake!" she chirped at us.

In rolled Aunt Vera reclining in the hospital bed. She'd been changed into a white gown with blue polka dots—the kind that never quite closed on your backside. An IV tube snaked out of her arm into a clear bag attached at the head of the bed. Her gray-haired bob, greasy from lack of washing, was pushed behind her ears, and a gauze bandage was taped to her forehead. The white bedsheet pulled up to her chin matched the color of her haggard face. Still, in the midst of the tubes and dirty hair was one of the most beautiful sights I'd ever seen: her bright blue eyes blinking coherently at us.

"You two are a sight for sore eyes," she rasped and raised a shaky hand.

We jumped to our feet, and the boys helped the nurse wheel Vera's bed into place.

"Aunt Vera! You gave us quite the scare."

"Well, Jillian, it was no picnic for me either," she returned cheekily.

"My name is Becca." The nurse wrote her name on the wipe board next to the letters LPN. "This works your bed. You see the arrows, up and down." She laid the remote next to Vera's hand. "And here's the call button for the nurses' station." She wrapped the cord around the upper part of the bed, leaving the button near Vera's ear. "Press the red button if you need something."

"Can you tell us, what did the CT scan show?" I asked.

"The doctor will be down soon to give you an update." Her gaze flickered over the four of us. "Visiting hours end at six and are restricted to no more than four. If anyone else arrives, one of you will have to leave." She picked up a piece of cardstock sitting on the counter that ran along one wall and turned to Vera. "Now, the doctor has you on a liquid diet for the time being. Would you like chicken or beef broth? Orange or green Jell-o?"

"Chicken and green Jell-o please." Vera sank into the pillows. "Is there anything to drink around here? I'm positively parched."

A small pink cup with a lid and plastic straw rested on the wheelie table, and Becca rolled it within arm's reach. "Here you go. And here's the television remote as well. Bethany will be in soon to check your vitals." She ducked out of the room as cheerfully as she'd arrived.

In the nurse's wake loomed a uniformed police officer in the doorway. Her hair was pulled into a low bun, and she must have been at least six-foot-two.

I'd forgotten my request to have Aunt Vera guarded, and her presence initially jarred me.

"Hi, Officer Jordan." My sister heaved herself off the sofa to make introductions. "This is my sister, Karina, and Rick."

We shook hands and did the niceties.

I smiled at her. "Thank you for keeping an eye on my aunt."

Her chocolate features remained serious, and she spoke in low tones, "It's my job. I've been informed that Detective Lang would like to get a statement from the patient if she's up to it."

I glanced over my shoulder. "I'm not sure—"

Aunt Vera watched our little group. "What is she saying? Are you talking about me? Speak up, so I can hear."

"A detective is coming to talk to you." I fiddled with my earring.

Jillian went to Aunt Vera's bedside, solicitously taking her hand. "Are you up for it, Aunt Vera? Maybe we should wait until tomorrow," she cooed softly.

With a shaking hand, Vera sipped her water before responding. "No, Jillian. I'm quite ready to speak to the police. It's time for the truth to come out."

I wasn't so sure I wanted my aunt talking to the police until we'd heard her side of the story. She might need a lawyer. "I don't know, Aunt Vera. I think we should hear what the doctor has to say about your condition."

"I'll be right outside the door." The officer exited.

Rick shut it behind her, and I pulled the ugly red recliner to her bedside. "Aunt Vera, I think it would be in your best interest to have a lawyer present when you speak to the cops."

"Why? I have nothing to hide."

"I need to tell you; they found the Paul Revere creamer in your house this morning."

Her face crumpled. "In *my* house? But ... I ..." She muttered unintelligibly under her breath.

"What did she say?" my sister mouthed.

I shrugged. "It would be best if we had a lawyer present when the detectives come. I can try to locate one for you."

She placed a hand to her temple and squeezed her eyes shut in concentration. "I don't think you understand. *I* am the one who uncovered the plot. *I'm* the one who noticed the missing pieces. And *I'm* the one who found Norman sneaking into the security room to cover up his thefts." The numbers on the blood pressure monitor next to her bed increased.

"Calm down, Aunt Vera." Jillian made shushing noises. "You're in no condition to get worked up over this. Karina's right, it's best that we wait to speak to the police until you're feeling better."

Vera shook her head, and her eyes remained closed. "They won't find anything. *I* have video evidence of him stealing from the case. Exiting the server room where he was able to override the security footage. On my computer."

"Yes, we found your computer. The police have it. They'll find the evidence. Norman's been captured. It will all work out," I assured, stroking her arm in an effort to calm her down. I didn't imagine having a concussion and surging blood pressure would be a good thing—seemed like a direct line to a brain aneurism.

Her eyes popped open, and, with unexpected strength, she gripped my hand. "The files and my flash drive?"

"We found the files. Rick's company identified Norman's motive for the thefts."

Her face relaxed; she let out a restorative breath and released my hand. "You got it. Good girl. I always knew you were a smart cookie, Karina."

"I had some help," I said, tilting my head at Rick, who'd stationed himself at the foot of the bed to keep an eye out for anyone who might be entering the room.

Jillian sputtered, "What about me and Tony?!"

"Of course, Jilly. You and Tony *also*," I confirmed.

Loud voices from the hallway interrupted our little discussion.

"What is that?" Jillian asked.

"I'll find out." Rick quickly went to the door to assess the situation.

Jillian rose to follow but paused when the raised voices subsided.

A moment later, Vikram rushed into the room, practically shoving Jillian out of the way. His clothes were grass-stained and wrinkled, with spots of blood on the yellow polo shirt. He sported scratches on his hand and a black eye.

"Vera, sweetheart! You're alive!" He scooped up her hand and held it to his cheek. "I feared I'd never see you again! What would I do without you?"

My aunt's gaunt cheeks colored with pleasure, but her features wrinkled with concern. "Ah, Vikram, it's good to see you. But what is this?" She reached out, her hand hovering next to his bruised eye.

"It is nothing, darling. I have seen to it that swine you call a boss was arrested."

Vera's face softened into a wobbly smile.

The door opened again. This time, a man wearing green scrubs and a lab coat entered. His gray hair receded high onto his forehead, and he had a pair of reading glasses perched up there. "Well, this is quite the crowd. I'm Doctor Westbrook, and you are Mrs. Wagner?"

I pushed the chair away from the bedside, so Dr. Westbrook

could shake Vera's hand.

"Hello, Dr. Westbrook, this is my family, and my ... beau, Vikram."

Vikram and the doctor shook hands across Vera's bed. "What can you tell us, Doctor?"

Rick's phone buzzed. He quietly excused himself and stepped out of the room.

The doctor ran down Vera's health concerns, which included a concussion, dehydration, UTI, and some other blood levels that were off due to the lack of food and drink. Considering all the issues, it was a miracle Aunt Vera was awake and coherent, which the doctor felt was a good sign. Tony asked a lot of medical questions that I never would have thought to ask. Some, the doctor could answer; others were met with a "wait and see" response.

Aunt Vera primarily listened and watched. Her eyes glazed over while Tony and Dr. Westbrook got into a friendly debate over particular chemistry numbers in Vera's bloodwork and her kidney levels. I may have zoned out too.

My sister gazed raptly at her fiancé's finesse with the medical jargon. Honestly, I had to give her credit: my sister's choice of future husband impressed me. He was a good guy, and, before this, I hadn't realized how useful it would be to have a paramedic in the family. She picked a good one.

Vikram asked a few questions, primarily about when Vera would be released from the hospital, to which the doctor responded, "We'll see how she's doing tomorrow."

I raised my hand in the air to garner the doctor's attention. "Dr. Westbrook, a detective is coming over to interview my aunt. I'm concerned her health is not up for such an interrogation and wondered if it would be best to put them off ... at least until tomorrow."

Aunt Vera's mouth dropped, but before she could protest,

the doctor replied without hesitation, "Agreed. I'll let the police know they'll have to return on another day. In the meantime, your aunt needs her rest. Don't stay too much longer." He wagged a finger at the five of us and exited.

Vikram spoke softly to Aunt Vera, who yawned and allowed her eyes to drift shut.

Rick waved Jilly, Tony, and me outside the room for a pow-wow. The police officer in the hallway had gone. I assumed she'd been called off due to Norman's capture.

The nondescript beige hallway wasn't busy; however, so as not to disturb patients in nearby rooms, Rick kept his voice low, "The doctor is right; there are too many of us. Your aunt needs her rest. I think it's best if I head back to her house."

Tony bobbed his head. "I'll go with you."

"Maybe we should all go and give Vikram time alone with her," Jillian suggested.

Shaking my head, I responded, "No. You and I need to wait for Mom and Dad to arrive. I'd rather not have them walk in to find Vikram, a total stranger, with Aunt Vera. We should be here for the introductions. Also, I need to find a hotel or bed and breakfast nearby, since it's clear Vera's going to be staying the night, and things are a bit crowded at her house. Not to mention it's still a bit topsy-turvy." I looked significantly at Jillian.

"Oh," the light dawned in my sister's noggin, "yeah."

"Don't worry." Tony kissed Jillian's forehead. "Donovan and I will put the house in order. And, if you can give me a ride," he directed at Rick, "the two of us will head back up to D.C. in the morning. That way, your parents can move into Vera's place tomorrow."

Rick nodded at Tony's suggestions, and his hand slid around my waist. "If you prefer, we can bug out tonight after straightening up."

At the mention of Tony leaving tonight, my sister's features became crestfallen.

Taking pity on her, I leaned into Rick. "Thanks, boys. I appreciate your help. Tomorrow morning will be early enough."

Okay, my motives may not have been completely altruistic. I was hopeful, now that we'd located Vera, the ghost would leave me alone, but I might have wanted the comfort of Rick next to me one more night in case he appeared. "I'll book my parents a place and tuck them in for the night before we head back to Williamsburg."

"Of course," Tony replied. "Jilly, can Donovan and I take your car?"

While she retrieved her keys, Rick leaned in for a kiss. "See you tonight."

****

Either the doctor or nurses must have put off our two detectives, because they didn't show up in Vera's room. Instead, I received a text from Riggins.

Hope your aunt is feeling better. Lang and I will come by tomorrow to get a statement.

I surmised, since the police officer no longer guarded the door, and no one had come to cuff Aunt Vera to the bed, they didn't plan to charge her with the theft of the Paul Revere creamer.

At least not yet.

Thirty minutes before visiting hours ended, my parents arrived. Jillian and I met them in front of the building. Mom climbed out of a white four-door sedan, and Dad drove around to park.

"Girls, it's so good to see you." My mom wrapped us in a joint hug, squeezing the two of us together.

"Unh," Jillian grunted.

"Good to see you, Mom," I wheezed.

Releasing us from her constrictor-like clutch, she said, "Sorry we're late, but your father and I decided to rent a car since we don't know how long we'll be here, and I'm sure you two will need to go back up to northern Virginia. Originally, we were going to get one from Budget, but they kept trying to upgrade us to a large SUV, which we certainly didn't need. I refused to pay for an upgrade. It was a hundred more *a day*! Then, your father remembered he had points with Avis, so we moved to the Avis counter, but there was a bit of a wait. However, they had just what we needed, and we get two free days with your father's points," my mother babbled on, nary taking a breath.

By this time, we'd reached the elevators. I knew it was a quick ride, so the moment she paused, I inserted, "That's great. Listen, I wanted to tell you that Vera's got a man friend, and he's here."

"Oh, you mean Vikram," Mom replied. "He's here? Wonderful, I've been dying to meet him."

"Wait a minute—" My sister pivoted. "—You know about Vikram?"

"Why, yes. Vera told me—" she tapped her chin in thought, "—oh, about a year ago, I guess. She said he's quite handsome. What do you girls think?"

My sister snorted.

I elbowed her. "I think he's a perfectly nice-looking fellow."

"Yes," Jillian agreed, "rather ... pleasant in a Mr. Rogers style."

"You're young." Mom waved her hand dismissively. "Your definition of handsome will be different when you're in your sixties."

So relieved I wouldn't have to make further explanations about Vikram, I simply smiled and nodded at my mother's assessment. "You're right."

The elevator doors opened, and Jillian led the way to Aunt

Vera's room. All the overhead lights were on, Vera's dinner had arrived, and Vikram was solicitously peeling open the applesauce cup.

Aunt Vera's eyes lit on my mother, and her face suffused with joy. "Sarah!"

"Vera!" Mom dropped her purse and fluttered across the room.

Vikram scuttled out of the way so Mom could envelop her sister-from-another-mister in a gentle embrace.

"I'm sorry, I didn't call you about the cruise," Vera apologized.

"Shush. Don't be silly. It'll get sorted out later." Mom plopped into the recliner. "Now, introduce me to your friend."

Chapter Thirty-One

That night, Jillian and I returned to Aunt Vera's home to find it cleaned and vacuumed in ship-shape condition.

"We even remembered to feed the cats," Tony bragged.

Tears of gratitude filled my eyes. "You boys are lifesavers. I don't know what I would've done without you." I grabbed Tony's face and kissed him on the cheek.

"Hey," Jillian cried and shoved me off her man. "That's *my* job."

I turned to give Rick a smackeroo on the lips. Meanwhile, Jillian and Tony were snogging like nobody's business, with Jillian making all sorts ridiculous of lip-smacking sounds. Not to be outdone, Rick dipped me to the side, reincarnating the famous WWII photo of the nurse and the sailor in Times Square on V-J Day.

"Enough." I laughed, and after one more kiss, he righted me. "C'mon, you two!"

"How about a drink?" Rick suggested.

"Sounds like heaven," I replied.

"There's some wine left from last night, and, of course, there's booze." He pulled open the liquor cabinet.

Jillian finally pulled her face off Tony's and piped up, "I'll have a glass of wine." She grabbed the green wine bottle off the counter and held it up to the light. "Uh-oh, there's only enough for one glass."

"You can have it. I need something harder. I think a Jack and Coke will do," I said, opening the fridge to get the soda. "What are you boys having?"

"I saw a nice bottle of single malt scotch in there. Do you think your aunt will mind if we drink it?" Tony went over to peruse the cabinet with Rick.

"Nah, she's a wine girl. Like me." Jillian poured the last of the red liquid into a stemless wine glass. "She keeps the scotch around for guests. Sometimes Dad drinks it."

Both the boys decided to enjoy a Scotch on the rocks.

Jillian stuck her head in the pantry. "I could use a snack. How about some popcorn?"

"Sounds good to me." I gathered a glass of ice, a can of soda, and the bottle of Jack Daniels, placing them all on the table. A reusable grocery bag sat in the middle. "What's in the bag?"

"That's your mail. I keep forgetting to give it to you." Rick splashed scotch over top of two ice cubes.

Jillian monitored the corn as it snapped and popped in the microwave, while Tony debated the merits of the scotch.

After fixing my own drink, I tugged the half-filled bag in front of me, dumped the contents on the table, and sorted the material into piles. Junk. Bills. Catalogs. Packages. I tossed the junk mail into Aunt Vera's recycle bin. Put aside the bills and got down to the good stuff—the packages.

Jillian tossed a handful of popcorn in her mouth and plunked down next to me. "Whatcha got there?" She tapped a package marked with the famous mail order logo known worldwide.

Distracted, I replied, "Should be a silk top, for work." It wasn't the brown package with the arrow on it that held my interest, but a white USPS envelope with Aunt Vera's return address. "What in the world is this?" I murmured beneath my breath.

Tearing it open, I shook out a piece of paper and a small black flash drive. The note read:

Dearest Karina,

When you get this, call me, and I will explain everything. Until we speak, please do not tell anyone, and keep this safe for me.

Love, Vera.

It was postmarked Monday.

"Holy shit."

All eyes turned to me.

"What?" my sister asked.

I held up the flash drive. "Does anyone know where my computer is?"

"In the parlor," Rick supplied.

I handed him Vera's note.

His eyes darted over the handwriting. "I'll fetch it for you."

Jillian snatched the note Rick had dropped on the table. "Jesus. It's from Aunt Vera." She passed it over to Tony. "What's on it?"

Rick placed the laptop in front of me.

It booted up, and I stuck the flash drive into the USB port. "It's password-protected. Did she write anything on the note?"

Tony read the note out loud and flipped it front-to-back and front again. "I don't see anything."

"What about her Google password?" Rick suggested.

Sure enough, it worked. "Looks like there are jpgs, document files, and video files."

I clicked on one of the video files labeled *October 18.*

An office hallway appeared, and Vera's voice could be heard whispering, "Today is October eighteenth. The time is—" a ladies watch appeared onscreen, "—ten-oh-seven PM. This is Vera Wagner, and I've just witnessed Norman Hedgewell enter the security room after business hours. This is not normal. I'm placing my phone in the doorway across the hall from the security room to record what happens."

I fast-forwarded until the door opened. Norman surreptitiously peeked out of the door, glancing back and forth as if making sure the coast was clear, then quickly exited while sticking something in his pocket. A few minutes later, we heard rustling, and the video jounced around to the floor and the ceiling.

Vera's voice came back on, and she was breathing heavily. "It's now ten-twenty-one." The watch flashed in front of the camera. Then the camera moved over to the security door, which had a card-key access swiper next to it and a red sign on the door that read AUTHORIZED PERSONNEL ONLY.

"What was that?"

The video jerked and then went blank.

"That was odd," Jillian said.

I had to agree with her. I wasn't sure why Aunt Vera was showing us a video of Norman leaving the security room. I clicked on an audio file marked *October 4*. We were looking at a rolling desk chair and a wall with a bookcase loaded with large texts.

Vera came into focus and sat down in the chair. "This is Vera Wagner. It's October fourth at eight-fifteen PM, and I have identified two missing pieces from the ceramics collection. My boss, Norman Hedgewell, claimed he had sent one of the items out to a specialist. However, I have contacted all the specialists who work with these materials, and none of them have the Japanese teapot in their possession. The missing silver saltshaker is listed as having been removed, by me, for cleaning. Which I have not done. It is my belief Norman has stolen these items and is selling them on the black market. I have not determined his motive for doing this, and I have yet to prove he is the one who has removed the items. I am fearful these thefts will be laid at my feet because, one of the times the display case must have been accessed, he used *my* passcode to check out the key to access the case. However, there is no video footage of the case being accessed."

"There's an audio file marked *October 19*." Rick pointed to an icon. "Let's hear what's on it."

"This is Vera Wagner, October nineteenth. I have just learned Norman's card should only have access to the security room between the hours of seven AM to seven PM. After those hours, he needs a security override by either the Head of Security or the Director of Museum Operations. I believe that Norman has altered the video feed to cover his tracks. I have just ordered spy cameras, which I plan to place in the ceramics rooms so I can get video footage of any future thefts."

"Are there any more video files?" Jillian laid her chin on top of my head to see the monitor.

Shaking her off, I moused around the screen. "Nothing."

"There was a video file in her Google cloud. It was labeled TEIN," Rick said.

I pivoted my head around. "Did you watch it?"

"No, I had no idea what TEIN stood for. I figured it was for work, or something she'd downloaded from the internet. Here, move aside."

I scooted off the chair so Rick could sit in front of the computer. A dozen keystrokes later, he clicked on the file.

The camera angle was from down low, but I recognized the location. "That's the museum room where the teapots are displayed. You can see it right there."

"This footage is from Monday. See—" Rick pointed to a running time clock in the lower corner, "—twenty-three-hundred sixteen. Eleven sixteen at night."

We could see shadowy movement, then Norman came into the picture. He quickly unlocked and opened one of the cases.

"He's taking Lucretia's silver cream pot!" Jillian exclaimed.

Norman shifted the other pieces around to hide the missing one, relocked the case, and quickly exited the room. The footage continued for five more minutes before it went dark.

"What happened?" Jillian asked.

"The cameras are probably motion-activated and turn off after five minutes of inactivity," Rick explained.

"There's not much more damning evidence than that," I commented dryly. "What else is on the flash drive?"

We went through the rest of the files. Documents similar to those in the blue file folder. A list of dates, times, phone numbers, names, and titles of antiquities specialists. A list of key card access times linked to a seven-number digit, several of which Aunt Vera had highlighted—most of them after hours. Two more audio files of Aunt Vera talking about Norman's activities on particular days, and notes from conversations she had with him. All of it, her evidence against him.

"Rick, go ahead and download all the files onto my computer. We'll give this flash drive over to Detective Riggins."

Chapter Thirty-Two

Monday

I would like to say Rick got some special love that night for his good deeds. However, between the lack of sleep, stressful day, and liquor, the moment my head hit the pillow, I zonked out and slept like the dead.

The alarm went off at seven. The boys got dressed while Jillian and I cooked them a hearty breakfast before sending them on the road.

While Jillian was in the shower, I wandered into the parlor to find Nightshade and Smokey staring pointedly at the chair in the front window.

"We found Vera, and she's at the hospital now. She got kind of banged up. I'm not sure when the doctors will let her come home. Hopefully soon. Norman is in custody," I said to the empty chair.

Nothing happened. I checked the cats.

Their attention remained riveted.

"Um, thank you for your help. We couldn't have done it without you."

Patchouli filled the room, and window curtains fluttered. The cats slunk away in opposite directions. I retreated upstairs to get dressed.

We washed the sheets and remade the beds. I pulled the striped backpack out of the closet and loaded Aunt Vera's toiletries, a sweatsuit, and a nightgown with a snuggly robe into it. Then Jillian and I headed to the hospital. We arrived shortly past nine when visiting hours began.

Vera had eaten and was watching a morning television show. Her face didn't seem so sunken, and her bloodshot eyes had cleared up. "Hello, girls. What have you got there?" she asked in a firm voice, pointing to the striped backpack Jillian carried.

"Some things from the house." My sister laid the bag in her lap.

Vera unzipped the top and peeked inside. "Wonderful. Oh, you brought my cold cream. Thank you." She piled the items around her. The nurses had given her a sponge bath this morning, which she said made her feel nominally better.

Jillian dug into the makeup bag. "We didn't bring a mirror, so I'll do your hair and face."

Silently, I held the flash drive in front of her.

"You got it. Thank heavens!" she exclaimed. "You must keep it safe. I'll give you the password, so you can see everything."

"Oh, we've already seen everything, Aunt Vera," Jillian chirped, dusting blush across her cheeks.

Vera pushed the blush brush aside, leaving one red cheek and one white. "You unlocked it? But ... how?"

My mouth twisted. "Vikram knew your Google drive password. You should really use more than one password."

Aunt Vera sniffed. "It's worked for years so far and never been compromised."

I seriously doubted that, but I didn't argue.

She continued, "Did you find the video file in the cloud?"

"I assume you mean the file from your little spy camera?"

"We did; we found it," Jillian said, finishing Aunt Vera's blush to match the other cheek.

"Why don't you tell us what happened?" I suggested, sitting on the ugly recliner. "I'm going to record it on my phone, if you don't mind."

She nodded and began to unravel her story. "It all started in July. Norman had transferred me to the new exhibit opening at Christmastime. I was happy to take it on because many of the items are coming from the Smithsonian, and it allowed me to work with my former colleagues. However, I still kept an eye on the ceramics collection. One day, I noticed a teapot was missing from the display case. As the conservator of this exhibit, keeping track of the items is my responsibility, even though I'd been tasked with another project. After speaking with Felicity, the curator of the ceramics exhibit, I went to speak to Norman."

"Close your eyes," Jillian directed.

Vera closed her eyes. "He told me the piece had been removed and sent to a specialist for reparations. He insinuated that *I* was at fault for not noticing the damage."

Jillian finished the eyeliner.

Vera opened her eyes and said sharply, "Of course, he did it to embarrass and disconcert me. Which it did. I doubted myself. Over the next two months, I noticed an additional piece go missing. Or at least, I thought it had. Only when I went to check the files for it, there was no record of the silver saltshaker. When I asked Norman, he told me he'd no idea what I was talking about. I thought I was losing my mind." She shook her head.

Jillian nodded with comprehension. "He was gaslighting you."

"Exactly, I even went so far as to check the security footage in the exhibit rooms, but the piece is not in the camera line of sight. And there was no footage showing the case being accessed. However, I found out my ID had been used to access the keys for the glass case."

"Yes, you mentioned that on one of your recordings," I said.

"I finally located old copies of the collection I had in a file at home and found the exact piece missing from the case and our computer files. I came to the realization: someone was tampering with the video feed."

Jillian dug through the makeup case. "On the flash drive, we saw video of Norman coming out of the security room where the camera feeds are stored."

"It's also on my computer," Vera stated.

"Norman had both your phone and computer. Do you use thumbprint identification, passcode, or password?" I asked.

Vera frowned. "Thumbprint. Why?"

I grimaced. "It's possible he wiped everything while you were knocked out."

"Well then, it's a good thing I sent you the flash drive and backed everything up to the cloud!"

Indeed, it was. I had to give my aunt credit; she'd covered her bases. "I'm glad you knew to back everything up to the cloud."

"Oh no. I don't know anything about backing up to the cloud. I simply went to the computer store and told the boy what I needed. His name was Tyler. Such a helpful young man. He did it all for me."

"Thank the lord for those computer store geeks," my sister drawled, pulling a brush through Aunt Vera's hair.

"Why don't you tell us what happened on Monday? That was the last day anyone saw you."

"I'd placed my little spy cameras around the exhibit. Such nifty little things," Vera said as an aside before continuing, "They were set to turn on when movement was detected. I felt as though Norman had been cagey with me that day. I began to wonder if he'd spotted my cameras. I was at home watching the news when my phone pinged a notification that one of my cameras activated. It was Norman."

She straightened her sheets and shifted position. "So, I hopped in my car and sped over there. I saw Norman's SUV in the staff lot and parked behind a dumpster so he couldn't see me. He came out carrying a box. I saw him put it in the car and expected him to leave. I planned to follow him."

I wondered how Aunt Vera thought her Karmann Ghia was unobtrusive enough that Norman wouldn't notice its noisy engine following behind, but I remained silent on that point.

"He must have forgotten something, because he turned and went back into the building."

Jillian had laid down the hairbrush, and I leaned forward on the edge of my seat.

"Of course, I had to take a peek. Norman forgot to lock the car, so I opened it. When I checked in the box, I found the Revere creamer. I was about to take it out of the car when I heard something behind me. I turned, and the lights went out."

"Aunt Vera, what you did was so dangerous," Jillian chided. "You should have phoned the police."

"Yes, dear, in retrospect," she admitted, "I should have done exactly that."

Jillian picked up the hairbrush and continued her grooming.

"What do you remember after that?" I prompted.

"When I awoke, I could tell from the little bit of daylight, and the gentle rocking, that I was on a boat. My hands were bound in front of me. I was so thirsty. My throat was dry as dust. And my head was spinning. He'd left a water bottle next to me, and I thought nothing of drinking it all down. That was a mistake."

"Why a mistake?" I asked.

"He'd drugged the water. Instead of clearing my head, it made it worse, and I conked out." She shuddered at the thought of Norman doing things around her unconscious body.

I didn't blame her. I wrinkled my nose in disgust. That was creepy as hell.

"That's horrifying!" my sister exclaimed.

It was rather dreadful, but very clever on Norman's part.

"He checked on me at some point. I have these jagged, swimming memories." She crunched her eyes shut. "I remember him feeding me. I didn't want it, but I was too weak to push him away. I think it must have had more drugs. The next time I awoke, my head was absolutely pounding and so incredibly heavy."

"I don't know how you survived it," I murmured in dismay.

"I knew I had to do something to try and get off the boat. I feared he was planning to sail out and dump me in the river."

Jillian's features turned south, and she looked like she might throw up. Aunt Vera spoke the very words I'd wondered myself ever since we found out Norman had a boat.

"I found a knife in the galley. But my head was so dizzy, it took forever to cut my bindings. I kept slipping in and out of consciousness. When I was finally free, I tried to escape, but he must have locked the cabin doors. I didn't have the strength or energy to bust them open … and I was so thirsty. My head was spinning. I must have fallen down…" her voice petered off.

As she recounted the story, her body wilted deeper into the pillows. Her hair and face were now made up, but the energy we'd witnessed upon our arrival had been depleted.

I wanted to leave her alone to take a nap; however, there was still one more question that needed an answer. "Do you know how the silver Paul Revere creamer got into your kitchen?"

She sighed. "He must have planted it. I'd left the keys in the car."

I nodded. "That's my theory as well."

My parents arrived full of smiles and bearing pastries.

"Good morning!" my mother cheerfully chirped. "We've brought a coffee cake!"

Chapter Thirty-Three

By the time Detectives Lang and Riggins arrived, Aunt Vera had fallen asleep from all the activity. My sister and parents had gone to check out the cafeteria.

I lay in wait for the detectives and detained them at the door. "I'm sorry, Aunt Vera is asleep. I've advised her not to speak with either of you until she has legal representation."

Lang stood, awkwardly shifting from one foot to the other. Riggins, deadpan, fiddled with a blister pack and stuck a piece of gum in his mouth. Today was the first day he didn't reek of smoke.

"Detective Riggins, this is for you." I handed over the flash drive, along with Vera's note and the packaging.

"What's on it?" he growled.

"All the information the prosecuting attorney needs to put Norman behind bars. She didn't steal the silver creamer."

Riggins gave a rueful smile. "I know."

"You know?"

"Norman made a plea deal," Lang explained. "Confessed to stealing the items from the museum and planting the silver in your aunt's home."

My lips pinched. "What was the deal?"

Lang crossed his arms. "We took attempted murder off the table, leaving him with second degree assault, felony abduction, and kidnapping."

I wasn't thrilled with the removal of attempted murder. "What about the larceny?"

Riggins shifted the gum to the other side of his mouth. He harrumphed. "Because Hedgewell sold the items illegally, the museum should be able to get them back *if* they are located. His lawyer is working on a deal. Hedgewell's offering information on the buyers. If the museum pieces are recovered, the DA will reduce jail time."

I grunted in disgust.

"The rest are all felony charges. It'll add up," Lang stated.

I wasn't thrilled with the deal, but if Norman confessed, it would mean the case wouldn't go to trial, and Vera wouldn't have to testify. "So, you're not here to charge my aunt?"

Riggins' face split into a smile. "No, ma'am. We wanted to see how she was doing."

"That's mighty kind of you," I intoned with disbelief.

Lang cleared his throat. "I will need a statement from what she remembers of the abduction."

I speared him with my gaze. "You know, I'm not thrilled you took attempted murder off the table. What was Norman planning to do with my aunt? Take her out and dump her?"

Riggins crossed his arms and stared at Lang, who shifted uncomfortably. "We're not sure. He claims it was all a miscommunication. Says he had no intention of hurting her; he just needed time to recover the items."

My brows went sky-high. "A miscommunication! He bashed her on the head, tied her up like a prize calf, and drugged her."

Lang blushed. "As I said, he's being charged with assault and kidnapping."

I chewed on that for a moment and finally decided to lower my hackles. "Aunt Vera will probably be awake after lunch. Why don't you come back in an hour?"

I walked with the two men to the elevator.

"By the way, where is the rest of the Scooby-Doo gang?" Riggins' gum snapped.

"They left for D.C. this morning. But we've brought replacements."

"Oh?" Lang said with interest.

"My parents," I clarified.

Riggins rolled his eyes at me. "The formidable Mrs. Sarah Cardinal. You'll have your hands full with that one, Lang."

The elevator arrived, and Lang got on. But Riggins put his hand over the door to hold it open. "You realize, I had Norman in my sights since we found his fingerprint on your aunt's vehicle."

"Why didn't you arrest him earlier?" I asked in an accusing tone.

He grinned. "You're a lawyer, you tell me."

I crossed my arms. "You didn't have enough evidence."

"That's right. Unlike the Scooby-Doo gang, I've got to go by the letter of the law, or cases get thrown out of court." He chomped his gum for a moment then confessed, "I'll admit, for a little while, I thought your aunt might have been working with him."

My eyes turned to slits.

"I'm glad it was a different story." Riggins stepped onto the elevator and pressed the ground floor button.

The doors closed.

My phone rang, and Rick's face popped up on the screen.

"Hello."

"Hey, beautiful. Calling to let you know Tony and I made it home in one piece. How's your aunt doing?"

"Better. The doctors expect her to make a full recovery, but she'll be in here another few days." I meandered over to a tucked-away bench in front of a window that looked out over the giant air conditioning units. "They're concerned about her kidney functions. Apparently, Norman drugged her."

"Jesus. What are they doing with Norman? Have they charged him?"

I told him about my interview with the detectives and Aunt Vera's story.

When I wound down, he said, "Your aunt is lucky to be alive."

"I know."

"When do you ladies plan to come home?"

"Jillian took a personal day, but she's got to drive back tonight," I explained. "I'm speaking at a luncheon on Wednesday, so I plan to drive home tomorrow. Aunt Vera will have my parents and Vikram at her beck and call until she's released."

"Why don't I bring dinner over to your place tomorrow?"

Delighted at the suggestion, I allowed a grin to split my face. "I would love that."

"Shall we say seven-ish?"

"Perfect." The phone line went silent as I formulated my next thoughts. Rick had been a rock over the past few days, and I needed to tell him how important it was to me.

"Karina? Are you still there?"

"Yes." I drew in a deep breath and dove in, "Listen, I wanted to tell you how much I appreciate everything you did this weekend. I don't know what I would have done without you. Not just the Silverthorne stuff, I mean the simple things, like taking care of the meals. Cleaning up the house..."

He guffawed. "Well, I had help. Tony—"

I cut him off. "No, it's more than just what you and Tony did. I'm trying to say something important here."

"I'm listening," he replied with sincerity.

"You're always there, talking me off the cliff. It's the fact that I know you've got my back. Look..." I drew in a deep breath and continued, "I don't know where this relationship is heading, but I want you to know ... I-I ... c-care deeply for you..."

Chicken! Just say it!

"Your generosity and-and forbearance ... I mean ... the way you take care of me ... I just..." Emotional feelings crawled up my throat, and I choked on the last few words.

"Karina—"

"S-sorry." I fanned my face with my hand and breathed deeply. "I don't know what's wrong with me..." I sniffed.

"Sweetheart, it's straightforward."

I wiped a tear away from the corner of my eye. "What is?"

"I love you," he said in the simplest of terms. "Don't you realize that?"

My heart leapt in my chest, and the tears started in earnest. "I love you too," I bawled.

Jillian walked off the elevator, and, spotting me weeping on the bench, she ran over. "Omigod! What's wrong? Is it Aunt Vera?"

I shook my head and pointed at the phone. "Rick s-said ... he—" gulp, "—l-l-loves..."

She rolled her eyes. "Of course he does, you nincompoop." Jillian took the phone from me. "Richard, is that you? My nitwit of a sister is blubbering on the bench. I'm assuming it's because, after all these months, you've finally said the words I knew you felt that day long ago when I was in the hospital. You remember?"

I didn't hear Rick's response, but Jillian snickered. "Well then, you're both nincompoops. Now, I've got to get my sister cleaned up before my parents arrive and wonder why she's turned into a watering pot. Say your goodbyes. You can talk to her tonight." She passed the phone back to me.

I sniffed a deep breath.

"Go get something to eat, beautiful. We'll talk about it later."

"Um-hm," was the most I could get past the lump in my throat.

"Love you." And with that, he hung up.

Author's Notes

When I began the sixth installment of the Karina Cardinal mysteries, it looked very different from the book you see before you. A third of the way into the other novel, I realized the book simply was not coming together the way I'd envisioned it. Karina was unhappy. I was unhappy writing that story.

After three months of banging away at a failing idea, I decided to chuck the manuscript. Which left me at a loss. Griping to my husband about my roadblock, he asked me, as a Halloween queen, why I'd never written a ghost story. Yeah, why hadn't I? From there, my scrappy little research brain went wild. In two weeks, I had an outline, and *Spectral Revelations* was born.

Williamsburg, Virginia, is one of Colonial America's first planned cities. The city is also known for having plenty of ghosts in and around the district. Aunt Vera's ghost was inspired by Lieutenant Disosway, a ghost who is said to haunt the Palmer House, near the Capitol Building at the end of Duke of Gloucester Street. I read about Lieutenant Disosway in *The Hauntings of Williamsburg, Yorktown, and Jamestown*, by Jackie Eileen Behrend.

In her book, Behrend recounts a haunting tale told by the Tuckers, a family who once lived in the Palmer House during the late 1800s. The Tuckers recounted a gentle soldier in Union garb who would turn up sitting in their parlor smoking a pipe. Further research led the Tuckers to identify the ghost as Lieutenant Disosway, who was appointed as a federal provost marshal to oversee the city of Williamsburg at the ripe age of twenty-four. He was billeted to Palmer House. However, one-night, inebriated Union soldiers began harassing some of the local ladies. Disosway ran to Market Square to put a stop to the threats. Unfortunately, this angered one of the drunk soldiers. He pulled a pistol and shot

Disosway on sight. The lieutenant was carried back to Palmer House, where he died two hours later.

In addition, Behrend's book discusses accounts of various ghosts she calls "walk-throughs," of starving Confederate soldiers fleeing through Williamsburg on their way to Richmond. One such story describes a family staying at a cottage in Colonial Williamsburg who experienced a ghostly visit. The ghost opened their freezer door multiple times, and the family's three cats spent the day watching an invisible spirit tromp through the house. The cats' reaction to the "walk-through" ghost inspired the scenes of Nightshade and Smokey watching the invisible Lieutenant Cabway.

On a different note, the "ceramics exhibit" overseen by Aunt Vera is based on an exhibit called *Revolution in Taste* and can be viewed in the *Henry H. Weldon Gallery* at the Art Museums of Colonial Williamsburg. According to the Colonial Williamsburg website, the exhibit is described as follows: "made of ceramic, glass, and metal, items like coffee cups, teaspoons, and dinner plates offered stylish and exciting new forms, improved materials, and dazzling colors. Elegant dining, tea drinking, and the consumption of alcoholic beverages became the focus of social life in early America, leading a revolution in taste that is still underway even today."

Acknowledgements

This Karina Cardinal novel couldn't have been completed without some help. First, I'd like to thank Jan Gilliam, Manager of Exhibit Planning and Curator at the Art Museums of Colonial Williamsburg, for giving me her time and sharing her knowledge of the museum exhibits and the Dewitt Wallace Collections and Conservation Building, an annex for materials not on display. Jan gave me valuable information that helped shape the storyline and allowed me to understand the value of collection pieces. In addition, Richard Hadley, Director of Museum Design and Operation, provided me with insight into the development of the museum.

Thanks to Mark Bergin a former Alexandria police officer who helped me formulate the interactions between Karina's gang and the Williamsburg police and detective. While Karina can find evidence through some very questionable tactics, the police must play by the book in order to keep the case above board. Poor detective Riggins had no idea what he was coming up against when he began his investigation.

I'd also like to thank Jeffrey James Higgins, a former DEA agent who gave me his valuable time to discuss a plotline for Karina, which did not come to fruition. This story initially started as something vastly different from the one in front of you. Midway through the writing process, I simply had to throw in the towel, because I could not develop it to my own satisfaction. Moreover, while I didn't use Jeffrey's insights within this story, I have no doubt they will come in handy in a future book.

Finally, thanks to my team members, Carolan Ivey, and Krista Venero for her editing skills and pointing out my plot mistakes. I don't know what I'd do without my team.

About the Author

Ellen Butler is the internationally bestselling author of the Karina Cardinal mystery series. Her experiences working on Capitol Hill and at a medical association in Washington, D.C. inspired the mystery-action series. Book critics call the Karina Cardinal mysteries "intelligent escapism." Butler also writes historical spy fiction. Her WWII spy novel, *The Brass Compass*, recently won a 2022 Speak Up Talk Radio Firebird Book Award for historical fiction. The second book in the duology, *Operation Blackbird: A Cold War Spy Novel*, is inspired by true events. Reviewers are calling it "riveting" and "a thrilling adventure."

When she's not writing, Butler enjoys reading, spending time with family, working on home improvement projects, and attending car shows. Butler has a passion for classic cars, especially the bright colors of the 1950s vehicles replete with fins and bulbous lights.

You can find Ellen at:
Website ~ www.EllenButler.net
Facebook ~ www.facebook.com/EllenButlerBooks
Instagram ~ @ebutlerbooks
Goodreads ~ www.goodreads.com/EllenButlerBooks

Novels by Ellen Butler

THRILLER/SUSPENSE
The Brass Compass, A WWII Spy Novel
Operation Blackbird, A Cold War Spy Novel
Poplar Place

KARINA CARDINAL MYSTERIES
Isabella's Painting (Book 1)
Fatal Legislation (Book 2)
Diamonds & Deception (Book 3)
Pharaoh's Forgery (Book 4)
Swindler's Revenge (Book 5)
Spectral Revelations (Karina Cardinal Mystery, Book 6)

CONTEMPORARY ROMANCE
Heart of Design
Planning for Love
Art of Affection
Second Chance Christmas

www.ingramcontent.com/pod-product-compliance
Lightning Source LLC
Chambersburg PA
CBHW031004260626
47169CB00002B/694

* 9 7 8 1 7 3 4 3 6 5 0 6 1 *